# Forbidden
## *faith*

# Forbidden *faith*

## Mechel Wall & R. H. Roberts

BONNEVILLE BOOKS

An imprint of Cedar Fort, Inc.
Springville, Utah

ISBN 13: 978-1-4621-2202-8

Published by Bonneville Books, an imprint of Cedar Fort, Inc.
2373 W. 700 S., Springville, UT 84663
Distributed by Cedar Fort, Inc., www.cedarfort.com

LIBRARY OF CONGRESS CATALOGING-IN-PUBLICATION DATA

Names: Wall, Mechel, 1967- author. | Roberts, R. H. (Renee H.), 1971- author.
Title: Forbidden faith / Mechel Wall and Renee Roberts.
Description: Springville, Utah : Cedar Fort, Inc., 2018. | Includes
   bibliographical references and index.
Identifiers: LCCN 2018002197 (print) | LCCN 2018008841 (ebook) | ISBN
   9781462128976 (epub, pdf, mobi) | ISBN 9781462122028 (perfect bound : alk.
   paper)
Subjects: LCSH: Noah, King (Book of Mormon figure)--Fiction. |
   Kings--Fiction. | Abinadi (Book of Mormon figure)--Fiction. |
   Prophets--Fiction. | Good and evil--Fiction. | Peace--Fiction. | Book of
   Mormon--Fiction. | Religious fiction.
Classification: LCC PS3623.A35968 (ebook) | LCC PS3623.A35968 F67 2018
   (print) | DDC 813/.6--dc23
LC record available at https://lccn.loc.gov/2018002197

Cover design by Shawnda T. Craig
Cover design © 2018 Cedar Fort, Inc.
Edited by Melissa Caldwell and Erica Myers
Typeset by Nicole Terry

Printed in the United States of America

10  9  8  7  6  5  4  3  2  1

Printed on acid-free paper

*Mechel Wall*

To my husband, Barry, for telling me I just needed to finish
writing this first book, and to Shanan for being my faithful reader.


*R. H. Roberts*

To you, dear reader—May you be brave enough to be strong
even when life doesn't demand it.

And to Matt, for sharing your courage and enduring love.
You are my best friend and my joy.

———•◆•———

# Battle Cry

## *Tamar, 160 BC*

*Y*ou don't have to come with me. I think I can handle my father without your help." Noah paused at the base of the ramp leading to the palace.

"I want to be there for you. I'm your wife." Tamar reached out and grasped his hands, worn rough from years of drawing the bowstring. "I love you."

Noah flinched, pulling his hand out of hers, looking away. "You know how I feel about you."

But Tamar didn't know, not any more. A breeze blew her scarf and long hair around her face, hiding Noah's expression from her. By the time she tucked everything back in place, Noah was at the top of the ramp, heading toward the palace door.

Winter had loosened its icy grip, allowing blades of grass to emerge from their long sleep. Tamar didn't mind the walk, taking in the fresh scent of spring. As she entered the Throne Room, a difficult conversation was already underway.

Noah tossed aside the robes. "I won't wear them." They slid off of the simple carved wood throne and onto the floor.

King Zeniff quickly picked them up, brushing off a few particles of dirt and grass. Carefully, he folded them and placed them back on the table behind him.

He turned to face his son. "You must if you are going to officiate at Passover. It's expected. It's required."

"They're old. I want new ones if I'm going to stand in front of the people of Lehi-Nephi."

"Practice a little humility, my son."

"You're old, I'm young. People expect me to be different."

"Some things are supposed to stay the same, regardless of age or time. It's God's way."

"Noah, listen to your father," Tamar urged. "He's a wise man and the people love him."

"Not all."

"Noah!" Tamar hushed.

"I'm just saying that not everyone agrees with his ways anymore," Noah added.

"Who?" Zeniff asked.

"It doesn't matter who. What matters is how I present myself." Noah ran a hand over his cloak, woven with threads of gold, fingers pausing to trace the gems embedded in the silver clasp.

"Is obedience to God important or the perception of a few?" Zeniff asked.

"Far more than a few. And they don't like Jarom either."

"Who doesn't like me?" Jarom said as he entered the palace doorway, which had been left open to let in the cool spring breeze. "Why does it matter if some of our city doesn't like me? I'll be king one day and I'll lead like father has."

"See, that's part of the problem. You're just more of the same. People want new leadership, finer things." Noah's eyes lit up and Tamar felt a familiar flutter in her stomach. She loved this side of him, the dreamer. "I've seen palaces in other cities, and they're far more majestic than ours here in Lehi-Nephi. We could have wealth and beauty with the right kind of leadership."

"What kind of leadership would you suggest, Noah?" Jarom squared up to his twin brother, speaking directly to his face. "Tell us how you'd do it if you were king."

"You're the next in line, so what does it matter what I'd do?" He leaned toward Jarom. "A long life to you, brother."

"Noah!" Tamar said in a rough whisper.

Zeniff put his hand on Noah's shoulder. "It's Passover. It's spring. Everything is new and full, so let's not argue. Maybe I'll rule till my dying day. Although I am growing weaker."

"Nonsense, Father," Jarom said. "You're a fine king, a great leader, and a great man. I hope to be half as good as you one day. You've got many years ahead . . ."

Noah cut him off. "You do want to be king!" he blurted. "You want to be just like him, so you want to be king, right?"

"Nothing could be further from my mind." Jarom sternly replied. "It's you that covets that role."

"What's wrong with ambition and big ideas? You're envious of my visions of what this place can become."

Jarom looked for a moment at Noah, then slowly shook his head. "I'll be at the north tower if anyone needs me." He stormed out of the palace doors.

Tamar saw him disappear into the trees, headed toward the verdant pastures teeming with sheep and goats.

Zeniff extended his arms to embrace Noah.

Noah backed away. "This won't be solved that way." He threw aside a tapestry, which covered the side door that led to a peaceful courtyard. Before the cloth could fall back into place, bits of broken pottery flew through the air outside.

Queen Mera slipped into the Throne Room behind Tamar just as the tapestry swung shut. She placed her arm around Tamar's shoulder. "Noah's throwing pottery again?"

Tamar nodded, avoiding her mother-in-law's gaze.

"We will get through this," Mera said. "Was Jarom involved this time?"

Tamar nodded again. "He went to the tower."

"I'm not surprised. It's his refuge."

Zeniff sank to the throne, which was draped with a thick sheepskin. His eyes closed and Tamar thought he looked a little bit older than he had the day before.

He spoke nearly in a whisper. "Was it all a mistake?"

"What?" Mera asked as she knelt on the hard clay floor beside the throne.

"Coming here, from Zarahemla. Leaving safety. People believed in me, followed me."

"We have a good life here. I love our little corner of God's earth."

"The constant threat of Lamanite invasion weighs heavy on me."

"You've done your part. The watchtowers, city walls, and relying on God's protection and teaching our people to live God's laws. We've been blessed."

"I couldn't bear to see my children, grandchildren, and those I love hurt because of my blind ambition."

"Hush. No more." Mera put her hand on his.

He grasped it and opened his eyes. "I love you."

"And I you."

Tamar cleared her throat, as if she were intruding on a private moment. "If it helps, I'm glad to be here. This is home to me. My father didn't blame you, King Zeniff. He just couldn't stay here after my mother died. I couldn't leave. So you're my family, and not just because I married your son."

Mera rose and embraced Tamar. "You're the daughter I always longed for. Thank you for loving our son."

"He's a good man." A quick glance between Mera and Zeniff caused her to stiffen. "He is good. Not perfect. You taught him well, so he will come around."

"I'm not sure he learned what was most important. I wonder what we could have done differently for him. Jarom is . . ." Mera's voice trailed off.

The words left Tamar's lips before she could stop them. "Jarom is the good son. That's what Noah always says."

"I didn't say—"

"I know, but Noah thinks he's the bad son. I tell him he doesn't have to be, and that he's not bad, just that he makes different choices than Jarom."

Two little boys burst into the room, breaking the tension.

"Grandpa, please can we go with daddy to the tower?" the older one pleaded.

"Oh no, you're much too young." Zeniff took one in each arm and placed them on his lap. "A few more years and you'll learn how to watch over our city. If there's danger, you have to be able to blow the shofar horn. It takes big lungs to do that job."

"Limhi goes with Noah sometimes. When will it be my turn to try?"

"Well, Neriah, you're seven now, so I think you'll learn soon." The little boys began making blowing sounds, each one bigger than the last, spraying fine spittle all over the king's robes. Zeniff tickled them till their blowing turned to giggles. "Let us all have some of their childlike joy. It's Passover."

The shofar horn blast filled the air, echoing off the massive stone bluffs that surrounded the city on three sides.

Tamar and Mera ran to the door. Women were paused in the act of grinding corn, shepherds stood still, children clung to their mother's shawls. All eyes were on the tower, partially obscured by low clouds rising from the river. Jarom's unmistakable form leaned over the edge of the rail, poised with horn in hand.

"One long blast, danger," Mera said, thinking out loud, as Zeniff and the two boys joined them at the palace doors.

Everyone held their breath, waiting for the next blast to tell them how quickly the Lamanites were advancing.

Almost before the thought left Tamar's mind, the answer came in one long blast. Tamar felt weak with relief. "They're coming in a slow march," she whispered. "We have time."

"Zeniff, go," Mera said. "I'll keep the boys till Sarai comes. She'll be looking for them."

Noah came running around the corner to where Mera and Tamar stood with Neriah and Hiram. "Where's Limhi?"

"He was with the storyteller." Tamar scanned the faces coming toward them from all corners of the city.

"Find him and keep him safe. I'll get my weapons and join the others at the wall." Noah grabbed Tamar roughly and kissed her. "I'll be back."

Women, children, and those men too frail to fight were beginning to gather at the palace, awaiting instructions from the matriarch of their city. Jarom sprinted from the base of the tower ahead of the growing number of soldiers gathering at the potter's mound where both the kiln and the munitions were stored. Jarom heaved a stone away from the belly of the hill and men disappeared inside, passing swords and weapons out to the waiting army. Zeniff shouted orders to the soldiers, his robes flowing behind him as he walked.

The court storyteller, a hunched old man with hair like fallen snow, led Limhi and other youth to the raised earth platform where Mera stood giving instructions.

"We have time to get to the cave," she said. "Take what food and water you have and a few skins in case we are there for the night. Go quickly." Gently but firmly she grasped her grandson's shoulder. " Limhi, go from house to house and make sure no one is left behind. You're old enough to do this for me."

Sarai pushed through the crowd and climbed the hill to where Mera and Tamar stood. She stooped to embrace her sons. "What can I do to help?"

"Lead the people to safety."

"Why not me?" Tamar asked.

"This is not the time," Mera replied. "Go with Limhi and see if anyone needs help."

The crowd followed Sarai, making its way across the bridge that split the city of Lehi-Nephi. The people rushed through the pastureland, over a second bridge, and up to the place of safety. A cave hidden in the bluffs.

Tamar, Mera, and Limhi ran from house to house, ensuring that no one was left behind. As they completed their sweep and went to retrieve some skins and food to take to the cave, Jarom came running toward them. His personal bodyguard, Helam, trailed close behind, his long legs churning up dust, cloak flying behind the bow slung over his broad shoulders. The sharp angles of Jarom's face grew more pronounced as his eyes scanned the vacated city.

Most of the men had already positioned themselves outside the city walls, along the edge of the hills, where a catacomb of pathways had been built long ago to channel any intruder's advance, giving the Nephite archers and soldiers a perfect killing field. The only other method of invasion was the river that ran beside and through their city.

"I need Limhi!" Jarom barked between gasps.

Tamar grabbed Limhi's arm. "Why?"

"I want him to man the watchtower for me."

"He's not old enough!"

"I've seen him there with Noah. He can blow the horn."

Limhi wiggled out of his mother's grasp and turned to face her. "The storyteller and others will guard the cave. I'll protect you from the tower."

"Your Highness." Helam bowed his head toward Tamar. "I guarded that tower myself at his age. Do not fear. It is a safe place."

Jarom bent to look into Limhi's eyes. "We can't spare any soldiers and I need to fight, not watch. Today you become a man. Blow the horn when the Lamanites are close, when the battle begins, and when it is over and the Lamanites are leaving." With a few more quick breaths, he added, "God will protect you. Be careful climbing up and down. Go!" He pushed Limhi toward the retreating women and children. "Run!"

Like a bobcat in pursuit of prey, Limhi was gone.

"You have no right to do that," Tamar said to Jarom. "Noah will be furious."

"War makes some choices easy," Jarom said. "I need to be by my father's side."

"Your father, but not your brother?"

"He's an archer—he can fend for himself. Father is old. I need to protect him from Lamanites and . . ." He glanced at Tamar.

Jarom sprinted off to where the men, old and young, stood ready to receive the advancing enemy.

"Why at Passover?" Mera moaned. "Will we be forever hated, never able to experience peace?"

Tamar wrapped her arm around Mera's stooping shoulders. "Everyone is out. We will be safe in the cave. Let's join the others."

# 2

# The Fallen

## *Mera, 160 BC*

*M*era scanned the valley. Overturned carts littered the muddy street. Reed doors hung open, forgotten. In the distance, Zeniff marched at the head of the army, like so many brave kings before him. It wasn't the first time and wouldn't be the last. Not unless they could make peace with their brothers of old.

True to his word, Jarom marched at his father's side. He would make a fine king someday, once Zeniff grew old and tired. A mighty man of faith. If anyone could bring stability, it was Jarom. Mera wished he would hang back in a safer position. What if she lost Zeniff and Jarom both? The Lord would help her through it, but she hated to think what it would mean for the kingdom.

Her younger son was not like Jarom. Rumors swirled around Noah like morning fog, only they never quite drifted away. Mera didn't believe most. But there could be no question who would be the better king, even if Jarom was the eldest by only fifteen minutes.

Noah would wait near the back with the archers in a position of relative safety. Mera rubbed her arms, feeling a sudden chill. *Why couldn't the Lamanites leave them be?*

"Come inside." It was Sarai, Jarom's wife, resting her slim hand on Mera's shoulder. "Everyone's hidden now. Come in where it's safe."

"Not everyone's hidden." Mera cast one last look at the soldiers, wincing as she heard their battle cries, then ducked inside.

———— ◆ ————

Icy water dripped from clefts in the cave ceiling, spattering Mera's cheeks and leaving dark streaks on her scarf and sleeves. She'd given up avoiding the miserable wetness. It was impossible. She longed to peer outside to see how far the sun had moved, measuring the time since the battle had started. But she knew better than to give away their hiding place before Limhi signaled all was clear.

Tamar huddled beside her, her face set in fury. "Jarom never should've sent Limhi to the tower. How could you allow it?"

"Limhi will be safe." Mera reached for her daughter-in-law.

Tamar jerked away, spilling wax from her candle. It dribbled down her sleeve, ruining the fine linen. "Jarom had no right. He should've sent *his* sons."

Mera glanced to Jarom's boys. Hiram's face was buried in Sarai's skirts, his dark curls unruly as ever. Neriah, on the other hand, was playing with his cherished dog, the one Mera distinctly remembered forbidding him to bring.

"My boys are too young to be out there," Sarai said, turning back to Tamar, who had been watching with a mixture of anger and longing. "They've never even blown the horn. It's an honor Jarom would've gladly given our sons if they were older."

"Convenient that they're not." Tamar drew herself up. "At least my son wouldn't cling to my skirts or bring a mongrel along, endangering everyone with its bark."

"I know you're worried, Tamar," Mera said, determined to keep peace between her daughters-in-law. "But he's safe. Limhi's up on a tower, far from the battle."

A tittering laugh from a nearby group interrupted the disagreement. Several girls stood apart from the crowd, whispering amongst themselves, their gold bangles and earrings glinting in the candlelight. One with unbound hair the color of honey looked straight at Tamar and covered her mouth while she spoke to the others. Tamar's face darkened.

Mera stood to face the mockery. "Shouldn't you be helping with the babies?" she said while nodding toward the back of the cave where tired nurses struggled to calm several infants. The girl smiled and sashayed away.

---

Mera's candle flickered. Somehow, as the day dragged by, she came to see it as a symbol of hope. If the candle burned until Limhi sounded the all clear, her men would be safe. All of them—Zeniff, Jarom, and Noah. Limhi too, although she didn't worry so much about him, being up on the tower. She couldn't pretend the whole army would survive. That never happened. But as long as her candle shed light in the gloomy cavern, everything would be all right. Her loved ones would return.

She knew she was being silly, that God didn't determine the fate of armies and nations based on the height of their candles. Other strengths determined that, and it wasn't always physical. But still, she liked thinking that her light meant something, that the warm glow it provided was more than just comfort.

Now, her candle was little more than a puddle.

The warm pockets of light glowing throughout the cavern had dimmed. A few had gone out. The refugees were growing restless. Women held their children close, clutching each other's hands. Most sat on the cavern floor, too weary to stand.

Mera huddled together with Tamar, Sarai, and her grandsons, who seemed more restless than all the other children combined. Neriah had persuaded Hiram to part with his ball of knotted string, and they tossed it back and forth.

Sarai leaned against her mother, Avi, a wrinkled old woman with a simple faith. She attributed everything to God's will, as if He controlled every element of their lives.

At the moment, Mera wanted to believe that, she really did. If it were true, her men would come home safe. All the Nephites would. But Mera couldn't accept easy answers. She'd seen too many good men fall and too many good families hurt. As far as she could see, life was full of sorrow. Joy too, of course. Much of it caused by her own choices. But some—and this was the hard part—some of it completely out of her hands, like pain caused by others or the strange ways of nature. She refused to blame God for everything.

Beside them, Sarai's younger sister, Lisha, picked at the cave floor, gathering grit into tiny piles, then scattering it again and again.

Sarai bit her lip, shivering, despite her thick cloak. "I can't stop thinking about Daniel."

"Your brother?" Tamar's whisper came out harsh. "You should be worrying about Jarom."

"Jarom is the best swordsman we have. This is my brother's first battle," Sarai said. "I worry for them both."

"Have faith, Sarai." Avi tucked her daughter's wayward curls back beneath her scarf. "Jarom and Daniel are faithful men. The Lord will watch over them."

"And what about the good men that died last time?" Lisha asked, tapping the rocky ground with her fingers.

"It was the will of the Lord." Avi's mouth tightened into a firm line. "You must seek to know His way. Then you'll not fear."

"And what's His will now?" Lisha asked, blinking back tears. "Papa and Daniel are out there fighting! What if I don't like the will of the Lord?"

Avi took Lisha's hands in her own, squeezing them as if she could force her own faith into her daughter. Mera wanted to tell her it didn't work that way, that no amount of squeezing, wheedling, or threats could create faith, but she didn't think Avi would listen. "They will be safe." Avi touched her clawed fingers to her chest. "I feel it here."

Tamar stood and tightened her belt, as if trying to hold herself together. She shifted closer to the mouth of the cave.

"They won't be back yet, Tamar." Mera moved between her daughter-in-law and the entrance. "You only risk revealing us."

"I was only checking." Tamar cast her a disgruntled look as they settled back down with their little group. "I can almost see the tower from here."

Mera didn't bother correcting her.

The dog barked and lunged for the ball that Neriah and Hiram were tossing. Mera snatched it away, careful not to tip her candle and douse its flame. "Come now," she said, wiping slime from her fingers onto the edge of her cloak. "Quiet, Pup, and I'll tell a story."

Neriah tucked the dog under his arm, shushing her. He and Hiram trained their eyes on Mera, their faces wan and dirt-streaked under the fading light. A hush fell around Mera. "Once there were two princes and a puppy."

"Tell us a real story, Grandma," Neriah said, "not something about us."

"All right then." Mera set Hiram's ball aside. He scooted over, picked it up, and started teasing apart the knots, ready to make a new creation.

"Once there were twelve princes."

"Twelve?" Hiram repeated, looking up from his string.

"Twelve," Mera said firmly. "Well, there weren't twelve at the start, but there were by the end. This one is your papa's favorite. Noah's too," she added, her brow furrowing as she felt Tamar tense beside her. "One day the smallest prince had a dream. He dreamed all the other princes bowed down to him."

"Really?" Hiram said.

"Really," said Mera.

A long, low blast of the shofar horn vibrated the air, followed by a second sounding.

Mera gasped. The battle was over. Her candle winked out.

———— ◆ ————

Torches snaked up the path to the village as Mera and the others scrambled outside, searching the tattered army for their loved ones. Sunset cast a bloody pall over the soldiers, making the task that much harder.

Noah marched at the head of the army, triumphant, though his cheek was scraped raw. Tamar rushed down the trail to meet him. Just behind him, Helam and several other guards carried two litters, each bearing a still body. Mera clutched her chest.

Beside her, Sarai whimpered. "It's them, isn't it? Are they alive? Tell me they're alive." She ran ahead of Mera, who tried to keep up but couldn't. Instead, she clasped her grandsons' hands, one on each side. She didn't know who was helping whom most. Other younger women passed them as she hobbled down the hillside, afraid of what she might find.

Wails mingled with cries of relief as the women, the very young, and the old discovered what had become of their families. As Mera neared the ramshackle army, her chest tightened. Sarai was leaning over Jarom, kissing the crescent-shaped scar on his forehead, courtesy of an argument he'd had with Noah when they were young. He winced as her teardrops fell on his cheeks.

Mera's chest loosened, just a little.

He'd made it. Not unscathed, obviously, but alive.

But in the litter beside him, the one that surely held Zeniff, there was no movement. The soldiers bearing him looked grim, their eyes rimmed red. Mera felt like sagging to the ground, but she had to be strong. She tugged Neriah and

Hiram forward, pausing to squeeze Noah's arm as she passed. He'd thrown it around Tamar and was searching the crowd, probably for Limhi.

Sarai's sons ran to her, leaving Mera to face the truth alone.

Zeniff lay motionless on a blanket stretched between two sturdy oak branches. His skin was as gray as the empty cave. Mera reached for his hand, longing to feel his warmth, even if for the last time. His fingers twitched in hers, applying a gentle pressure. "Zeniff? Zeniff!"

He moaned—a low, weak sound, like the sigh of a dying wind. Out of the corner of her eye, Mera saw Noah wave someone down. Aaron, the court healer, left an injured soldier he'd been tending and pushed through the crowd.

"My father needs help," Noah demanded.

"No . . ." Zeniff stirred. "Jarom has lost too much blood."

Aaron took one look at Zeniff and swept past him to Jarom's stretcher.

"Can't you help him?" asked Helam. Though exhausted by battle, Helam's grip on the litter was sure, his face tight with concern.

Noah released Tamar and pushed between the healer and his brother. "See to the king first."

Helam turned an incredulous gaze on Noah.

"The king may be weak," Aaron said, "but he's stable." He pulled strips of cloth from a leather pouch at his belt and pressed them against Jarom's left shoulder. "I need to stop the bleeding."

"You need to save the king."

"Noah," Mera said, pulling on his cloak. "Aaron knows what he's doing. Let him work." She hoped she was right. Aaron was the chief healer for a reason and she trusted him.

Noah shook Mera off, jostling Jarom's stretcher. "The king lies dying and you're focusing on a flesh wound?"

Aaron raised his eyes to Noah, his expression just shy of deadly. "If I don't stop the bleeding, Jarom will die." Beside him, Sarai uttered a quiet cry.

Noah narrowed his eyes, looking more dangerous than Mera had ever seen him. "I am a prince of these people."

"And I am their healer. Now move aside."

Noah stalked a short distance away, his triumphant expression gone.

Mera felt a stab of pity for Aaron. If he didn't take care, Noah would try to banish him from the palace.

Tamar scurried after Noah, striving to be a good wife, though he didn't seem to notice. She dabbed at his scrapes, but he shook her off as if she were an irritating fly.

A moment later, Limhi pushed through the crowd, his cheeks flushed and his hair sweaty. He ran up to his father as if to hug him, then stopped a foot away, looking uneasy.

"Where've you been?" Noah demanded, his voice rising over the clatter of the weary men ambling along the path. He grabbed Limhi by the scruff of his neck. "I go to battle and you're not even here on my return?"

"Jarom sent him to man the tower," Tamar said. She pulled Limhi close.

An angry flush crept up Noah's neck as he glared toward his brother.

"It needed to be done, Noah," Mera said warningly. "And Limhi served honorably. You should be proud."

Zeniff strained to raise his head, blanching white with the effort.

Mera gently pushed him back. "Easy, love, Aaron will take care of Jarom."

"This looks like an exit wound," the medicine man muttered, turning Jarom onto his right side to inspect his back. "Yes, I can see the entry here. Went clean through."

Jarom flinched. "A haze rolled in. It was chaos. What's wrong with Father?"

"Exhaustion." Aaron shook his head. "He shouldn't be leading battles at his age."

Soldiers shuffled past, the injured receiving attention from the healer's assistants. Mera stood between the two litters, Sarai trembling beside her. "They'll both be okay, right?"

"Yes." Aaron raised his lined face. His fingers were bloody from stanching Jarom's wound. "The king will need time to rest. Perhaps many months."

Mera took a deep breath and gave a curt nod.

"This should do it." He released his pressure on Jarom's shoulder. "I'll stitch up the crown prince in his room." He nodded to the porters, who moved to carry Jarom back to the palace, Sarai at his side. Before they took more than a few steps, Sarai's younger sister, Lisha, rushed up.

Her face was filthy and tearstained, the front of her dress torn. "He's dead," she shrieked at Sarai. "You and Mother promised! You said God would protect him, but he's dead!"

Sarai shook her head. "I never . . . wait. What?" She stepped away from Jarom and grabbed her sister's shoulders. "Who's dead?"

"Daniel." Lisha buried her head against Sarai's chest, then collapsed to the hard clay floor, leaving Sarai's arms empty.

*3*

# Shiva

## *Tamar, 160 BC*

*M*ist hung heavy over the river, leaving the tops of the newly leafed trees shrouded in white, as if they had no roots or trunks at all, but were simply floating next to the towering cliffs that surrounded the city. Thatched rooftops loomed through the fog, barely visible atop their earthen platforms near the river.

Tamar stood alone outside the palace in the predawn light.

A torch glowed on the far side of the city, illuminating a mournful path. Like the shadows of Tamar's nightmares, faceless shapes moved slowly through the darkness, both human and beast. One by one, the animals—loaded with earth from the valley below—lined up along the path that led to the burial mound, preparing for the burials the next day.

Tomorrow it would grow taller.

Sarai's weeping, anguish for a wounded spouse and deceased brother, began again. Jarom's voice mingled with hers, hushing her, but Tamar could hear it all. Their palace compound was too small for mourning to be kept private.

Today the Shiva period would begin. A time of sorrow for each soul that was lost. Tamar shivered in the cold as her husband silently placed a soft wool blanket over her shoulders and wrapped his arms around her. His chin rested on her head and his breath hung in the chilly air.

"You didn't sleep much last night."

"Neither did you." Tamar turned to face him, still tight in his embrace. "My dreams are vivid and haunting. I needed reality." She laid her head on his strong chest and basked in his warmth. "I like this reality."

"Come back inside. The dead don't need you now. The living do."

"Is Limhi still asleep?"

Noah nodded and took Tamar by the hand, leading her back to their wing of the shared palace home. Tamar finally allowed herself to relax, safe in Noah's arms, his rhythmic breathing coaxing her eyes to close.

———————— ◆ ————————

The bleating of lambs echoed through the approaching dawn. On this day of death and mourning, life marched on.

Limhi cried out, jolting Tamar out of her rest.

She ran to where he slept on the opposite side of the room. "Son, son— it's okay. What's wrong?"

As Tamar smoothed her hand over his forehead, his eyes were wild with fear. He glanced over at his father. Limhi clutched his mother's hand. "I . . . I just had a bad dream . . . about the battle." He sat up and threw his arms around his mother. "I thought I saw Uncle Jarom when he was shot," he whispered in his mother's ear.

Before he could say more, Noah sat up, leaning on one arm. "What's this you said about the battle, son?"

"I . . . nothing. It was a terrible battle, but you fought well, didn't you?"

"Of course he did," Tamar soothed. "He's the army's finest archer. Someday you'll be just like him, won't you?"

Limhi nodded slowly. "Will we help with the burials today? I'd like to."

"That's not work for us to do." Noah's voice graveled from the shadows. "Others take care of those tasks."

"I want to help, to do something for Daniel," Tamar said.

Noah rose abruptly. "We have to prepare for Passover. There's much for the ruling family to do, and you are needed here." He pulled on his robes, slipped on his leather sandals, and ran his fingers through his dark wavy hair. "We have different responsibilities. With Father unwell and Jarom injured, it is up to us to make Passover what it should have been all along. A true celebration."

"We must mourn first, Noah." Tamar stood to face Noah.

"You mourn. I'll be at the weaver's hut getting proper robes made for us all." Noah reached for a loaf of bread on the table, slid the linen cover off, took it in both hands, and ripped it in half. He tossed the other half back into the bowl, uncovered.

Lifting the heavy tapestry that covered the door, he strode through it, slipping out as it fell back into place with a thump, sending a puff of ash from the fire pit.

Tamar turned back to Limhi. He was shaking, his eyes wide with fear. "Son, what's wrong?"

Limhi vomited on the baked clay floor.

As Tamar cleaned up and coaxed him back to sleep, she couldn't get his expression out of her mind. Once he was settled, she slipped out into the courtyard, where she saw Mera kneeling on the soft grass beneath the old maple tree. Its graceful sweeping arms appeared to be closing in to embrace her.

Slowly Tamar approached, careful not to disturb Mera's fervent prayer. Whispered words stumbled out between ragged breaths, and Tamar heard her pleading, sorrow, and promises. She intentionally stepped on an old dry leaf.

Mera's head swiveled around. "Oh, it's you. How are you doing?"

"That's just like you to ask how I am. How are you, Zeniff, Jarom, and poor Sarai?"

Mera stood and extended both arms. The women embraced. "We will get through this," Mera said. "I fear for Zeniff. He's grown so weak. I don't know what I'd do without him." Mera pulled back and looked intently at Tamar. "I'm not even sure who he will ask to be king. He's very unsettled. All night long, he murmured about Jarom's life being in danger." She stopped speaking and shook her head, trying to regain her composure.

Tamar looked away. "I'm glad Jarom's injuries weren't more serious. He should have been more careful. Is Zeniff reluctant to ask Jarom to be king because of his wounds?"

"I don't know." Mera sighed, glancing toward the tapestry door that led to Jarom and Sarai's chambers. "We must be with Sarai for Shiva and with the others who are grieving. I'll ask the healer to come early to dress Zeniff's and Jarom's wounds, then we will weep with those who mourn." Mera stood tall and regal.

"You are a wonderful queen. I hope to be . . . I mean, should I ever have to fill the role of queen, I would hope to be like you."

The opening of Jarom and Sarai's tapestry interrupted their conversation. Two little boys ran outside to where they watered the trees every morning. They were more subdued than normal, but they chattered like all little boys do.

Sarai was the next to emerge. Her eyes were puffy and red. She looked as if she'd not slept at all. "Did you finish making the candles?" she asked Tamar. Her voice was husky and tired.

"I did," Tamar said, "but they are for Passover. Do you not have any in your house for Shiva?"

"I wasn't expecting to bury my brother today, Tamar."

"Of course. I'm sorry. Truly, for Daniel and for Jarom."

Sarai stiffened. "I'm sure you are, you and Noah." Then looking directly at Tamar, she added, "Have you considered what would have happened if Zeniff and Jarom had died?"

Tamar looked from Mera to Sarai and back. "No . . . well, yes, but only for a moment. Zeniff and Jarom will both recover, right?"

"The healer has brought herbs and linens to wrap their wounds." Sarai's expression changed as she turned to face Tamar. "Jarom was shot in the back."

"Surely it was an accident. It was a heated battle," Tamar stammered, her face flushing. "You couldn't possibly be saying . . ."

Sarai looked one last time at Tamar, then turned back to her doorway, lifted the tapestry, and vanished into the darkness.

"I'll get one of the longest candles for Sarai, even if she doesn't deserve it." Tamar paused, then her face softened. "I'll make more later. In fact, I'll take all of my candles to the families who are mourning. That's what you would do, right?

Mera nodded and gave Tamar a light hug. "The day of mourning has begun. We must go gather our families."

———◆———

The fog slowly lifted, but the line of earth-laden baskets carried by man and beast continued. The burial mound, topped by shrouded bodies, soon was covered by a thick layer of rich brown dirt. Seeds were sown atop the mound to ensure a quick growth of spring grasses, and before the sixth hour of the day, the grim task of burying the dead was done.

Tamar took her carefully wrapped candles down from the shelf in their home, her fingers gliding down the smooth surface of each one. These were her finest candles yet. They were to be used in the temple for Passover. She had made them just the right size to fit in the silver candlesticks. Noah would have been so proud of her fine workmanship. She wrapped them back up and joined Mera on the terrace of the palace.

Together they walked from house to house, washing their hands at each doorway and giving a candle to burn for the departed family member. In each home, they sat on the floor on skins that had been placed there for mourners and wept with their friends, neighbors, and loved ones. As they neared the final house, Tamar whispered to Mera, "I don't think I can make any more tears. I'm weary."

As Mera and Tamar rounded the corner near the potter's mound, Noah emerged from one of the huts, followed by several young women.

"What brings you down to this side of town?" he sputtered.

"I could ask you the same thing," Tamar murmured.

One of the girls looked directly at Tamar, "We are fitting Noah with some finer robes for the Passover celebration. The old ones are . . . well . . . old." She tossed her hair, her bangles tinkling.

"So," Tamar began in a sappy voice, "you're out so often you must keep your wet nurse very busy. Your child rarely sees you anymore."

Noah avoided looking at Tamar. One of the other young women added quickly, "His shoulders are too broad and strong to fit in the old robes." Giggles followed. A smile curled at the edges of the girl's lips.

Mera took Tamar by the arm. "Let's finish our duties to the people. Tomorrow we prepare for the Sabbath. There's much to do." They began to walk past Noah. Mera reached out, grasped his arm, and whispered, "Please, go check on your father."

The girls disappeared like the chattering birds of spring startled from their foraging. Noah stood there, alone.

———— ◆ ————

The final Shiva visit was brief. Talk of the family member felt cursory, and Tamar sighed with relief that the task had been completed. There were no tears in her eyes left for weeping. Each candle had been received with appreciation. Each life would be remembered for the full week, and the candles, symbols of their lives of goodness, would burn bright until Passover. A fitting time.

As Mera and Tamar passed the burial mound, Sarai made her way carefully down the hill, helping her aging mother. The old woman stumbled slightly and Sarai caught her, steadying her descent to where a small group had gathered. Several of the high priests were speaking with great emotion, clearly not all in agreement. As the queen's presence was announced, they ceased conversing and asked how the king and Jarom were doing.

Mera gave a brief report, but suggested they go back to check on Zeniff personally. As they walked and talked, some movement on the tower far up on the bluff where Limhi had watched the battle caught Tamar's attention.

She paused for a moment to let her eyes focus. One man stood atop the tower. Taking Mera's arm, she casually suggested, "Let's check one more time at the temple to see what needs to be done to prepare for Passover.

"I'd like to get back to check on Zeniff and Jarom."

"This will only take a moment. I need to make more candles and will need much more wax. Limhi will need time to gather from the combs."

"That's fine, but I'd like to get back."

Tamar's eyes were fixed on the tower.

The man turned, his dark hair silhouetted against the blue sky, his cloak catching the wind and flying out behind him. It was Noah. He looked like a huge bird ready to take flight. A shudder rippled down Tamar's back.

After a brief stop at the temple, Mera and Tamar entered the royal chambers where Zeniff lay, gray and still. The healer was there, rubbing oils and herbs on his chest. She watched him work, fascinated with his skilled hands and obvious knowledge of plants.

Zeniff's voice, gravelly and deep, called out to Tamar. "Please, my daughter, go bring the priests."

Tamar nodded and slipped silently out of the chamber to complete her task.

It didn't take long to locate the high priests and deliver the urgent request to gather in the king's private chambers. She then ran to the bridge, gazing up at the man she loved, the one who, if Jarom did not survive, would be king. She shouted and raised her arms, calling Noah's name. Her voice echoed off the bluff walls, climbing through the trees to the top of the tower where Noah stood. He turned. She shouted again, signaling for him to come. He turned and began his descent. She waited for him to arrive at the bridge, then together they returned to Zeniff's chambers. Tamar called to Sarai through the courtyard, asking her to come and bring Jarom if he was able to walk.

The high priests, Noah, Mera, and Tamar converged on the modest room, squeezing in one person after another, all standing around, looking down at the wounded king. Sarai and Jarom were the last to arrive. Sarai supported Jarom as he slowly moved through the somber group. He winced as his shoulder was jostled, letting out a grunt of pain. Those next to him gave a little more room.

Zeniff's words came slowly, painfully, and deliberately. Although his eyes were closed, it was evident that he was very much aware of who stood by his bedside. "Let me say thank you for all who have stood by me, from Zarahemla, the long journey with great suffering and hardship, to this beautiful place—the land of our first inheritance."

He paused and drew in another shallow breath, struggling to continue. "My wife, Mera, a queen like no other, will be by my side in the eternities. God has promised me this. My sons—like Jacob and Esau or Cain and Abel of our forefathers—could not be more different one from another. Brothers raised the same do not always turn out the same. There is much good to be found in both, but the one who will rule this kingdom after me must be faithful if our people are to be protected and blessed."

After the whispers and murmuring voices calmed, Zeniff asked the high priests to stand together. "Jarom holds the birthright and rightfully should ascend to the throne upon my passing. Thanks be to God that his injuries were not fatal, but the ways of God are mysterious. Why He has seen fit to extend my life while taking young Daniel and others, we know not."

Sarai's lip began to quiver.

"I intend to bestow the crown upon Jarom," Zeniff said. "God's wisdom is eternal and our prayers are that he recovers fully. I have faith that he will be blessed to regain his full strength." He closed his eyes and took several breaths before finishing. "However, if God sees fit to take him home to his eternal rest, who among you will support my son Noah as the next king?"

Silence filled the room. No one raised their hands.

# The Throne

### *Mera, 160 BC*

*M*era stifled a cry of outrage. How dare they not support her family! The high priests fidgeted, but none spoke. And how dare Zeniff place the priests in such a position in front of Noah. Why would he even bring up such a horrible possibility, that Jarom might die, unless . . .

Mera threw back her shoulders. "You're all dismissed. The king and I must speak alone."

None of the priests met her gaze as they filed out of the royal chambers. Noah left the room behind them, his face a blaze of fury, oblivious to Tamar, who was clinging to his arm, whispering something in his ear.

The tapestry swung shut behind them, leaving Mera with Zeniff, whose eyes were closed, and Jarom, who reclined awkwardly in a wooden chair, favoring his bandaged left side. A breeze stirred the still air, setting the linen curtains swaying.

"You too, Jarom." She nodded toward the door.

"I need to stay."

Zeniff nodded and Mera tightened her lips.

"Prop me up a little," Zeniff said, shifting in his bed. "We have much to discuss."

Mera settled him with several pillows behind his back before confronting him. "You're considering conferring the kingdom on Noah." She folded her arms against the chill breeze.

Zeniff's dark eyes gleamed. "I said no such thing. I simply asked if he'd have support should the worst happen."

Mera glanced to Jarom, but he only listened, his expression unreadable.

"You're playing a dangerous game, Zeniff. The priests will believe you're changing your mind. Noah will too. And those priests that didn't support him—" She stormed across the room and closed the reed shutters in the windows.

Zeniff's lips were parched and he reached up to moisten them with a damp cloth. "They'll come around. I can convince them."

"We won't need to convince them! Jarom is fine, or he will be. There's no need to start an uproar." She narrowed her eyes at her husband. "You're not being completely honest with me. When the time comes, you think Noah should be crowned."

Zeniff sighed. "The time is coming faster than you might think, Mera. Look at me." He gestured down his weakened body. "Aaron says I mustn't march to battle again. That means it's time to crown a new king."

"I . . ." Mera sank into a cushioned chair by his bedside, picking up Zeniff's wrinkled hand. Sometimes she forgot how much older he was than her. "But if that's the case, surely Jarom . . ."

"Yes, Jarom is eldest. He is strongest in faith. His character . . ."

"So it was a test?" Mera said. "To see which priests were loyal to him?" Zeniff hesitated.

Jarom cleared his throat and leaned forward, his expression pained. "I cannot be king."

"What?" Mera stood, gathering her shawls against her chest. "Why?"

Jarom shook his head. "You'll think I'm a coward."

"It's the arrow wound, isn't it?" Zeniff said, his expression grave.

Jarom nodded.

"What about it?" Mera hurried to Jarom's side and tried peeling back his bandage. "It's not festering."

Jarom and Zeniff exchanged a glance, and Zeniff's expression darkened.

"What is it?" She placed her hands on her hips, looking between them. "What's going on?"

"I believe it was Noah who shot me." Despite what he'd just said, Jarom's voice was strong and sure.

Mera sank back in her chair. *This couldn't be. Jarom must be mistaken.* "He wouldn't."

"His head guard has kept close watch on me ever since the battle. Amulon even sent Aaron away when he came to check on me." Jarom's right hand clenched. "Noah's motives are not good, Mother, I'm certain of it."

"And you suspected this?" She turned to Zeniff, who sighed and gave a single nod. "But this is all the more reason not to crown Noah. What kind of king will he be if he's willing to kill for power?"

Zeniff looked up at her. "But Jarom will be alive."

Mera gave a sharp exhalation.

"You'll have to guide him, Mera," Zeniff continued, "and Tamar too. She might be the only one who can reach him. Between the two of you, perhaps you can keep him from destroying what we've built here. And Jarom, you can sway him, if only by example."

Jarom remained still. "I won't be staying in Lehi-Nephi. Noah will hunt me down. He'll never feel secure as king unless I am gone. And my sons. I'd live in constant fear for their lives."

"But Jarom—" Mera looked from her broken husband to her sweet, injured son, who rejected power to protect his family. How would she guide Noah without them? "Sarai can't leave so soon after her brother's death. She'll have to sit Shiva. She needs to be with her family. She . . ." Mera's voice shook. "Jarom, what would I do without you?"

------◆------

"The servant will return with Noah soon," Zeniff said, his face grim. "The sooner we tell him, the safer you will be, Jarom. Your family can leave after the coronation."

Jarom flicked the tapestry aside to peer out the doorway before turning a white face back to his parents. "He can't know I'm leaving. He'd throw me in the dungeons. He'll fear I'll rally resistance against him."

"You won't, though," Zeniff said. "You won't tear apart this family."

"Of course not." Jarom returned to his seat, then met his mother's worried look with a somber expression. "I've made the decision to leave here. Since then, the Lord has made it clear to me that I must return to Zarahemla. Like our fathers before us, Lehi and Nephi—our city's namesake. I will obey."

Mera folded her hands in her lap. "I have friends in the city. They'll help you escape, if . . ." She hesitated. "If it's really necessary."

The tapestry rustled and Noah strode into the room, already looking more kingly than Zeniff or Jarom. "What is it? I left Tamar up to her elbows in wax and I've just commissioned new plates for the feast. The potters will work their fingers bloody to finish in time for Passover, but they'll do it." He smiled.

"That's not reasonable," Mera said, unable to stop herself. "Rachel already works long hours. Alma's been stoking the kiln every day. All the apprentices are exhausted. You don't have any idea what you're asking."

Noah shrugged. "They'll manage. How old is Alma anyway?"

"Alma? He's thirteen, almost a man."

"He's always taken a shine to me." Noah brushed the front of his cloak. "I think I'll ask him to join my guard. He's probably strong enough now, with all that work."

Mera threw her hands in the air. How could she support Noah as king? The very idea went against all she believed in. She loved Noah. He was her son. But he was too self-absorbed to be a good leader.

Jarom caught Mera's eye, a pleading look on his face. He always seemed to know what she was thinking.

She glanced down at her hands. Her two boys had clung to them when they were young, one on each side of her. She couldn't let them destroy each other now. She sighed. "Noah, we have some important news."

———— ◆ ————

"You want *me* to be king?" Noah froze where he stood, his crimson cloak swinging to a halt around his legs. "That's not what you said earlier."

"I changed my mind," Zeniff said, looking more weary than ever.

Noah's gaze darted to Jarom, and Mera felt like she'd swallowed a sour persimmon. Noah lowered himself into the chair usually reserved for Zeniff. He surveyed the room before narrowing his eyes at Mera. "Why? Jarom's not dying and you don't think I'm half the man he is."

"That's not true!" Mera gasped. She knew her cheeks were flaming. Noah would take that as confirmation enough.

"I don't want to be king," Jarom said in a reassuring voice, folding his free arm across the one in the sling.

"The responsibility will be good for you, Noah," Zeniff said. He reached for a drink on a small table by his bed. His hand trembled and he shook his head. "Isn't it obvious? I can't do it anymore. You're the only one of us who came home still strong."

Noah's face darkened. "Jarom's strength will return. And the priests want him. They refused to support me, Father, even if Jarom were dead!"

Jarom rose slowly to his feet. "I *won't* be king. Take the throne, Noah. You've always wanted it. It's yours."

"So you refuse the kingdom, just like that?"

"Yes, I do." Jarom resumed his seat and gazed at an empty wall.

"See?" Mera sidled over to Noah. "Jarom will help you. You don't need to worry."

"You're saying he'll be the power behind the throne." The look Noah gave Jarom was so full of loathing that Mera shuddered. "That I'll be a figurehead."

"I'll leave, if that's what you want," Jarom said.

Noah stormed across the room, grabbing his brother by his collar. "You're not going anywhere."

"Stop!" Mera tugged at Noah's shirtsleeves. "You're hurting him."

Zeniff cried out, clutching his chest.

"Father!" Noah turned, releasing Jarom. "Someone call the healer for him."

Mera stepped into the hall and sent a guard after Aaron. When she got back, her sons were arguing at Zeniff's bedside.

"I never realized you felt so close to Father," Jarom said, cradling his sore arm. His clothes were a disheveled mess. "Or are you trying to keep him alive until he can make the announcement? That's what matters to you, isn't it?"

"Jarom!" Mera said. "Don't say such things."

Zeniff pushed up on his elbows. "I'm all right," he said. "I got overexcited."

Jarom leaned down and kissed his father's brow, then left the room.

Noah wiped the kiss away with the edge of his cloak.

"You can be a good man, Noah," Zeniff said, a tear tracing a deep crevice down his cheek and mingling with his gray beard. "I'll talk with the high priests. They'll come around. Just promise me you'll be a good man."

"Oh, I'll try." Noah's face hardened again. "But I'll never be as good as Jarom."

# 5

# Passover

## Tamar, 160 BC

Tamar stood in the courtyard outside the royal chambers and saw every-one exit soon after the healer arrived. The breeze calmed her nerves. Too much had happened in too short a time and the jumble of thoughts careening through her head caused it to throb. She massaged her temples and closed her eyes. The sounds of the evening were deafening—crickets singing, wood being split for dinner fires. Over it all, Tamar heard the voices of her son and his two cousins coming from the woods near the palace.

She opened her eyes long enough to see the three boys sitting together, chatting on a low branch overhanging the river. "Be careful boys. It's getting dark."

In unison, they responded, "We will."

After a time, the healer also slipped out, revealing the darkness of the room. Zeniff would be resting. She felt reluctant to interrupt him, but they needed to speak.

She leaned back against the cool wall, feeling the roughhewn stone with her fingers, tracing the chisel marks as her thoughts wandered back through her day. Taking a deep breath, she slipped into the room.

Zeniff's long white hair had been smoothed back and fell in cascades over the skins that pillowed his head. The room was pungent with the smell of herbs.

Zeniff slowly opened his eyes. "Tamar, come closer." His voice was hoarse and quiet.

She placed her hand on his arm. "I'm so sorry to wake you."

"You didn't. My mind will not rest."

Zeniff took a slow breath, filling his large chest, then said, "Noah will be the next king." He grasped Tamar's arm with unexpected strength. "Guide him. Help him find a way to rule in righteousness. He needs you, Tamar."

The words echoed in Tamar's ears. She hadn't heard much past "king."

"Tamar, did you understand?"

"Yes, oh yes, I understood and certainly will . . . I need to go find Noah."

Before leaving, she grasped Zeniff's weathered hand. It was strong and rough. She squeezed it, then slipped outside. With a mixture of elation and nerves, she passed through the courtyard to where her son and his cousins were still playing, pretending they were battling Lamanites. This thought turned her joy to fear—the thought of these little boys being men and facing the dangers of grown up life in this city. She shuddered.

Loud whispers emerged from the shadows of the palace, far from the king's private chambers.

"He said he doesn't want to be king, that he'll just leave it to me."

"Impossible. Didn't Aaron say he would recover?"

"He just said I could have it, as if it was something he could throw back at me like a discarded play thing. Disgraceful. Watch him for me. He said he would leave the city. I want to know his every . . ."

Tamar pressed herself to the wall, looking for the nearest place to hide. She slipped back inside the courtyard and knelt by the tree where she had seen Mera pray. *Please Lord, I know I have been silent for too long, but in my heart I've known you were always there. Help me. I'm afraid . . . my faith is weak . . .*

A hand rested on her shoulder. She acted surprised.

"Oh, it's you." Tamar stood to face her husband. "Are you all right?"

"I have some news." He spoke with a half smile. "Father plans to crown me king."

"What?" Tamar feigned surprise. "Why? I thought Jarom would be the next king."

Hugging him seemed like the right thing to do, so Tamar buried herself in his arms. "You'll be a wonderful king, won't you."

"Is that a question or statement?"

"A confirmation. I know you can be a great king. I believe in you."

"I'm not my father and I'm definitely not Jarom. I seek a different kind of greatness."

"Why?" Tamar still kept her fingers laced behind his back and arched her neck slightly to look into his face.

"When they're gone, their names will not be remembered. I want my name to be spoken generations after I'm gone. I'll live forever! I want the storytellers to repeat the history of my kingdom—to be talked about from the great sea to the mountains to the land of many waters. That's the kind of glory I plan to achieve." Then, almost as an afterthought, he added, "And you will be the queen of my greatness."

Tamar smiled. For a moment she envisioned what it would be like to be, as he'd said, "The queen of Noah's greatness." Then thoughts she'd kept buried for years came tumbling out. "I'll be that queen for you, the one object of your love and devotion." She paused to build up her nerve, then added, "And no other will share your passion."

Their eyes locked. Tamar felt strong. She didn't look away. She'd found the courage to confront him.

With sweetness reminiscent of their first night as husband and wife, Noah kissed her, pulled her close, and whispered, "You're the only one who shares my bed."

Tamar pulled back. "Are you saying there have been no others?"

"If there were, in the past, you must realize I could not turn them away now. They would be outcasts. The law says they should be stoned. You wouldn't want to be the cause of such a horrible, humiliating death. I'll respect your request but I'll not make them despised of society."

Tamar's stomach twisted.

"They'll be servants. Yes, you need a servant woman to help with the chores. I'll make them respectable in society by letting them be servants of the court." Noah was nearly frothing, his words were coming so fast. "Let them do the cooking, gather wood, grind corn, and do the demeaning tasks. I'll build a new palace for us, for just us, and they can live here in these quarters."

He grasped Tamar's shoulders and pushed her back, to speak face-to-face, away from her tight embrace. "In fact, we can all live in the palace together. I'll be better to Jarom. I'll be good to him and take care of Mother when Father dies. You'll see. I'll be a great king."

Then as if a light came on, Noah added, "I'll wear the robes of the High Priesthood and . . ."

At that moment, Limhi ran into the courtyard with Hiram and Neriah following close behind.

Before Limhi could speak, Tamar announced, "Your father has some wonderful news. He will be the new king!"

———— ◆ ————

Limhi sat quietly in the corner, breaking twigs into tiny pieces and tossing them into the fire.

Noah lay back on his pile of skins. "Sabbath is nearly over and tomorrow we finish preparations for Passover. The people will be expecting to have a new king named this year, since Father is not well—they just won't be expecting it to be me!"

His eyes were wild with excitement. Tamar's face flushed with admiration. "This is what you've always wanted, isn't it? Your dream is coming true."

"Passover will be the grandest ever. I'll see to that. You finish your candles and I'll get servants to do the rest. Mother is busy taking care of Father and no one would expect Sarai to help. She'll carry this Shiva for her brother as long as she can."

"True, but don't speak ill of her. Limhi can hear."

"I understand, but the mourning needs to end so we can celebrate!"

Limhi turned his head halfway around. "Does that mean I will be king someday when I'm older?"

"Well, yes, but I plan to live a very long time so you needn't worry about that. When you do become king, you'll have the grandest kingdom in all the land."

Limhi turned back to the fire, tossing twigs again, one after another. The snapping and crackling sounds of flames consuming the sticks filled the air. Limhi left the fire and curled up in his blanket across the room.

One by one, they drifted off to sleep. Tamar's dreams were horrifying, thick with shifting black mists. They reared up like serpents over a raging fire. The flames burned hot with an acrid stench Tamar couldn't escape. The visions left her exhausted and full of questions. Yet at the same time, she felt a swelling of peace. *How could this be? What did it mean?*

Agitated by her nightmares, Tamar rose earlier than Noah and Limhi. She tiptoed across the cool baked clay floor, picked up a heavy shawl, and slipped out of their quarters. Pulling the wrap tightly around her for warmth in the chilly air, she wished she had taken the time to put on her sandals.

Ribbons of smoke rose from a few of the homes. Chickens were already out scratching the ground for insects. Their heads bobbed up and down in time with their pecking, making them all look like they were dancing to the beat of some distant drum. The lambs were all awake and calling to their mothers. What could possibly be done to make this place better? It was perfect as it was.

No one else in the palace had wakened, so the courtyard was hers alone. She made her way to Mera's place of prayer and knelt down. Her knees quickly became cold and wet with the morning dew. *Lord, I know that all things are in thy hands. Please help me to be a good queen. Bless Noah to be a good king. Limhi is young but I've taught him thy ways. Please help me know how to teach him righteous leadership.*

A calmness came over her like falling leaves. One thought after another came, each laying gently over the one before, building up to a mound of understanding. Tamar knew she would have more to do than she had previously planned, now that she would soon become the queen. Making candles would not be her only task. She stood resolutely and tiptoed back to her life with determination she hadn't felt before.

"Limhi, son, it's time to wake up." Tamar stroked his hair, smoothing the cowlick that swirled up over his dark eyebrows. When his brown eyes opened, they revealed something Tamar had not often seen in them, fear. He rose up and wrapped his arms around her and squeezed tight, and whispered, "I'll protect you, Mom—always."

"I know. I love you."

Noah roused and announced, while still lying on his bed of sheepskin, "It's the beginning of a new day, a new way, and a new kingdom. I can see it now, a grand palace, robes of fine linen, and a throne fit for a king. We will have servants and grand celebrations, starting with my coronation . . ."

"Passover, my dear. The coronation is part of it but the purpose is to celebrate our freedom—"

"Yes, all of that," Noah interrupted, "but crowning a new king is a substantial part." He paused. "I know how important this is to you, to us, and to our people, so just remind me if I get too caught up in the excitement of my new place in society. I mean, our place in society, our family—Limhi, you too. This will be a big week for all of us."

"Well, let's begin by thanking the Lord that Jarom will recover and asking for peace and comfort for those who are still mourning."

Noah threw off his blankets. "Speaking of Jarom, I need to go check on him, so you go ahead and pray without me." He ran his fingers through his thick, dark hair, smoothing out some of the curls at the back. Those in the front just did what they wanted, making him maddeningly handsome, even in the morning. Tamar and Limhi knelt beside the fireplace where some warm coals still glowed bright, and they talked with God. Noah slipped out the door without a sound.

After the morning chores, Tamar sent Limhi out to the woods to gather wax from the old bee tree. "Remember to put the oil on your arms to keep the bees from stinging you. I don't want you all swollen for your father's big day."

"I don't really care," Limhi said in a soft voice.

"You don't care about being stung or about your father's day?"

"Both," Limhi said.

"Come, let me help you. I don't want you to be the cause of little bee deaths," Tamar said.

Limhi smiled. "Okay, to keep the bees alive, go ahead." Tamar smoothed the oil over his exposed skin and kissed his forehead.

"Be safe."

Limhi chuckled as he trotted down the trail and into the woods.

She watched him go, puzzled at the change that had come over him.

———— • ◆ • ————

Tamar made her way to the bridge that led to the pasture filled with sheep. Lambs were a few months old now and frolicked about, jumping over tufts of tender green grass and chasing each other. Tamar was not the only one heading that direction. Many of the women from the city were also crossing the river, some with children, some with husbands, and others alone.

Tamar found Mera in the throng and came up beside her. "How is Zeniff today?"

"He's sleeping. I don't think he will be up much today. He's physically drained and emotionally spent."

"How is Jarom?"

"Sarai said his wound isn't red, there is less oozing, and it appears to be closing up. He's in a great deal of pain still."

"Are you choosing a Passover lamb for them too?"

"We will share. I don't think Zeniff will eat much, so one will be enough for us all."

"There are fewer of us. We would be happy to share."

"Thank you. I think it would be nice for us all to feast together, but I'm just not sure everyone would enjoy that."

"I wish it weren't so. I'd love to spend more time with Sarai and Jarom and the boys. It's just so hard when . . ." Tamar's voice trailed off, letting the thought get lost in the jumble of others' conversations.

The crowd had moved across the bridge and the people fanned out, looking for their Passover lambs. It became quite a frenzy with little lambs bleating for their mothers, and ewes calling to their babies.

When it was all done, Tamar and Mera returned to the city, where an unusual excitement buzzed in the air. The feast and coronation celebrations had been taken over by Noah. He was surrounded by his friends, and every few seconds someone in the group would race off in one direction or another, bringing back artisans and craftsmen. The crowd grew by the minute, pushing ever closer to the center of activity, Noah.

The potter and apprentice ran past, stopping for a moment to congratulate Mera on what a fine leader Noah was becoming. "He's paying us handsomely for a whole list of new things. We will be busy for months!"

A new young weaver had set up his own shop and eagerly waved his cloth in the air until he got Noah's attention. The young man also took the time to congratulate Mera on the fine taste her son had. "I'll be weaving for a year to do what Noah wants for the new palace!"

As they neared the tight cluster, money was being exchanged, more money than Tamar had seen in a long time. Excited shopkeepers and artisans exclaimed how they'd be able to expand their businesses and begin trading with nearby cities with all of the new work Noah was providing. "What a blessing Noah is for our city!" they all said.

The group was comprised of some of the finest artisans the city had, notably, Yoseph, who carried the title of master weaver. Absent in this group were the high priests. Mera took Tamar's hand. "Let's go to the temple."

They arrived just as a number of the high priests were leaving, heading toward the palace. Mera stopped them. "What's going on?"

"Noah has taken money from the treasury. He says it's for Passover and necessary things. We tried to stop him, but he forced his way in and took what he wanted. Zeniff needs to fix this before it gets out of hand."

"He's sleeping. Please let him rest," Mera pleaded.

"This is important. He must stop Noah while he's still king."

Tamar slipped away as Mera and the high priests discussed the unfolding drama. The crowd around her husband had grown and included many of the pretty girls that always seemed to appear when she was not around. She slipped past the craftsmen who had returned with samples of their work to show Noah, others were scratching on rolls of parchment, notes and sketches. When she finally got close enough to Noah, there was no way to discuss anything privately, so she put her arm around him and gently squeezed.

"Hey now, ladies. One at a time. I'll get to you . . ." He swung his arm to embrace whoever had hugged him, turned, and saw it was Tamar.

Her face flushed with embarrassment. "Can we talk . . . in private?"

"I'm very busy. Can it wait?"

"Are you sure this is the right way to go about this? Shouldn't you be discussing this with the queen? This is more her responsibility."

Noah turned to the crowd. "It looks like my wife needs me, so I'll have to ask you all to give me a moment." He pulled Tamar close and matched her steps. They walked a short distance from the crowd and Noah buried his face in her scarf and whispered a curt message. "Stay out of my way. You're my wife and will be queen, but don't ever question me in front of my people again." He pulled back and with a huge smile, gave her a kiss on the cheek. "I'll see you at evening meal."

Tamar watched him stroll away, trying not to show the shock on her face. She had just been scolded and dismissed.

After this, Passover became a blur for Tamar. She went through the motions, not feeling the reason for the feast: freedom, deliverance, gratitude, and being led by God. Instead she felt captive, ungrateful, and lost.

When the sacrificial lamb burned upon the altar, the memory of her nightmare returned. The images were fuzzy, but what had not been lost was the image of an altar, piled high with branches, smoke ascending like the angry green billowing clouds of a whirlwind in spring. A sure sign of destruction.

# 6

# The Move

## *Mera, 160 BC*

*M*oist clay seeped through Mera's fingers, the soft glob taking shape as the wheel in front of her spun. She pumped her foot, working the lever that turned it. The clay rose, its middle growing slimmer with a little pressure from her fingers. Every touch, every gentle stroke shaped it. This was something she could master, something she could control.

Passover had ended, Noah's coronation had been announced, and Mera felt as if angry snakes had taken up residence in her stomach. She'd prayed, tried to find peace. But she still felt that Noah shouldn't be king. She wished she hadn't agreed. If only she'd pressed harder, maybe Zeniff and Jarom would have found a way for Jarom to rule in safety. Noah could have been his chief advisor.

But that would never work. One step from the throne, Noah would be more dangerous than ever. If only she could persuade Jarom to stay. He could influence Noah, mentor him.

Mera frowned, focusing on her vase. The only way she knew to work out her feelings was with her hands—weaving, gardening, or her favorite, pottery. Her handiwork may not be perfect, but at least it obeyed her.

Outside the studio, children rattled by, the closed drapes doing little to shut out their shouts. The sounds reminded Mera of her sons, how they'd laugh, fight, then laugh again. But that hadn't happened in years. Not the laughing part, anyway.

"Careful, Mera." Rachel leaned around her shoulder, covering Mera's hands with hers, giving them a slight pull. "You're squeezing too hard."

"Oh no!" Mera's vase wobbled, but Rachel's master touch made all the difference. Together they shifted the clay a bit at a time until it stood straight and tall.

"Keep pumping the wheel," Rachel said, wiping her fingers on her smock before moving to Naomi, another novice potter.

"Don't be smearing my masterpiece with Mera's brown clay, Rachel." She leaned forward, protective, and a strand of her long, dark hair caught in the clay. She shrieked as it spun in a hopeless tangle, slicing through her soft, white bowl.

A young man burst through the linen drapes, carrying with him a strong smell of smoke, fear etched into his sharply planed face. "Mother, I heard you cry out."

"I'm fine, Alma." Naomi pulled her hair from the clay. "What a mess."

Alma sank into the chair beside her, looking relieved. His long lanky legs blocked the only walkway.

"Don't get soot everywhere," Rachel chided, nudging him out of the chair.

He stood, then widened his eyes at Mera. "Queen Mera." Alma bowed his head in respect. "I didn't notice you there."

"It's all right, Alma." Mera looked up from her piece, which was finally taking shape. It was almost what she had in mind. "I've been making pots alongside your mother since you were five. You know I don't stand on ceremony. Not here, anyway."

"But, Your Majesty, I'll be in the palace soon. If I breach protocol there—"

"What's this?" Naomi said.

"Noah asked me to join his guard. I'm to be fitted with armor. I'll be using Father's old sword." Alma's face shone, but Naomi looked crestfallen.

"But if you finish your apprenticeship here, at the kiln, you could be a craftsman. You could make swords instead of going to battle. Then—" Naomi looked away.

Alma knelt beside his mother. "Don't worry, Mama. Father taught me to be strong. He would've been honored to see me serve the king. Oh!" He stood and glanced over to Mera. "Noah sent me to tell you that he and Tamar are moving into the royal chambers tonight instead of next month. That way he'll be ready for the coronation tomorrow."

"Tonight?" Mera's vase collapsed under the pressure of her fingers. "But Zeniff is still frail. If we move now he'll grow weaker. Attending the coronation is one thing, but changing quarters?"

"He said to tell you Jarom would help." Alma flushed, wiping his sooty hands on his pants.

"Jarom. With his injured shoulder." The clay weighed heavy in Mera's hands.

Rachel and Naomi shared a dark glance.

"Go ahead home, Mera," Rachel said and Naomi nodded. "We'll clean up here."

Mera scraped the ruined vase from her palms and rinsed her hands in a basin on the workbench. Already, Noah was growing more inconsiderate and self-absorbed. There was only one solution. Jarom would have to stay. They would confront Noah together.

———— ◆ ————

Mera swept aside the tapestry to find the royal chambers abustle with movement. Jarom directed servants laden with small tables and clay pots. Sarai was dusting and packing Mera's favorite wall hangings. Zeniff stood, leaning against the bedpost, sorting cloaks into baskets, his face the color of a pale gray brewing storm.

Mera gasped. "Zeniff! Sit down this instant."

All action in the room stopped. Zeniff turned tired eyes on his wife. "This must be done, however difficult it may be."

"Those things stay here." Mera took a painted flowerpot from one of the women, returning it to its place by the window.

The other servants looked to Zeniff, who sighed and nodded for them to exit. They set down their burdens and filed out of the room. "Helam—" Zeniff turned to Jarom's head guard, who'd been watching the courtyard for intruders. "Please see that they don't go far. We'll need their help again soon."

"Of course." Helam bowed his head. "I'll return shortly."

"We will *not* be needing their help again soon because we're not moving until next month," Mera said.

"He's a good man, that one," Zeniff nodded toward the doorway. "Have you thought to bring him with you, Jarom?"

Mera put her hands on her hips. "Don't pretend you didn't hear me."

Zeniff sighed and sank into a sitting position on the bed and before he could breathe in a sigh, Mera was there trying, without success, to force him to lie back. "You need your rest. We will move in a month, as planned. I don't know what Noah is thinking to spring this on us." Shaking her head she added, "He isn't thinking at all."

"He's thinking, but just of himself, Mother," Jarom said, a tinge bitterness underlying his voice. He'd found a stool and was sitting awkwardly, favoring his left shoulder as usual. Sarai started folding bed linens from a basket that had toppled. "It's Noah's way," Jarom said. "Always has been—only it's worse now."

"We must appease him," Zeniff said. "It's a simple request. Inconvenient, but simple. And I understand him laying claim to the royal chambers. He's about to become king."

"You never would have done this," Mera said.

Zeniff rubbed his forehead. "I promise not to overexert myself. Neither will Jarom. That's why we have servants and guards helping us." He took Mera's hand. "We'll be fine. It's just a move across the courtyard."

Mera stifled a sob. "That's not the point. How could Noah ask us to move now when you're both recovering? It's as if he doesn't care."

Jarom's face tightened. "Let's just get it done, Mother."

Mera took a deep breath, then nodded.

A dark-haired boy peeked through the tapestry, then stepped inside. "I hope we never move, Mama." Neriah surveyed the cluttered room with distaste. "Pup would tear everything up."

Sarai rose, piling the bed linens into their basket. "Pup's asleep. You should be sleeping too."

Neriah jutted out his bottom lip. "But what about Grandma and Grandpa? Why should they move? They've been here their whole lives."

"No, we haven't." Mera knelt in front of the boy. "We've only been here *your* whole life."

"That's the same thing." Neriah gave her a stubborn glare. "You shouldn't have to go."

Sarai shot a worried look to Jarom.

"I've moved many times in my life, Neriah," Mera said. "This time it's only across the courtyard."

"So you're not leaving the palace?" he persisted.

"No, but if we were, we'd still be together, in here." Mera placed a hand over her heart.

Neriah's small arms snaked around Mera's neck.

"No more dawdling, son." Sarai's voice caught. "Kiss your Grandma and Grandpa, then it's back to bed."

Neriah planted a wet kiss on Mera's cheek, then scrambled across the room to where Zeniff now lay resting on the bed. Zeniff's eyes twinkled at the sight of his grandson scurrying toward him.

Mera held her temper in until after Neriah left. "And you're still planning to leave the city, I suppose?" she said to Jarom. "Think what that will do to your sons. All they know is Lehi-Nephi. They'll be raised away from friends and family. You'll be alone."

"It will be far worse if we stay." Jarom leaned forward, then winced.

Mera turned on Sarai. "Have you told Avi and Lisha?"

"Of course. They're furious."

"Avi, furious?"

"Well, no. My sister's furious." Sarai's voice broke. "My mother's devastated. Oh, can't you see we don't have any other choice?" Her eyes shone. "I don't want to leave you or Zeniff or my family, especially so soon after Daniel's death. I don't want to leave at all." Sarai looked away, her cheeks flaming.

Zeniff pushed up on his elbows, struggling to sit upright. "Don't make this more difficult than it has to be, Mera."

"Difficult?" Mera cast an indignant glance around the disordered room. "I'm not the one making this difficult. I wouldn't have thrown over Jarom and put Noah on the throne. I would've listened to God. He doesn't want our kingdom led astray. He doesn't want—"

"The decision is made, Mother. My family is leaving," Jarom said. "With or without your help. I believe the Lord is calling me elsewhere."

Mera felt like a batch of bread dough that had just been punched down. She sank onto the cushioned stool beside the bed. Everyone's eyes were on her, Jarom's determined, Zeniff's resigned, Sarai's teary.

"It's the only way, Mother. We've announced Noah's coronation already," Jarom said. "There's no going back. If I don't leave, he'll kill me and my sons"—Sarai gave a soft cry—"or imprison us, at the very least."

"I'll help," Mera said in a soft voice. "I've already spoken to Rachel, in case it came to this. She's arranged safe places we can hide if Noah's guards spot us leaving."

"We? You're not coming with us, Mother," Jarom said firmly.

Mera gave him a steely look. "I'll see you to the city walls. Your father cannot. But I will, and don't try to convince me otherwise."

"Wait until after the coronation, when Noah is drunk from celebrating," Zeniff said.

Jarom nodded, thoughtful. "We'll bring Helam along to escort Mother safely back to the palace."

"If Noah's men find me, they'll think I went to the temple."

"In the dead of night?" Zeniff raised a brow. "When the temple is closed?"

"I could walk the temple grounds at night, seeking solace. That's why I'd bring a guard."

Jarom's lips pursed. "Better be rejoicing instead. Noah wouldn't like the idea of you grieving when he's just been crowned."

Mera nodded.

"You could bring an offering," Sarai said, her forehead wrinkled with concern. "That would make sense." Her dark eyes fastened on Mera. "Thank you for coming with us. I can hardly bear this as it is."

"Come with you where?" a deep voice boomed as Noah pulled the tapestry aside and entered the room. "You can hardly bear what?" He looked from Sarai to Jarom, his eyes narrowing. "Don't even think of leaving here, brother. You'll bow before me like everyone else."

# Coronation

## Tamar, 160 BC

*T*amar shifted in her seat and the stiff robes, with all the newness of freshly woven linen, didn't shift with her. She looked out over the faces of those she had grown up with, learned from, loved, and even a few she distinctly disliked. The tall wooden menorah, carved long ago by a very old friend of Zeniff's, held the largest candles she had ever made. Their light flickered, casting dancing shadows across the faces of the high priests who stood behind it.

People made their way to the temple where the altar smoldered with glowing coals from the evening sacrifice. Now the people waited anxiously to see the new king crowned.

Zeniff rose slowly, using a shepherd's crook for support.

"Many years ago, I used this crook to guide our little flock through miles of pastureland, forest, and field. We came to this place, the land of our first inheritance, to reclaim what was once ours. The journey was difficult." He turned to look back at Mera. "I felt like a shepherd, leading a flock of like-minded people. Some of you remember that journey. Others have gone to their final resting places. Newcomers may be learning this part of our history for the first time.

"Many have given their lives to protect and preserve our freedom. God has granted me a long life. I thank Him for that. Soon I will stand before Him." With a somber expression, he said the words the crowd anticipated. "Before that day comes, I will name a new king."

A hush settled over the crowd. Even the little children seemed to be holding their breath. Eyes moved back and forth from one end of the row where Jarom sat to the other end of the row where Noah sat.

Zeniff held out his left hand, pointing to Noah. "My son Noah will be your new king."

Tamar moved to grasp Noah's hand before he stood, but he leapt out of his seat, knocking her hand away, oblivious to her gesture. She quickly tucked it back in her lap. Then she reached over to clutch Limhi's hand. They watched as Zeniff removed the crown from his own head and placed it on the head of his younger son.

There were whispers, then someone from the back of the crowd shouted, "Long live King Zeniff!"

A few others joined him.

Before things got too far out of hand, a group of Noah's friends stood and shouted, "Long live King Noah!" The shouts rang out. The nervous crowd joined in until those cheering for Zeniff were drowned out by everyone else.

Zeniff took his staff, turned, and slowly sat down. Tamar saw the look he exchanged with his wife. Some in the crowd were looking expectantly at Jarom and Sarai, who sat stone-faced, watching the proceedings.

Noah rose to his full height. His new robes, woven with golden threads and adorned with jewels, shimmered in the firelight, sending flashes of light into the crowd at every turn. He slowly pivoted and scanned the crowd.

A flash of memory, a horrible lifelike dream that lurked in the back of Tamar's mind, caused her to cry out. Her hand flew to her mouth to cover the sound. Tears sprang to her eyes, followed, yet again, by the strangely familiar sense of peace.

"My people!" Noah began. "We will see this city grow to become the greatest in the land. Greater than Zarahemla!" His eyes were on fire as the glow of the menorah reflected on them. He spread his arms wide, letting the full effect of his new robes and crown fill the people's view. "We will embark on a journey of greatness unlike any other journey before. The name of this great city will no longer be Lehi-Nephi, but will now be Shilom."

A gasp escaped the lips of many in the crowd and everyone else seated behind him. Zeniff raised his hand briefly, as if he wanted to stop what was now happening. Then his hand fell into his lap, and his eyes closed, head bowed, as if in prayer.

"Shilom will have only the best of what the land has to offer. The finest craftsmen will be employed to build a new palace!" His voice boomed across the crowd. More than before, the people cheered wildly. "I'll give everyone work and pay you well!" Now the crowd was in a frenzy. Only a few remained still, watching this spectacle unfold. "Everything will be new, including the high priests."

An audible gasp escaped many lips. A hush fell over the crowd. Shock and surprise passed over the faces of the sitting high priests as they turned one to another, then all at once, to Zeniff.

"Come forward, those whom I have invited to be our new high priests."

Hesitantly, a few men exchanged glances. "Come now, don't be afraid. The people will love you as they love me!"

Tamar felt her heart sink. One by one, men who were friends of Noah, who stood to gain by his position, who traveled with him on trading expeditions and cheered loudly with each new announcement, now surrounded him. The light from the menorah no longer cast its glow upon Noah. He stood shrouded in darkness as he stood with his new leaders.

Tamar waited for her introduction as the new queen. She had braided her hair in Noah's favorite style and worn the gown he gave her as a gift for this night. He just kept talking. All of the dreams she had heard him speak of for years were now being shared publicly. The words came out in ribbons as colorful as the weavings Mera created. Noah had a gift for words and he mesmerized the people with his vision of this new kingdom. He whipped the people into a cheering, dancing, reveling mass.

Someone added wood to the altar near the temple and before long, the crowd had left the palace and moved to encircle the growing flame, led by Noah. The rest of the royal family had been all but forgotten.

An old weathered man slowly made his way to the line of stunned family members, still seated behind where Noah had been crowned. It was the storyteller, who kept the history of this people, and who was nearing the end of his own story. The tales of ancient Israel had fascinated Tamar all of her younger years. She leaned forward in anticipation of another story.

He rose to his full height, as straight as he could, and said, "This day will live in infamy like the day Moses found the children of Israel worshipping the golden calf." The storyteller turned and walked slowly back to his humble cottage, far from the now raucous group of people dancing and shouting around the blazing altar, oblivious to the prophetic words that had just been uttered.

Those who had cheered for Zeniff as well as others close to the royal family remained in the shadows. Tamar watched with trepidation as several in the celebrating group brought in the firkins of wine that Noah had specially prepared for his coronation—stronger than what was normally consumed. The people cheered and began passing goblets around, filled with the potent wine. It didn't take long for the gathering to become vile. The women tossed their scarves in the air, gripped their skirts in their hands, and danced. Higher and higher their hems were flung until Tamar turned in embarrassment. She couldn't help but see the similarity between Moses's people and hers.

*These are my people. I am their queen. Lord, help me be like Esther of old.* Tamar squeezed her eyes closed for a moment, willing the jumbled images of her nightmare and the reality of what was unfolding in front of her to vanish. *I don't know what is real anymore. Lord, help me find my footing.*

A hand rested on her shoulder.

Limhi.

She could feel the weight of his young hand. She reached up and covered his hand with hers. After gripping his young fingers, Tamar stood to face him. "You are a gift to me. A gift from God, and I love you." She stepped around her chair and wrapped her arms around her son, holding him tight, shielding his eyes from the unusual display of defiance to the laws and practices that had been kept under Zeniff's rule. "Let's go home."

Suddenly, the fire flared, casting dancing shadows into the darkness. Although her back was to the altar, flames illuminated the buildings and trees, sending a long shadow of her and Limhi standing together. She turned. What Tamar saw next made her blood run chill. Those whom Noah had appointed as new high priests were tearing the holy robes from the shoulders of Zeniff's old high priests and tossing them on the fire. The royal family had not interfered, until now.

In a few strides, Jarom stood behind Noah, grasped his shoulders, leaned forward, and spoke into Noah's ear. In a flash, Noah spun around, flinging his brother's hands away. Jarom winced in pain, grabbing at his shoulder.

Before she could stifle it, Tamar's voice rang out with a cry of, "No!"

Noah called to his guards, "Take him to his quarters. Confine him there." Two soldiers rushed to secure Jarom's hands. "Never lay hands on me again," Noah sneered as they took Jarom away.

Mera was running toward the old high priests, who, one by one, were being stripped of their robes. There were but three left when she pushed her way through the crowd. Tamar was frozen in place, unsure of whether she should, or could, get involved. *His own mother . . .* Tamar feared what would happen next.

Mera stood in front of the last remaining men with her arms outstretched.

"I'll not stand by and watch this any longer. Stop. Now."

Noah, fully drunk, leaned over and kissed his mother. Then he gently moved her aside as he methodically removed the cloak from another high priest, never letting his eyes leave hers. It was a dangerous dance. The singing had stopped as the drama unfolded.

Melek, the eldest of the high priests, said in a calm voice. "I don't need a robe to know that my authority comes from God. You can take mine." He handed his own robe over to Noah. "But you cannot take away what God has given."

The remaining priest did the same. Mera's eyes were ablaze as she watched her son cast the remaining three cloaks on the fire. It roared, the flames soaring higher.

"Now that everyone"—he looked at Mera—"understands who is in charge, let's begin a new tradition. You all like traditions." Noah stood in front of the remaining people and stretched his arms out once again. "From now on, when the sun rises on our city of Shilom, all will bow to the throne, whether I'm sitting in it or not." Noah scanned the crowd. He teetered and Amulon grabbed his shoulders. "Go get the throne, Amulon. Let's put it right here by the altar."

Amulon and a few other men disappeared into the darkness while Noah continued his drunken rant.

Tamar pushed Limhi behind her. "Go home. You don't need to see any more." Limhi resisted for a second, then obediently vanished into the night. Tamar turned back as Noah took each priest that had been stripped of his robe and forced them to kneel. "You now bow to me. I am your new king." Then Noah looked around as if searching for someone. "Where's my family?"

"Noah, they've gone to bed." Tamar eased closer. "We can work through all of this tomorrow."

Noah laughed a deep, long laugh. "They will learn to show obeisance to me, as they have to their God."

Amulon and the others returned with the throne and placed it at the head of the altar. Noah swirled his colorful glistening cloak and in one sweeping motion landed himself squarely in the throne.

"Tomorrow, all will bow to me!"

Rachel stood in the shadows near the temple. As Tamar and Mera stepped out of the chaos, Rachel reached out to embrace Mera. They spoke in whispers until Tamar grasped Mera's arm. "We need to get back to our families. Sarai was left to help Zeniff to his bed and our children are probably frightened." Rachel nodded with a worried expression, still clinging to Mera's arm. "We must go, now." Rachel released her grip.

Tamar and Mera retreated to their disheveled living quarters.

This was going to be a long night.

# Betrayal

## *Mera, 160 BC*

*M*era waited several hours after Tamar left for the royal chambers. She lay in bed beside Zeniff in their new, smaller room, his grunting snores reassuring her that he was still alive. She stared at the dark ceiling. Their place was still a mess, baskets unpacked and strewn haphazardly about. But that wasn't what kept Mera awake. The image of Noah tossing the high priests' robes into the fire burned in her memory. How could he take such a drastic step just moments after being crowned?

*Thank heavens Melek didn't resist.*

There was no telling what Noah would've done. Mera shuddered, not wanting to think on it. One thing was certain, Jarom must leave tonight. Mera had already set the plans in motion. Noah would be livid if he ever found out she'd been involved. But what choice did she have? Clearly Jarom could hold no sway over Noah, not without ending up imprisoned—or worse. It would be up to Mera and Zeniff, and hopefully Tamar, to rein Noah in.

She pushed her furs aside and placed a gentle hand on Zeniff's shoulder. She hated waking him, but she'd promised.

"It's time?" Zeniff whispered mid snore. He rolled over and stroked her cheek.

"Yes. I'll be back as soon"—Mera's voice hitched—"just as soon as I can." She picked up a small bundle and tucked it into her robes.

Zeniff sighed and pushed up on his elbows. "I should come."

"We've been over this. Jarom knows you'd do anything for him. This time that means staying here. You've said your goodbyes?"

Zeniff nodded. "Be safe. I pray the Lord watches over you."

———— ◆ ————

Jarom's wound had reopened from Noah's rough handling. Mera pressed a linen dressing to it while Sarai hovered in the background, gathering the remaining essentials. Neriah and Hiram slept in the corner, curled around their dog.

"I'm fine, Mother," Jarom said, though he sounded tired. "It doesn't matter if it scars."

Helam, the guard, slipped in through the tapestry-hung doorway, scanning the room, vigilant as always. "The guards outside Jarom's quarters are passed out with drink. Everyone in the courtyard is asleep too, including the king. It should be hours before they wake. I doubt even if the sun will rouse them with all the wine they've had."

"Then the time has come," Jarom said in a sure voice. He squeezed Mera's arm, then shouldered his pack, heavy with tools, bedrolls, dried meats, and breads. His face tightened with pain. "Wake the children, Sarai, but keep them quiet."

Sarai raised her brows, then proceeded. The boys moaned and burrowed deeper in their covers. "Come along," she said softly.

Neriah rubbed sleep from his eyes. "It's nighttime."

"I know. Don't wake Pup. We're taking a walk. I have packs for you and Hiram."

Hiram climbed out from under the bedding, blinking in the dim candlelight as he accepted his bag. Mera pressed his favorite ball of string into his hand—it would help him pass the time on the long journey. He looked confused but didn't comment.

Mera swallowed. She would miss him. She'd miss them all.

Neriah studied Jarom's huge pack, his small face growing sober. "We're going away, aren't we?"

Jarom paused in adjusting his straps. "This place is not safe for us anymore. We'll find Zarahemla. There are prophets there, and a good king. At least that's what your Grandpa always says."

Mera nodded. "Come now, before the guards wake."

Neriah bit his lip, looking over at the dog, who was whimpering in her sleep. "It's not fair. Why should we have to leave now because Uncle Noah's king? Grandma and Grandpa only had to move to different rooms." His voice rose. "And what about Pup? I'm not leaving Pup."

"Hush, Neriah, we must keep quiet," Sarai said, kneeling before her oldest son. She looked strained, as if living the last few days had taken all her strength. "Pup's too loud and wild. I wish we could bring her. But we can't."

Neriah wiped a grubby hand across his eyes.

"Grandma and Grandpa will care for her like she's their very own," Sarai added.

Mera tried to look earnest. It was difficult because Jarom was rolling his eyes.

Slightly mollified, Neriah picked up his pack, then paused. "If we leave here, I'll never be king."

"That's right, son," Jarom said, "but you'll be alive. I can't promise as much if we stay." He glanced at Helam, who nodded, then Jarom snuffed out their candle and the small group crept into the courtyard.

The night was chill, the moon as thin as pounded iron, shedding almost no light. Men lay sprawled wherever they'd dropped during Noah's celebrations. In the darkness, it looked like the battlefields Mera experienced in the many conflicts with the Lamanites, bodies everywhere, splattered in blood. This is what she was saving Jarom from, and his family, too.

"We'll need the oil lamp so we don't tread on someone and wake them," Helam said in a hushed voice. Sarai passed him a lamp, which he lit, then prowled ahead of them as they picked their way through the sleeping forms, his hand on his sword.

Mera paused as she skirted Noah. In sleep, he still looked innocent, the way he had when he was young. He grunted and rolled over, mumbling a strange girl's name. Mera froze. What if he woke now, with her bending over him and Jarom's family creeping through the courtyard? He moaned again, throwing his arm across his face, then fell still.

Mera hurried off, catching up with the others. With the Lord's help, maybe she could teach Noah new ways. Different from what he had in mind, of course, but she was his mother. She'd make him listen.

The little group reached the edge of the courtyard, escaping into the city beyond. They hurried through the shadowy market where buildings loomed like hulking beasts. Something clattered behind them and Mera and the others whirled around. It was only a rat picking through garbage, its scratching magnified in the still night.

About halfway through the city, Helam darted ahead, searching for dangers.

The moment he was out of sight, a huge figure emerged from behind one of the stalls, blocking Jarom's path. Amulon, Noah's head guard. "I knew you'd try something like this." He swayed a little, blinking bleary eyes. "I warned Noah and he told me to watch you."

"King Noah, you mean," Jarom said evenly. "You ought to show some respect."

Amulon's face twisted. "We'll see how you respect Noah after he's taught you a lesson." The guard made a grab at Jarom's injured shoulder but missed, snagging his fingers in Jarom's robe.

Jarom whipped away, clubbing him in the side. Amulon grunted and stumbled backward, uttering a low, repulsive laugh. Then he plunged his fist into Jarom's stomach.

Jarom doubled over.

"I'd kill you," Amulon said, fingering a dagger at his belt, "but Noah wouldn't want you dying in a dark alley." He chuckled again, grabbing Jarom and pounding his wounded left shoulder. "Something more public, now that's another story."

"Stop!" Mera hissed. She spotted Helam creeping up behind the fighting men. If she could just keep Noah's guard distracted. "Amulon, you're better than this. Think of Jarom's family."

Sarai and the boys huddled behind her. Neriah struggled against his mother's grip. "Let me help!"

"I am thinking of his family," Amulon said, eyeing her strangely. "His brother. The king." He yanked on Jarom's pack, dragging him back toward the distant courtyard. Jarom kicked at Amulon's knee. The blow connected and Amulon howled in rage. He pulled out his dagger.

Helam was close now, carrying a heavy stone. Mera forced herself not to look at him. She scrambled closer. "Put the knife away, Amulon."

"Grandma!" Hiram cried, watching the scene from between fingers pressed to his face.

Amulon turned an ugly glare on her. He darted forward, his knife hand swinging. But before he reached Mera, Helam rose up behind him and slammed the stone into his head. Amulon collapsed to the ground, unconscious.

Helam drew out his sword.

"Wait," Jarom commanded. He drew himself upright. "We don't need to kill him."

"He could wake and rouse the others," Helam said, holding his sword tip near Amulon's exposed throat. "He doesn't deserve your mercy, my lord."

"I'm not granting him mercy," Jarom said. "I'm protecting you. I'd never best Amulon with this lame shoulder. If he dies by the sword tonight, Noah will suspect you. He knows you're my head guard. When I'm gone, I need you to protect my parents and Limhi. He's done nothing to deserve a father like Noah. But if the king thinks you had a hand in this, you'll be hanged."

Helam's hand quivered.

"He's right, Helam," Mera said. "Amulon may not have seen you with us. We need you. You're one of the few guards we know we can trust."

Helam met her gaze for a moment, as if he were measuring her somehow. Then he sheathed his sword. "Between the wine and the blow to the head, most likely Amulon won't remember what happened. But if he does, I'll be there to protect you."

———— ◆ ————

The little group spent the next hour hiding in a safe place Mera's friend Rachel had arranged for them, in case they'd been followed by other guards.

"Thank you," Mera told her before they slipped away for their final destination—the city wall. "I will never forget what you've done this night."

Rachel's round face softened. "I'd do anything for you, my queen, you know that."

They hugged, and then Sarai embraced Rachel as well. "I wish I'd be here to see your Gideon grow up. He'll be a fine man, someday."

Then, without any more words, they slipped away to meet Sarai's family at the farthest gate from the palace, where Helam had stationed guards loyal to Jarom. This little band of refugees waded through the thigh-high waters of the river that ran through the city, to throw Pup off their trail. The sky had lightened to dim gray at the horizon, but sunrise was still hours away.

"I always thought you'd be queen." Sarai's younger sister twisted the edge of her robe. Her eyes shone in the frail lamplight. "I envied you. Now you're leaving."

"Be quiet, Lisha, or they'll discover us," their mother said, "and Sarai will be killed."

Mera couldn't remember Avi looking so old. She seemed as if she'd aged a century in the last few weeks, her skin thin and gray as crumbled slate. "No one's killing Sarai," Mera said.

Lisha's eyes hardened. No one so young should look so desperate. "If they do, then it's only me left to tend Mama." She pulled her black scarf a little tighter, as if its presence would make her forget her loneliness. "You told me God watched over the righteous," she said with an accusing look at Avi. "But He didn't watch over Daniel. I fear He won't watch over Sarai either."

Sarai squeezed her sister's hand. "You must be strong, Lisha. You're our family's future here. Don't let grief destroy your faith."

"The Lord's word and His ways *do* protect us, Lisha," Mera said, "but He will never control us. He will never take away our choices. Ours or our enemy's. But He will bring you comfort, if you let Him."

Lisha's unsure gaze lingered on Mera, and then Lisha turned back to her sister. "Find a way to send me letters, Sarai. Or better yet"—she gave a half-laugh half-cry—"find a way to come back. You can tell me what they wear in Zarahemla."

The sisters embraced.

Neriah tugged Mera's shirtsleeves. "Grandma? Will you rub Pup's ears? She really likes that." He hiccuped. "I don't want her to miss me too much."

"I'll take good care of Pup, I promise." Mera slipped a small bundle from inside her robe. "And I brought this for you." A tiny puppy rested in her arms, snuffling softly in his sleep. "He's too young to make any more noise than that. I know it's not Pup, but—"

Neriah grabbed the puppy tight against his chest. "Thank you," he whispered.

"Are you sure you're strong enough to carry the puppy and your pack?" Jarom asked with a weary smile.

"I can help," Hiram piped up, absently turning his ball of string in his hand. "And when he gets bigger, I'll make him a leash out of my string."

Mera let out a long, low breath. The boys would adapt. They were young. They were strong. Jarom and Sarai were too. But oh, how she'd miss them.

"We'll cross the river again to hide our scent," Jarom said. "Noah will use Pup to try and find us." A light breeze lifted his hair away from his face, then fell back, covering the old scar from his childhood. Mera reached up and let her hand brush across the crescent shape. "What will I do without you?"

He pulled her into a tight hug and then kissed her cheek. "I'll find my way back someday, Mother, when Noah's grown used to ruling and no longer sees me as a threat."

Mera swallowed a sob. She squeezed Jarom and then let him go. "Be safe, my son."

The little family made their way through the gate into the darkness, leaving Helam to stand watch. Lisha slipped her fingers into Avi's hand. The three women stood side-by-side, blinking back tears as Jarom's tiny lamplight disappeared in the night.

———— ◆ ————

Mera waited alone, atop the cliff behind Shilom, the rock beneath her cold and unyielding. She had climbed the stone steps that led to the tower, desperate to watch Jarom and his family for as long as she could. The flame from their oil lamps wove through the pasturelands before disappearing into the forest.

Mera pulled her wrap tight around her shoulders, but it didn't shield her from the chill or the dark. Her breaths came tight, hanging in the air. She knew she should've returned to the palace instead of dismissing Helam. Avi and Lisha were long gone. She should've rushed back to reassure Zeniff that they were safe, but he was sure to be sleeping. She needed these few moments alone.

The moments stretched into hours.

She sat there the rest of the night, praying, pleading. Now she waited, quiet, with nothing left to say and the darkness feeling endless.

When Zeniff first journeyed to Lehi-Nephi, they built the city from nothing but crumbled ruins. When Mera was young, she helped clear the land. She gathered tall grasses to make bricks for the walls. As she grew, she caught the eye of the king. His first wife had died childless and he'd remained alone many years. But something about Mera had called to him.

He claimed it was her gentle spirit. She teased him that it had more to do with her fine weaving. Either way, after four moons of courtship, they united in marriage. She became queen. The people rejoiced. Every night the people gathered and told ancient stories. The stars smiled down upon them.

Now Noah had forbidden those stories. Even the name of the city had changed.

*Dear Lord, I can't live like this forever. Noah was such a good boy. Please remind him. You have to remind him. He doesn't listen to me.*

No answer. Just the cold distance of the stars, fading as dawn came—a seeping spill of gray, navy, and indigo, then fiery pink, orange, and gold.

*God won't force Noah,* Mera thought, *but I will persuade him. He has to listen to reason.*

She stood with an aching stretch, brushed off her skirts, and began the slow, weary trek toward home.

# Discovery

## *Tamar, 160 BC*

*I*n her dreams, Tamar walked through tall grass, and a little creature kept nipping at her toes. Pup. She bent to pick her up, but the dog ran back to the woods, barking. She kept barking, and the further she got away from Tamar, the louder the barking became. Finally Tamar turned in her bed, pulling the soft sheepskin under her chin, its curly fibers tickling her nose. She was awake, but Pup's commotion from her dream continued.

She rolled over, seeing a crack of light slicing through the darkness of their new room. Disoriented, memories coming in slowly, she remembered the move, the coronation and the drunken state of her husband and the new high priests who celebrated long into the night. She lay for a moment, collecting her thoughts and rubbing sleep from her eyes. The barking continued.

"Goodness sakes. Limhi, can you go and see why the dog is barking?"

Limhi too rolled over and gave a sleepy, "Sure, Mom." He appeared as confused as Tamar for a moment as his eyes adjusted in the darkness to the new, larger living quarters. "I'll start the fire too." He climbed out of his bed and pulled his outer robes on, slipping sandals over his bare feet. Limhi had his routine and followed it. A quick prayer, splashing water on his face from the pot on the table, and running wet fingers through his hair. He poured a drink from a ceramic pitcher into a cup he had made with his grandmother at the potter's shed. He sighed a deep sigh. "Did Father ever come home?"

Embarrassed, Tamar responded with a quick, "No."

"Where does he sleep when he doesn't come home?"

Tamar didn't answer.

Without saying another word, Limhi went into the courtyard to gather wood for the fire and to quiet the dog.

Tamar also followed her typical morning routine, but hastened to try and find Noah before the people of the city awoke to find him drunk, or worse, in someone else's bed. Tamar pulled her outer robe on, fastening it around her slender waist with a pretty woven ribbon Noah had ordered for her. It matched her favorite shawl, which she pulled over her head and around her neck.

She slipped out through the heavy tapestry door and into the early morning light. The air was fresh and cool. She inhaled deeply, taking in the beauty of this place. Anxious to find Noah, she surveyed the quiet street and descended from the palace platform. As she rounded the corner to the courtyard where the temple altar and tower stood, she stopped. The scene disgusted her. Bile rose in her throat.

She hurried to where her husband lay, unconscious in the grass. As she stooped to brush the hair off of his face, he muttered a name she didn't recognize. His hand flew up and grabbed hers. His bloodshot eyes opened and he stared at her.

"Noah, get up. Come home and get cleaned up for your first day as king."

Recognition registered and he quickly rolled over and sat up. Both hands flew to his head and he groaned.

"I'll get some herbs to help with your head and stomach. Try not to move quickly, but let's get away from here before the city wakes and sees you in this condition."

Noah laughed roughly. "Half of the city was with us last night. Not you though. You're too good for us. Good little Tamar. Queen Tamar." His words were still slightly slurred. He patted her roughly on the head.

Tamar flushed as she helped Noah rise. Together they walked arm in arm toward the palace.

Pup was now running at full speed away from the palace with Limhi in full pursuit.

"Pup!" he cried as she ran toward them. "Come back here!"

The barking was too much for Noah's head and he shouted, "Somebody kill that dog!"

"Noah!" Tamar breathed.

He swung a leg to kick Pup as she ran past, and instead of connecting with the dog, his leg wound around Tamar and both tumbled to the ground. While they untangled themselves, a few people woke. The reveling masses from the night before looked like rising spirits of the dead. The sober townspeople were also waking and coming out to see what the commotion was about. Tamar helped Noah to his feet and brushed the grass and dirt from his heavy woven royal robe and from her colorful shawl. "Just walk with me."

Noah's arm draped over Tamar's shoulder and they walked slowly toward their new living quarters, nodding to people as they passed, trying to appear as though they were out for a morning stroll. The gazes of sympathetic friends confirmed Tamar's fears. They knew.

Pup's barking had woken the town. Everything was moving, albeit a bit slower for some. Limhi caught the puppy and was carrying and soothing her as they walked. He reached Tamar and Noah as they began the climb up to their quarters.

"Where are Hiram and Neriah, Mom?" he asked.

Noah froze and looked directly at his son. "What do you mean, where are they?"

"They're not in their quarters. Sarai, Jarom and . . ." Before Limhi could finish, Noah was scrambling up the grassy slope to the palace, stumbling over his new robes and falling a time or two. He ran headlong to the wing where Jarom and Sarai lived and tore at the tapestry, revealing the empty interior of their home.

"Amulon!" Noah roared. "Where are they?" He spun around and saw two guards passed out, leaning against the courtyard wall. "Guards!" Noah kicked them, hard. They both jolted awake.

Wheeling around, he looked at Tamar. "Do you know where they've gone?"

"No, I was in our room all night long. I have no idea . . ."

Noah grabbed Tamar's scarf and pulled her close. "If you had anything to do with them leaving . . ." His hot breath smelled of foul grapes. "I'll have you thrown in prison, or worse."

Tamar was shaking and pulled away. "Don't threaten me. You're drunk."

He released his grip and pushed her away.

"Amulon! Guards!" Noah's voice echoed from the bluffs and rang through the city. Soldiers came rushing toward him. Clearly, not everyone had partaken of the wine from the night before. "Find Jarom. Bring him to me." They fanned out and began searching the streets and homes.

Noah made his way to the palace and stormed into his room, tearing the tapestry and knocking over the table. A pot crashed to the floor, spilling water everywhere and sending shards of pottery across the room. Noah cursed and ran his fingers through his hair, pacing across the room. The water left a blood-like stain as it soaked into the clay floor. Tamar began picking up the pieces. She was always picking up the pieces.

"Why does it matter to you if Jarom and Sarai left?"

"I wanted to establish once and for all that I was the king. I was successful. I was right. I was first." Noah continued pacing. "I've never been those things and I wanted to see Jarom's face as he bowed to me. Just once, I wanted to be better than him."

Tamar's heart hurt for him. "You don't need to do any of that. You're good in many ways. You don't have to prove it to him; you just need to prove it to yourself." Tamar paused as words flooded her mind. "Do you believe me, that you are good, and that you can be better? You don't need to compete with him. Just be yourself. Be the man I married. Be the man I love." She slipped her arms around him, stopping his pacing for a moment. "You're not perfect. I'd say you could do some things better. But you'll never be Jarom, so be the best you."

Noah's eyes took on a flame of anger and he took her hands from behind his back and pulled them roughly away, gripping her fingers tightly, more tightly than Tamar thought was necessary. "You still love him, don't you?"

"No!"

"You liked him first, before me, and now you compare me to him. I'm your husband, not him. Don't ever bring his name into this room."

Tamar, shocked by his reaction, tried to undo the harm from what she thought were helpful words of encouragement. It seemed that nothing she did was right. He was always angry.

Soldiers interrupted their moment with cries of Amulon being injured and calling for Noah to come. Noah freed her hands and rushed from the room.

By the time Tamar got back outside, a group of soldiers carrying Amulon made their way up to the palace grounds and carefully laid the injured advisor on the grass. "Call for the healer," Noah said. "Tamar, bring your herbs."

"He's been hit on the head, we found him beside one of the homes near the river."

"Search the river, cross the river, search the . . ." he paused. "Limhi, bring me Pup!" Noah chuckled. "That dog will lead us to Jarom."

Limhi emerged from Jarom's quarters holding the now quiet dog.

"Give me the dog, son."

"Why?"

"Let her go so she can find Hiram and Neriah. I'm sure she misses them."

"You said you'd kill her."

"I'd never kill an innocent beast or person. Just a guilty one. I've forgiven Pup now and want her to go free." Noah's voice took on a hard tone. "Let her go."

Limhi stooped, not taking his eyes off of his father as he slowly placed the dog on the ground. The barking began again and the dog, confused, began running back toward her old home, then to the altar and zigzagging from structure to structure, almost as if she were tracing each step Hiram and Neriah had taken over the past week. Noah didn't need to ask. All of the soldiers followed, which was a rather humorous sight, soldiers chasing a frantic dog.

The healer arrived and began dressing Amulon's wounds, which caused him to rouse. He mumbled a few sounds, nothing discernible until he managed to say, "Mera."

A wave of panic washed over Tamar.

# 10

## Desecration

### Mera, 160 BC

The morning sun warmed Mera's face as she made her way home. As she crossed the bridge over the river that divided the city, she wondered if she'd always feel split in two. Half of her heart with Jarom and half with Noah.

The city was starting to wake, smoke unfurling from small dwellings as women stoked their fires and prepared the morning meal. Dogs barked and a few children were already tossing sticks in front of their homes. Mera picked up her pace. It wouldn't do to arrive back at the palace after Noah woke. She didn't have much to worry about, of course; he was rather drunken from his celebrations.

Mera was just passing the burial mound when she heard it, the stomp of a hundred feet, the shouts of the palace guard, and Noah bellowing orders. Soldiers poured into the open space between the burial grounds and the palace. Without thinking, Mera ducked behind the mound, her heart fluttering in her throat. If Noah found her now, she'd lose any chance she had to influence him. A cold chill ran up her arms. She might lose more than that.

Keeping low, Mera crept around the burial mound, making her way to the temple. It was her only hope. Noah would believe she'd gone there to worship. That was her way.

While the soldiers fanned out to search the city and check both gates, Pup lollopped among them, howling and yipping. Mera groaned. Why hadn't they thought to tie Pup in their quarters? At least Jarom's scent would be long gone.

Guards marched between Mera and the temple, their swords gleaming in the morning light. She crouched behind one of Rachel's safe houses, wondering if she dared dart around front and slip inside.

"When you find Jarom, send me word," Noah barked. He stood just feet from where Mera was hiding, Tamar at his side, looking disheveled. "I'll search the homes around the palace."

"Noah, be reasonable." Tamar tugged his arm, but he threw her off. "No one will be hiding Jarom in the city."

"I'll not be undermined by my brother."

"If you search these homes, you'll undermine yourself," Tamar said, and Mera felt impressed by the girl's nerve. Tamar didn't usually stand up to Noah, not that Mera had seen. "The people will hate you if you ransack their homes. None of them are fool enough to shelter Jarom. Make a show of strength at the gates."

Noah nodded, rubbing his brow. "That blasted sunlight is killing my head." He looked around. Mera ducked a little lower, sweat running down her back despite the cool morning air. "Pup headed toward the far gates, didn't she? Come." He beckoned to Tamar, who swallowed, her expression tight as she took his offered arm.

Mera waited until they disappeared around the burial mound before rushing across the clearing toward the temple. Reaching the palace would be impossible at this point, with all the soldiers running around. She took the temple steps two at a time, forgetting to look worshipful. As she closed the wood door behind her, she thought she heard a crunch of boots on gravel. Had the soldiers seen her? Would they report what they'd seen to Noah?

She leaned against the door, her chest heaving. A priest sat at a table, his head bent as he studied scrolls by candlelight. Mera's throat itched. She hadn't thought of this complication. Had Noah's new priests already taken over the temple?

The priest raised his head, then gave her a respectful nod. "My queen."

Mera felt a rush of relief. "Melek. I didn't know you without your robes."

The former high priest wore a grave expression. "Until Noah forces me from the temple, I will serve, high priest robes or no." He rose, carried an armful of scrolls to the wall behind the altar, pried loose a great stone, and hid several scrolls inside before wedging it back among the others.

"What are you doing?" Mera asked.

Melek's expression was grave. "We must preserve our records. Noah's priests will destroy them and write their own." His gaze roved over Mera, lingering on her hair, which had come loose as she ran. "You came here for comfort."

"Oh . . . yes."

"You're welcome to stay as long as you need. Many saints stay the night at the temple in times of great sorrow or rejoicing. I am certain Noah will honor the way you've passed his first night as king."

Mera opened her mouth to say she hadn't been here all night, but of course, Melek knew that. He was granting her sanctuary and was willing to brave the wrath of the king. "Thank you, Melek. Rachel is blessed to have you." She crossed the room, lit a candle, then knelt to pray.

*Dear Lord, please protect Jarom and his family. Soften Noah's heart and help him change his ways. Help him know we love him and that he can be a great man if he can just manage to be a good one.*

Barks filled the courtyard outside the temple. The wooden doors flew open, clattering against the stone walls.

"Mother!" Noah burst inside, not bothering to close the doors to keep the dog out. Pup bounded up to Mera and licked her full in the face. "You think to hide here in the temple?"

Mera rose to her feet, trying to maintain what dignity she had left. "I have no need to hide, Noah. I simply came to worship and to rejoice as you took the throne."

Noah's face twisted, as if his fury were a bottomless pit. Tamar stumbled through the temple doors, breathless, too late to stop him from stepping toward Mera, grabbing her by her cloak. "I smell night air on you, Mother."

"That's impossible," Melek said, setting aside the scrolls and moving toward them. "You can see for yourself the queen has been here in prayer. Perhaps it is the incense you're smelling."

Noah's eyes narrowed at Melek. "You're no longer a high priest and have no business being here interfering."

Mera hadn't moved. She remained two inches from Noah with his hands fisted in her cloak. "Since when do you treat me with such disrespect?"

Noah thrust her away from him, as if touching her were somehow painful. "Since you helped Jarom escape! I know you were there. Melek chose wrong in hiding the truth from me. Now he'll rot in prison."

Mera stumbled against a table, toppling a candle. It snuffed out, spilling wax along the linen tablecloth. "I didn't . . . he didn't lie."

Noah overturned several other tables, then tore away the curtain between the main chamber and the Holy of Holies, striding inside and knocking down the altar. "These relics mean nothing. My priests will commission new, better ones. New king, new ways." He spun around and glared at Mera. "Amulon saw you in the city last night before Jarom attacked him." He advanced on her, spit flying. "He mentioned your name. You'll rot in prison, with this false priest." He gestured to Melek, who several guards now held by the arms.

"Noah!" Tamar pressed up against him. "Amulon was raving. He was fevered or drunk. He didn't know what he was saying."

Noah turned on her. "Everyone heard him, Tamar! What army would follow me if my own family is against me? If I don't take care of this"—he flung an angry hand toward Mera—"they'll never respect me!"

"The *people* will never respect you if you're cruel to your family," Tamar said. "They love your mother. They'll follow her lead. Let her stand beside you. She can tell them you sent Jarom away. That was all the commotion this morning, not that he escaped. If they see your parents stand beside you and they know Jarom is long gone, the people will rally behind you. And those that suspect the truth will see this as an act of mercy. You'll win their hearts today, Noah. This will set the tone for your reign."

Not once did Tamar look at Mera. What was going on in her daughter-in-law's head was a mystery to Mera. Was she trying to retain power or was she protecting the former queen?

Noah huffed out an angry breath, deflating just a bit. Could it be that Tamar could sway him? Mera's hopes rose, not just for herself, but for her family, for her people, and for her son.

He turned pleading eyes on her. "Why, Mother? Why are you against me?"

Mera sat on the table she'd ruined, too exhausted to consider how irreverent that was. The temple was in shambles anyway. "I'm not against you,

Noah. Jarom wanted to leave. He sought a different life." She looked around the demolished room, her eyes skipping from one disaster to the next. "I thought to strengthen your reign, Noah, not undermine you."

Mera tried not to flinch at the half truth. Her true purpose had been to protect Jarom, the rightful king, the man who should be leading their people, even if by protecting him, she ensured that would never happen. She'd given no thought to Noah at all, except to deceive him. But some deceptions were good, weren't they?

There she sat, in the ruined remains of the temple, misleading the highest leader of the land. It didn't feel like a good omen.

# 11

# Riotous Living

## *Tamar, 157 BC*

Tamar moved silently, stepping quickly like the squirrels that scurried around the grain storage hut waiting for an errant kernel to fall to the ground. Noah had come home angry, but she managed to coax him to bed, giving him herbs to soothe his aching head and sick stomach from all of the wine he had consumed. In his years of being king, this was a regular occurrence.

He had fallen fast asleep and she didn't know what his demeanor would be when he wakened, so she drew out the silence as long as she could, fearing at any moment he would emerge like a whirlwind in a spring thunderstorm.

She managed to fill all of the water pots, empty the old ones, refill the grain bin, and brush dirt from the floor all before seeing Noah's body shift beneath the skin blankets piled high on the bed. He groaned.

Tamar put a pot over the fire to heat water for tea. He was going to need some chamomile and lavender today. She put some dry leaves and stems into a cup, awaiting warm water. Limhi had already left, his morning routine complete.

Noah drew in a deep breath. "Tamar, what are you doing at this hour? Come back to bed."

"It's long past morning. I tried to be quiet to let you sleep."

"I know when a Lamanite walks too close to our city. I can hear every step you take."

"How are you feeling—your head?"

"My head is fine. I'd like some food. There's much to do today."

"I can't imagine you'd be hungry after such a night of feasting."

Noah groaned again. "Passover is better every year. Coronation year was the beginning of my greatness and with a celebration lasting all night. Look at what we've done with a new palace, nearly complete."

"Remember the first Passover as king?"

"If you're asking if I remember Mother's betrayal at my coronation and her constant meddling ever since, yes, it's burned into my memory. It's the last Passover Mother and Father attended with me. I'm reminded of it every day as mother goes to the old temple instead of my new one."

"Your temple in the new palace is certainly impressive." Tamar knew she could divert his anger if she could get him to talk about his achievements.

"Egyptians built larger structures, but my palace is the finest in this land. I've seen every city from the mountains to the great deep. There's nothing to compare with what we've built in Shilom."

Noah's voice rose. "Mother won't even go in to see the carvings, the gold candlesticks, the forged hinges, doors that open and close with the slightest touch, thin leather to let in light, and actual altars of gold. The high priests will each have their own place of honor, high above those who come to worship the gods of Shilom. Travelers now come just to see my fine structures. People know my name, Tamar!" He spread both arms out wide. "This is my dream." Noah began placing heavy gold rings on his fingers and suddenly shifted his focus. "I'm missing one of my rings." He looked on the bed, stooped down, and looked on the baked clay floor.

"Maybe you left it . . . where you were last night."

Noah paused, rubbed his head and wrinkled his forehead, then grinned. "Oh, possibly, yes . . . likely it is in the guest wing here in the old palace." He sat back on the bed.

Tamar closed her eyes and her shoulders drooped just a bit as she cast her face toward heaven. *Lord, how long must I endure this?*

"Pray elsewhere. Not in this house. No more prayers from you or Limhi. No public praying unless it's in the new temple. Anything other than that will be a betrayal." He paused. "Just like Mother."

Tamar opened her eyes and sighed. "Your mother didn't betray you. If anything over these years, it's you who's betrayed her. Your parents will never pray in your temple. Now you threaten to not allow us to pray at all. Noah, it's who we are, down to our very center we look to God for guidance and peace. You know that; it's how you were raised. Do you truly not believe?"

"I don't. I stopped believing when I saw that God didn't speak to me like everyone else. Father, Jarom, and even Limhi claim to hear or feel God's voice. For me, there is nothing. I believe in myself."

"He's there. I know it. If you'd but listen—"

"He's not and we won't talk of this again. No prayers. Not here, not in the city, not in the temple—"

"Noah! You cannot destroy this people's faith!"

"Watch me."

Tamar trembled as the man she once loved rose up from his bed, stood at his full stature, and vowed to crush what she held dear.

"I'll not accept this." Tamar's heart raced. She could feel each beat thumping in her chest. "I'll not stand by your side if that is going to be your path."

"That's a bold statement. Do you not wish to be queen any longer?"

Noah had moved slowly toward Tamar with each exchange till he stood directly over her, hands on his hips, bare chest rising with each breath. In her mind she heard the words of Zeniff, *You can influence him to be better.* Then, as if all other sounds in the room faded in the morning sun, another sound entered her mind. It was a voice almost like her father's and it said, *Teach Limhi the ways of righteousness and help him see the consequences of wickedness. I will be with you through your trials. Be still and know that I am God.*

". . . and then we will build the new tower next to the new temple."

"You're building a new tower?"

"Didn't you hear anything I said?" Noah's voice tightened.

Tamar stumbled over her words. "Yes, I mean, not that last part, but the rest, yes."

"I said, I'm not destroying the religion, I'm just going to improve on it, making changes to suit our new city and make it fit our new name. The old ways will be done away, but I won't leave the people without something to worship. A God needs to be visible, not imagined. I have built a temple to our God, and all who go there will be able to see Him, feel Him, and touch Him. He will be real to them."

Tamar whispered her response. "God *is* real to me. That you can never take from me." She turned and left Noah standing in his loincloth and bare feet.

Tamar hurried to the wing of the palace that used to be her family's quarters and called for Mera.

Mera's tired face peered from behind the tapestry.

"How are you?"

Mera's eyes teared up.

Tamar reached through the doorway and drew her into an embrace. "It'll be okay. We have each other." Tamar took locks of Mera's hair in both hands, drew the long greying tresses to the front of Mera's gown, and let them fall. "I may be the queen, but you left mighty big sandals for me to walk in. I still have not filled them. We must lead our people, help them stay in the way of truth."

"You're doing well."

"So many are falling into the paths of sin and becoming more like Noah." Tamar's hands knotted in worry. "I don't know what to do."

Mera smiled. "I think you do. You're already doing it."

Tamar closed her eyes for a moment, then took in a deep breath. She reached out and grasped Mera's hands. "How is Zeniff today?"

"He had a bad night and is still sleeping. When he wakes, I would love to get him out of this room and into the warm sunlight."

"I'll ask Limhi to help. Maybe he can stay with him. I need for you to come with me somewhere." Mera's puzzled expression didn't deter Tamar. "Please just come for a walk with me."

"Send Limhi and we will go."

———— ◆ ————

Tamar walked through the city, calling for Limhi, looking in all of the usual places.

As she gazed over the green pastures of Shilom, she recognized his brightly woven cloak. The man standing next to him wore the robes of a royal guard. Helam.

Tamar crossed the bridge and watched the interaction between them. Helam appeared to be showing Limhi how to use the atlatl. She could see Helam's tall form reach back with the long spear-like arrow and then lunge forward in one smooth motion, launching it far across the pasture. Limhi retrieved several before Tamar reached them.

"Limhi, I need to speak with you." Tamar moved through the green grass, her robes grazing the tops of the clover. Limhi ran to greet her. She put her arm around his shoulders and turned back toward the city. "Zeniff would like to spend some time out in the spring sunshine. Would you take him for a short walk and sit with him?"

Before Limhi could even answer, a voice from behind interrupted their conversation. "I couldn't help but overhear. I would be happy to accompany them, lending my arm to Zeniff as well." Helam came and placed his hand on Limhi's shoulder. "Your son has a natural skill with the spear. He'll make a fine soldier one day, like his father. "

Tamar cringed, not wishing Limhi to follow in any of Noah's footsteps. Helam quickly added, "He's a faithful young man with a good heart."

"Thank you. I'm glad you see the good in him too."

"Did you see him throw the atlatl?" Limhi asked. "He's incredible."

"I did."

"Can I teach him?" Helam asked. "He desires to learn."

"That would be wonderful. Yes." Tamar tousled Limhi's hair. "Now please take your grandfather for a walk. Mera is waiting."

Tamar watched Helam and Limhi walk together toward Shilom. *Lord, why couldn't Limhi have had a father like Helam?*

———— ◆ ————

Tamar's solitary walk back to town was pleasant. She pondered what to say to Mera, knowing the words would add more weight to an already unbearable burden. It had to be done. When she arrived at the palace, Mera was waiting near the long walkway that led to their three living quarters. Jarom and Sarai's wing was usually vacant, except for when the frequent travelers and guests of the king came to stay. Tamar chose not to think of that now. She felt something akin to courage rising in her bosom, and she felt she now had purpose but lacked a path. Mera would help with that.

"It's such a lovely morning," Tamar said as she neared Mera. "I've enjoyed the peaceful walk. It gave me time to think."

"What's on your mind?"

"Let's go where we have some privacy."

Arm in arm they walked through the woods, past groves of trees, vines clinging to the trunks, and tendrils of the same vines hanging like dry snakes from the branches. "It's amazing what light does. What seems dark and dreary at night, with light is graceful and beautiful."

Mera nodded, evidently deep in thought.

They followed a well-worn path along the river for some time, and in the distance the trees cleared out. The sun's rays drilled shafts through the shadows, setting the surface of the water on fire. The ripples of the spring-fed pond glittered like gold.

"I love this place." Tamar's words came out in a sigh.

"It's a shame Noah has never come with us to see this." Mera waved her hand through the air as if gently brushing the branches. "Truly this is almost as beautiful as the temple—but adorned with God's majesty, not man's."

"I agree." Tamar nodded.

The two women sat on a boulder near the water's edge, letting the sun warm their faces. "You asked me to come so we could talk," Mera said. "Are you ready to tell me what's on your mind?"

Without meeting Mera's gaze, Tamar let the words flow. "Noah has refused to let us pray in our home. He's already made changes with his new temple and he lets us do what we wished with the old one, but I fear that our lives are about to change in some very painful ways. What will we do if we cannot pray?"

Expecting a very different reaction, Mera didn't seem as upset by the news as Tamar expected. After a moment of thought she spoke. "Do you always pray out loud, kneeling?"

"No, why?"

"Do you feel that words must be spoken for God to know our hearts?"

"When you say it that way, I do ask things from time to time, not in the kneeling and bowing head kind of way, and feel that the Lord guides me. I never really thought of those conversations as prayer."

"I believe they are prayers of the heart. We can also sing the songs of our ancestors. I know God hears our songs of praise and knows our desires." Mera's eyes teared up. "He hears them." She breathed deeply and grasped Tamar's hands, facing her as they sat in that beautiful place. "If, indeed, Noah will make his will law, and forbid us to pray, then we go to the Lord in our hearts and minds. Noah cannot take that from us."

# Uprising

*Mera, 155 BC*

Mera felt sick seeing row after row of clay idols lining the shelves in the master potter's studio. She knew Rachel hated making them. Her assistant, Naomi, hated it too, and so did the apprentices. Mera flat-out refused to do it. Of course, she only crafted pottery as a hobby, and as the king's mother, she wasn't likely to be thrown in prison for defying his orders. It wasn't right, though, that he forced Rachel and the others to violate their conscience and create false idols for worship.

She settled herself at her usual table and turned to the master potter's son. "Gideon, would you fetch me some of the red clay?" A light-haired boy of about eight scurried to the stores against the wall. "He's grown so tall, Rachel."

At the table across from her, Rachel lit up. The light in her face disappeared almost as quickly as it had come. "Melek would be proud of what a good boy his son is. But we haven't been allowed in to see Melek since Passover."

Gideon's hazel eyes darted to Mera's and away as he placed a slab of clay on her work surface, taking care not to soil her aproned dress with stray flecks.

"It isn't right, Mera," Naomi said as she placed the final touches on a figurine of a howling wolf.

Lisha worked beside her, carving a lump of clay into what, Mera couldn't tell. Sarai's petite younger sister was now nearly seventeen and determined to show her worth as a future potter. Mera had encouraged her, if only to help keep the girl's mind off Sarai and Jarom. It helped Mera. At least she thought it did.

"Noah shouldn't have kept Melek in prison this long," Naomi continued.

Rachel's mouth tightened.

"Of course he shouldn't," Mera snapped, gouging her smooth clay with a stone knife. "All these idols aren't right either." She waved the knife at the overburdened shelves. "But the more I correct Noah, the more he pushes me away. He's replaced all the priests with his friends."

Rachel stiffened. "He did that years ago, Mera. That's why Melek's in prison."

Mera sniffed. "Melek's in prison because of me. Because he protected me. And now Noah's replaced even the lesser priests."

"Alma's a priest now," Lisha said, a gleam in her dark eyes. "You should be glad for that, Naomi, having a son as a priest in Noah's court. Not everyone can claim that kind of honor."

Naomi carried her finished wolf to the shelf of pieces awaiting the kiln, setting it down with more force than was necessary.

A cool breeze gusted through the stall, setting the linen walls dancing. Naomi sighed as she returned to her seat with a fresh ball of clay. "I'm not certain that's a good thing, Lisha."

"But why?" the girl asked. Her sculpture was looking even less like any sort of shape Mera could recognize.

"What we need are real priests, who truly believe," Mera said. "I don't mean to speak harshly of Alma, Naomi, I know he does what he can—"

Naomi's pitch increased. "He listens to Noah now and Amulon. Not to me. It's like all the things I taught him since he was a small boy don't matter. Like everything I've done didn't matter. Why won't he listen?"

Mera shook her head. "I don't have the answer to that. I wish I did. Should I throw a water pot, Rachel, or do you need more cups?"

"Cups," Rachel said. "These idols have put me so far behind on my regular work that people will soon be using turtle shells for their drink."

"Mama?" Gideon tugged at his mother's rolled up sleeve. "If Daddy were here, he'd teach us the true ways, wouldn't he? We'd pray together."

"Hush, Gideon." Rachel cast a terrified look toward the swaying curtains. "No one must hear us speak of prayer."

Mera gritted her teeth, her brow furrowing as she crafted a perfectly symmetrical cup, as good as any the master potter had ever made. "This is why I love coming here," she said under her breath. "Because I can make a good, useful cup. And if the clay doesn't do what I want, I just crush it down and start over."

Naomi raised a brow but didn't say anything.

"And for all of you, of course," Mera said. "I don't know what I'd do without you."

"You'd talk to Tamar, for starters," Rachel said, without looking at Mera. "From what I hear, she's more of an ally to you than you realize. You're not alone."

Mera leaned back in her chair. "You shouldn't be alone either." She lowered her voice. "And you're right." She nodded toward Naomi. "Melek's been in prison far longer than is reasonable. All he did was stand up for me."

"He's a threat to your son," Rachel said. "That's his real crime." She picked a glob of clay off the ground. "I'm sorry, but it is."

Mera paused, her mind working furiously. "Noah is wrong to demand idol worship and to imprison the priests."

Rachel gave a curt nod. "He shouldn't be trading with the Lamanites either. He seems inspired by their ways. Sometimes I wonder if Zeniff's choice to lead us here and make a place right alongside the Lamanites has condemned us."

"Don't say that." Mera fingers tightened on her cup, her nails cutting into its sides. She pursed her lips as she tried to smooth over the damage.

Rachel looked up from her work. "How many concubines does Noah have now? Too many to count, and half of them Lamanite women, whispering in his ear. It's a dangerous situation, and not just for the king."

"You can't lay all that on Zeniff. Even in his weak state, he teaches Noah." Mera folded her hands in her lap. "We both do."

Rachel sighed. "I know. I'm sorry. I don't mean to cast blame. It's just, on top of everything else, Noah's taxing us one-fifth of what we own. Not what we earn, but what we own, all that we've sacrificed to build."

Mera glanced to Naomi. Without a husband, how could Naomi support her family if Noah took so much from her? While his palace rose, his people starved. It wasn't right.

"What if I found a way to set Melek free?" Mera said, surprised at how calm she felt. "He could remind Noah of the truths we've taught him." *The high priest is almost like a prophet,* Mera thought. *If anyone could reach Noah, it would be Melek. He just needs a chance.*

Rachel froze, her hand hovering over a partially sculpted bobcat. Gideon leaned against her side, a question growing in his eyes. "But how? Won't Noah be angry?"

Mera wanted to shrug, but her shoulders felt too tight. "I'll speak with Helam. We'll come up with something. Zeniff will smooth things over with Noah when it's done."

Rachel raised her hand to her mouth, her eyes shining.

"You won't tell Alma, will you?" Mera said, looking at Naomi. "It's not that I don't trust him, but . . ."

"Of course not." Naomi slapped her moist clay with unusual vigor, flattening it into a smooth, thin circle. "I'd do anything to persuade him to listen to real priests, even if it means keeping secrets from him. And you won't tell Alma either."

Those last words were meant for Lisha, who'd started coming to the studio ever since she'd noticed Alma's broad shoulders and warm smile a few months before. Win the mother, win the son. Sometimes it worked.

Lisha flushed. "I won't say a word. Alma's nothing like Noah. You'll see." She bit her lip while scraping clay out from under her short fingernails. "When the time comes, leave Gideon with me. Alma will stay with us too. Noah ordered him to create firkins for the royal wine since he has experience here. He's been carving the king's seal into wooden stamps. Should be done by now."

Naomi turned to Mera at once. "It's a good idea. That gives Alma a reason to be away from the palace. Because if he's there when you set Melek free . . . I mean, anything could happen."

"Nothing will go wrong, Naomi." Mera paused, examining her cup, the best she'd thrown so far. "Well, nothing that will harm the guards. In fact, if Alma were there, I might be able to persuade him to unlock the prison. It would make my task that much simpler."

"And endanger my only son." Naomi's face set with the firmness of a protective mother.

"Alma will stay here with Lisha and Gideon." Rachel strode to the basin with a handful of dirty brushes and awls.

"Any word from Jarom and Sarai?" Lisha asked without looking up from her lumpy creation.

"You'd be the first I'd tell, after Zeniff, of course," Mera said.

Lisha squeezed her sculpture back into a ball, her expression unreadable. "Well, I know you're all worried about Noah's influence, but I'm glad Alma's on his good side."

---

Helam carried a small oil lamp to the dark corner of the temple courtyard where Mera and Rachel waited. "I asked Tamar for a sleeping draught," he said. "I told her I couldn't sleep."

Mera raised her brows.

"I know that wasn't honest, but if Noah found out she knew . . ." Helam's voice trailed off and he shook his head. "I don't want to endanger her."

"I agree," Mera said.

"The draught won't kill the guards," Helam added, "but mixed with their wine, it'll keep them asleep long enough."

Mera rubbed her arms. "Thank you Helam, for helping us, and for what you do for Tamar. I'm glad you check in on her from time to time."

Helam nodded. "I promised Jarom I'd watch over you all."

"Will Noah hang the guards when he finds Melek is gone?" Rachel asked in a soft voice.

Helam shook his head. "They're too valuable. Amulon will whip them."

Rachel winced, then shook herself. "Let's go."

They crept north of the temple and through the wide pastureland. They were out of breath as they reached the summit up the switchbacks and long steep trail to where the prison overlooked the river. Climbing this at night was a challenge. Sure enough, four guards lay slumped at their posts, snoring. Helam removed the wooden slats barring the door.

"Wait here," he told the women, then stepped inside.

Several long minutes later, there was a shuffling sound and Melek poked his head out the door. In Mera's lamplight, his features were barely discernible beneath his snarled beard. He looked filthy. "Rachel! Mera?" He hovered in the doorway, unsure. "What's happened? Why . . ."

Rachel pulled him out of the jail, wrapping her arms around his neck. "Mera planned it all." Her voice hitched. "You can live with me and Gideon again. Zeniff will persuade Noah."

Even in the dim light, Mera could see Melek stiffen, see the dark shadow cross his face.

"Noah didn't order my release? After five years, he still won't set me free?"

Helam barred the door, then glanced toward the palace. "We shouldn't stay here. Zeniff and Mera can reason with Noah if you're out, but if the guards find you here, like this . . ."

With a disgusted look at the sleeping guards, Melek started away from the prison, his arm around Rachel. "So what's the urgency, Mera? You never even came to see. After what I did to protect you, I would've thought—"

"Noah forbade it. He only allowed Rachel and Gideon."

"Yet you've found a way to set me free."

"I . . . it's not right, you being imprisoned here, Melek. And it's gone on long enough." They were passing the old temple now. It loomed up in the darkness, blotting their view of the stars.

"What do you want from me, Mera?"

Mera's cheeks warmed. "I . . . I want you to be free. I want you to be with your family. And . . ." She sighed, then the words rushed right out of her. "I want you to teach in secret. We promised Naomi . . . I mean, Naomi hopes you'll talk with Alma. He's grown confused. And . . . I need you to influence Noah. You don't know what he's become!"

"You'll do no such thing," Rachel said, flaring up unexpectedly. "You'll be a peacemaker, lay low, so the king has no cause to imprison you again. Don't even speak with the king or the former priests. I forbid it." Her voice trembled.

"Rachel!" Mera said. "He must visit Noah. Maybe not immediately . . . but Noah needs Melek to set him right."

"Oh, I'll set him right," Melek said. "But he won't like it."

Mera swallowed. "What does that mean? Melek?"

They'd reached the dwelling behind Rachel's studio. Gold light seeped through the reeds covering the windows. Melek paused and bowed his head to Helam. "Thank you." The soldier gave a curt nod and strode into the night.

As Melek reached for the door, Rachel caught his arm, "Alma's still there. He mustn't know you've escaped. That could put him at odds with the king."

Melek shook her off. "The king will find out, one way or another." He pushed inside and the others followed. A loud squeal erupted. At the sight of his father, Gideon dropped the tablet he'd been drawing on and ran into Melek's arms.

Across the room, Alma looked up from his work on the firkins. Lisha sat beside him, her hands white with clay dust.

Normally Rachel would chide them for taking unfinished pottery out of the studio. Tonight she kept silent, her face unnaturally pale.

"Melek?" Alma squinted up at him.

"Alma, you've grown." Melek crossed the room with Gideon on his hip and clapped Alma's shoulder. "A man now."

"King Noah set you free?" Alma searched Mera's and Rachel's expressions. "He didn't." He set his tools on a small table.

Rachel crossed the room and knelt beside Alma. "Your mother will be so angry with me for asking this, but please, Alma, please don't tell the king."

Alma opened his mouth and looked to Mera.

"He will know soon enough," Mera said. "And he had no right to keep Melek so long just for trying to protect me."

"He's punishing you," Alma said to Mera.

Rachel gave a soft cry.

"Alma, I've always loved you like a son," Melek said, setting Gideon down and resting a hand on the boy's head. Gideon clung to Melek's leg. "When your father died, I . . ."

"Alma?" Gideon's hazel eyes glistened. "Please don't tell on my daddy. Please don't let King Noah take him away again. You know what it's like to lose your father." His voice broke.

Lisha stroked Alma's arm.

"I'll do what I can," he finally said, his expression guarded.

———◆———

Mera sat inside the new temple near the doors with the rest of the family, close enough to Noah so he could lord over them, but far enough away to keep out of his way. He loved to hold court in the main part of the temple, as if that were its intended purpose, to glorify him instead of God. And he relished ordering his family to attend, oblivious to the pain it caused them to see his harsh judgment of petitioners, not to mention the agony written on Tamar's face at the stream of scantily clad women flitting in and out for Noah and his high priests' entertainment.

The latest in a long succession of new concubines and wives was a dainty Lamanite girl of barely fourteen, the same age as Limhi. When the guards brought her to the temple, Tamar went an icy white and called for Helam. "Please take Limhi out for some practice with the atlatl." Obediently, he grabbed the lad and invited him to go to the pasture.

"Helam's a good role model for Limhi," Zeniff said quietly as they exited the palace. For a moment, Mera thought Tamar had flushed. But when she turned toward them, Tamar's eyes were alight with fury.

"Helam is what Noah should be, what he would be if he'd ever listened to you."

"It's not Mera's fault," Zeniff said even quieter than before, looking older today than usual.

Mera's lip quivered. "Of course it's my fault," her voice cracking with strangled emotion. "I'm his mother. I must've gone wrong somewhere."

"And Jarom? Where did you go wrong with him?" Zeniff said.

"I . . . Jarom's perfect, but that's him, that's just how he is."

"Well then, if you can't take credit for that, you can't take blame for Noah."

Tamar fidgeted in her seat, her eyes on the door through which Limhi had just left. "I wasn't implying . . ."

Mera put her hand on Tamar's. "I know." She sighed. "It's just hard not to blame myself."

"The Lord gave us each the freedom to choose," Zeniff said, shifting his walking stick to the other side of his chair. "It was His greatest gift. The only way we could learn and grow." Zeniff paused for a thoughtful moment. "Let me rephrase that. His greatest gift is the Savior, second is our agency."

Mera sniffed and blinked hard.

The temple door flew open and Amulon stormed inside, his armor jangling. He paused for a moment for a quick bow in Noah's direction. "My lord, the false priest Melek has escaped."

Whispers filled the room as Amulon strode forward at Noah's signal to confer with the king in private. Mera and Zeniff exchanged wary glances.

Beside them, Tamar gave a little moan. "Was this your doing, Mera?"

"I though he could teach Limhi the old ways—the truth—instead of what Noah wants us all to believe."

Tamar looked as if she'd been slapped. "You don't trust that I can teach him?" Then her expression softened. "You're right, of course." Her eyes were grave. "Noah will know it was you. No one else would dare defy him."

Mera nodded and Zeniff squeezed her hand.

Noah and his priests sat in angry discussion at the head of the chamber, just outside the Holy of Holies. His face was growing redder by the moment.

"The guards must be beaten," Noah ordered. "See to it personally, Amulon."

Amulon gave a sharp nod. "And what of Melek? Shall we drag him out of his home?"

Mera stood before Noah could answer, capturing the attention of the court as she approached the throne. "He's no threat to you, my son. He's a relic, a broken-down relic of the past."

Noah's eyes narrowed. "You and your infatuation with the former priests and the old ways. I don't know why Father doesn't put you aside."

"Noah." Zeniff's voice was strong and rang through the court. He stood, leaning heavily on his walking stick. "You dishonor your mother."

A hush fell over the temple and Noah removed his arm from the waist of the Lamanitish girl at his side.

"Please, Noah," Tamar begged him, ignoring the girl. "Your mother meant no harm."

Mera moved closer to her son, feeling as if she were goading an angry bear. She lowered her voice so only he could hear. "Melek only meant to protect me, Noah. He never intended to defy you. Five years is such a long time. Think of Rachel and Gideon. Think how you would've felt to lose your father at such a tender age."

Noah hesitated, looking somewhat lost. Mera pressed her advantage. "Just listen to Melek. Give him a chance. The old ways, they can be your ways too. You can still be a strong king . . ."

"I *am* a strong king!" Noah said, loud enough for the others to hear.

Mera shook her head. "I wasn't saying . . ."

A loud commotion in the courtyard outside the temple interrupted them. Jeers and shouts filled the air as a large crowd gathered outside.

"What in the name of . . ." Noah said.

A guard burst through the door, saluted to Amulon, then gave a confused bow to the king. "It's the false priests." His face was red and sweaty. "They've rallied the people. They're storming the temple and the new palace."

Noah roared in rage.

Amulon raced outside, calling for his men.

*Has Melek done this?* Mera turned to follow, but Zeniff stopped her. "It's not safe out there," he said, holding her back. Instead, they peered through a reed window. Tamar did the same.

"Limhi!" she cried.

"Is he there?" Mera said, scanning the crowd. She saw Naomi and Rachel just behind her with Gideon at her side, holding a small scroll, a child's version of the scriptures. Sure enough, Melek stood at the front of the irate crowd, chanting something about Noah and judgment. She couldn't spot Limhi anywhere. "Don't worry, Tamar. Helam will keep Limhi away from this."

Guards marched between the growing crowd and the temple doors. Alma stood with them, looking shaken. While Mera watched, Noah strode outside, swelling in fury. With one fluid movement, he grabbed a sword off a nearby guard and plunged it into Melek's stomach.

A thin wail rose above the crowd and Mera saw Gideon crumple like the scroll in his hand.

# 13

# Protection

## Tamar, 153 BC

Tamar heard Noah before she saw him. Their arguments had become lines in the sand, Tamar insisting that all of the other wives have their own homes and Noah insisting that they all live in the new palace, together.

"Limhi is heir to the throne and must live in the palace!" He was arguing with Mera and Zeniff again. Tamar slipped out of her quarters and into the courtyard where Noah stood with hands outstretched, shielding her view of his parents.

"This is between us," Tamar said, "not them."

Noah spun around, his expression scornful. "I thought my mother might talk sense into your head, but I can't reason with her either."

Tamar stared at the man she had married and realized he was a stranger to her. "You've spent the last two years traveling to every city known to the Nephites. You've filled Shilom with strangers you've brought back from your travels. The new palace is filled with women you bring back as gifts to your high priests. You've broken your promise to me that I alone would share your bed and now there are a dozen children who bear your name."

In a move of frustration he ran his fingers through his silver-streaked hair.

"You're the queen. You must move to the palace. I still love you." His eyes revealed not love, but hurt pride. The one woman he wanted didn't want him back. He reached for Tamar and wrapped his arms around her. She responded with a weak embrace, but could no longer lock her fingers behind his back. He had new robes made every few months to fit his expanded girth.

"The palace has been finished nearly two years. We are expected to live as a royal family there. I've been patient, but the people are talking. These old quarters will be torn down and new homes will be built." He spoke in a surprisingly gentle tone.

"Maybe all of the women in your life have softened you. I, however, have become stronger. Your words mean little to me. I don't wish to dishonor you, but I will not be moving to the palace. I choose to stay here. Limhi will remain with me. If you destroy my home, I'll simply find a different place to live."

Noah's color changed. Gone was the pleading, and in its place was the old familiar anger. "You'll not take my son from me."

"You have other sons," Tamar said flatly.

"The palace celebration begins at sundown. You will all be there." Noah had the last word as he thundered out of the place he once called home.

———— ◆ ————

The city streets were filled with visitors and guests of the court. Noah had invited everyone to celebrate the new palace and temple. His vision certainly was grand. The new structures lined the crest of the hill overlooking the river. Standing on the palace grounds was almost like standing atop the bluffs or the tower. Tamar had visited the palace while it was being constructed. Once she realized that the design was intended to provide rooms for many wives, concubines, and others, she knew she would never be a part of that life with Noah.

As she passed by the small shops she had grown up with, now dwarfed by those selling all manner of fine-twined linens and idols designed by Noah himself, she stepped inside to visit with an old friend.

"Welcome, Queen Tamar!" Hagar said affectionately. "It's been such a long time since you visited."

Tamar embraced her. "I should have come more often. How are you?"

"The Lord provides. We cannot complain. Although, the tax . . ." She paused. "Many of the smaller shop owners are ready to close, like ours. We sell simple necessities. The new stores have the king to back them. He gives them our tax money to make their goods while we struggle. We cannot compete. We're going to try to make it back to Zarahemla."

Tears sprang to Tamar's eyes. She tried to push back the loneliness of the past seven years since Jarom and Sarai had escaped and the isolation and separation from those who shared her faith.

"We miss them too," the woman whispered.

"It's hard to hide true feelings from those we love." Tamar embraced Hagar again. "I can offer you a few coins." Tamar pulled a pouch from her dress and dropped several gold pieces into the woman's hand.

"You don't have to pay taxes on this. No one will know." Tamar closed the woman's fingers around the coins. "Those who are struggling, send them to me. I'll do what I can to help. One more thing, is your husband here?"

"Yes, one moment, I'll get him."

A tall, graying man came from the back of the shop, wiping his hands on a leather loincloth. "I'm not clean enough to shake your hands, my queen. What can I do for you?"

"You served with Melek. He kept the scrolls at the temple. Where are they now?" Tamar asked in a whisper.

"The king would see it as treasonous to possess or read the scrolls." Micah glanced about. "The king won't be using the temple for court now that the new palace and temple are complete. We are hoping to obtain the scrolls that Melek hid within the stone walls."

"They've been there this whole time? Did Noah even know?"

"No, my lady, he didn't. If he did, he would have destroyed them. During the celebration, we plan to retrieve them."

"Would there be a chance for Limhi to see them. Possibly read them?" Tamar hesitated. "It is difficult to recall the stories of our people. It's been too many years. I wish . . ."

Hagar stepped quickly to the door, looked up and down the street, then pulled it tightly closed. "We cannot speak of the records here. Remember Melek's fate. I'm sure the king would not hesitate to do the same to any of us if he finds us teaching the old ways."

"It's for my son. Please?"

"If we find the records, I'll find a way." He added, "My lady, you're rais-ing him to be a good man. You've taught him well. I must caution though, you mustn't come here any more than you have in the past. Nothing out of the ordinary."

Tamar shook her head. "I cannot teach him all he needs to know. He must not become like Noah. I couldn't bear it."

Hagar pulled Tamar close, whispering in her ear. "He mustn't say a word to the king. Please make sure he knows our lives would be in danger, my queen."

"Would you start teaching again, the words of Melek and the stories of our people?"

Micah's words came out in a whisper. "It would be very dangerous, for everyone."

"For Limhi?" Tamar glanced around to make sure no one else could hear. "He wishes to learn the old ways."

A smile turned up the corners of Micah's lips. "That is good to know, my queen. We will find a place to gather. Others have been whispering and desire to learn from the old high priests again—the king will never know. I'll send you a message when we find a safe place."

"Thank you." Tamar picked up her goods and slipped out into the street.

---

The grandest party Shilom had ever seen commenced at sundown. Women adorned in the most beautiful gowns, with gold and silver ropes woven through plaited hair, glided in and out of the candle lights. Noah spared no expense on food. The new temple altar was filled with meats of every kind, being offered to the new gods Noah had created for the people, giving the people of Shilom a way to see and speak to the object of their worship. Gold adorned the comfortable seats built to the size and shape of each high priest.

In elegant ceremonial fashion, each priest was escorted to his seat by a beautiful woman, who then spent time feeding, caressing, and showering affection on her assigned priest. As the evening wore on, the women rotated around the room, giving each high priest the same treatment. Tamar could only stand so much. She left before the men became drunk enough to take advantage of the company of women.

It made Tamar's stomach turn. She let her mind focus on the new day ahead. A promised meeting at the spring. Dawn would come. She looked forward to the light.

"Can I stay, Mother?" Limhi whispered the question in her ear.

Tamar wouldn't have been more shocked if he'd slapped her.

"Father asked me to stay. I'd like to, even though this won't be our home, it's still a celebration for our family."

Tamar glanced at the faces of the women of the court. Her mind raced, worried that the influence of the unfolding night would be the beginning of the end for her son's righteous life. One of the youngest of the concubines kept looking over at Limhi and smiling.

"Son." Tamar took both of his hands in hers. "None of this will bring you lasting happiness. I've done my best to teach you. But you're a man now." She took in a deep breath. "I am leaving. What you see happening in and throughout this place brings pain to me and shame to you. But I'll not force you to leave."

Limhi glanced back at the pretty young girl. She looked younger than him. He looked around at his father, surrounded by several beautiful women. Tamar could sense his inner struggle. She touched his arm, to let him feel her support and strength.

"I'll tell him I'm going home."

"He'll try to stop you."

"Yes, but he's drunk and won't remember it tomorrow."

Several of the women Tamar had been watching over in the corner were summoned by the nurses. Their children, all having forms of the name of Noah or named after his gods, were ready to be fed and bed down for the night. Some of the other women whose bellies expanded beyond their inter-locked fingers were clearly with child. Tamar buried the pain—the ever-present knife in her heart—and began walking toward the massive carved doors that led to the stone portico.

She felt a hand on her shoulder. Limhi.

"Can I walk you home and then come back?"

Tamar slipped her arm through his. "That would be wonderful. The walking part, anyway." The words came from her mouth, but in her head she was begging him to leave the wickedness in the palace and never return.

"Don't you see how much worse things have become?" Tamar asked, willing herself to not say anything unkind.

"What's the danger in just being there? I'm not doing anything wrong."

"Being where there is such wickedness is a danger to you, to your spirit."

"Really, Mother, do you think I'd ever become like that?"

"Noah was once young like you. He was good and kind." Tamar felt a pain seize her heart. "I loved him, and still do, in a way." She continued, "I'm not sure I could take it if you started . . . became . . . were affected in any way by his example."

*Lord, please help me know what to say. I fear for my son. Noah's pull is strong.*

They had moved away from the palace, and the noise from inside faded. The crickets were deafening as the twilight sky rang with their songs. There was something pleasing about the cacophony of night noises that felt like music, yet the tinkling cymbals and drums of Noah's party irritated like the grittiness of sand in a shoe. Tamar wanted to be free of it.

"Can I ask what makes you wish to return?" Tamar asked in a calm voice, devoid of any anxiety, which surprised her.

"There's a young lady that came from the eastern lands with her father," Limhi said. "He came to set up his trade here, and Father took her into the palace." Tamar winced. "She's a nice girl and I wanted to ask Father if he would let her live apart from the palace, here in Jarom's old quarters. I can't see her being happy as one of the many women there. She's not like them."

A warm peace flooded Tamar's chest. "So you've taken notice of this young lady. Let's see what can be done. Maybe if you asked Noah yourself, he would agree."

"She doesn't deserve to live in that place."

"Have you spoken with her?"

"No, I just feel in my heart that she shouldn't be there."

"What will you say to him?"

"I'd love to tell him I'm embarrassed at how one after another of the women become heavy with child and name their innocent children after him or his gods. I'd say how I avoid him and love spending time with Helam instead. I know I can't say any of these things. I'm not sure he even knows I can throw an atlatl across the pasture and hit my target. He doesn't know me."

A soothing breeze rippled across Tamar. She had anticipated an argument and instead found a window to her son's soul. "It's his loss. He may not ever see it. For that, I am sorry that you've not had the kind of father you needed."

"Oh, I've not lacked for love or instruction. Grandfather, Grandmother, you, and so many others taught me the way I should be. I imagine myself like Moses in the court of Pharaoh. Maybe God has a work for me to do one day. I must be prepared." Limhi gave Tamar a quick hug. "You've taught me well."

*Thank you, Lord, for helping me not be angry with him. He's a blessing to me.* Tamar hugged her son and held him a little bit longer. "You've become quite like your grandfather and you look more like him every day."

"Will he live much longer?"

Another pain twisted in her chest as she realized that someday soon they might be bidding farewell to this great man, leaving Mera to live the rest of her years alone. "He's not well. Spend time with him. Now that Noah will be busy with more building projects, he may not even be aware of how feeble his father has become."

They reached their home and shared an evening prayer. Afterward, Limhi turned to his mother. "Do you believe we will see Jarom and Sarai again?" He asked. "I pray that God will watch over them. I just wish we could know somehow if they ever made it back to Zarahemla."

"There are others that want to return."

"Would we ever leave here?"

"I don't know. I wonder the same thing. I don't know if Noah would allow us to leave."

"If we can't leave, will we ever get to pray or hear the old stories that used to be told to the children? Remember, the ones you learned as a child?"

"Possibly. I'm not sure how it will come about. You must not say a word to anyone. Lives would be at stake."

Limhi's brow wrinkled and he balled his fists. "Why?" He exhaled. "Why is Father doing everything you've taught me not to do? One part of me despises him. Another part of me pities him. Deep inside, my heart just hurts because I still love him."

Tamar went to stand beside her son, who was nearly a man now and as tall as Noah. "I feel the same. I fell in love with a man who loved his family. He had faith and trust in God. He was a visionary and had such dreams. I truly loved him once. I don't know what to feel anymore." Her arms gently embraced his strong shoulders and she lay her head on his arm.

"Mom, I want to give Father one more chance. If I go to the palace, stay there some nights and listen to him, won't he then listen to me?"

"He won't stop until he's won your mind, your heart, and your soul."

"I'm big enough to handle things, Mom. You've been the finest teacher."

"Would to God you could have a real teacher, like Melek." Tamar's voice wavered.

"Me too. God willing," Limhi said. "Please don't be angry. I'm still planning to return to the celebration. I know you disapprove. I'm strong."

"I know you're strong. None of us are strong enough to live around wickedness and not be affected. Loving someone doesn't mean you look past their sins. You love them in spite of their sins, and protect yourself from their influence."

After a quick hug, he left. Tamar spent hours tossing and turning in her bed. Partly because she knew that her life would change soon, and partly because she knew it wouldn't change enough.

———◆———

The next morning, Tamar chose to not think of where Noah was, but where she soon would be. The morning was cool and clear. Baby birds chirped in their nests, and the trees were budding out. Within a week or more, the canopy would be fully formed and the tiny spring plants on the forest floor would have their source of light snuffed out. She felt like that at times. Today though, there was light. Everywhere. In the sky, on this path, in her heart.

She heard a familiar voice call to her. She stopped, turned, and there Limhi was, looking much like the Noah she had fallen in love with. Anxiously she waited for him to catch up to her.

"I did it! I got him to release the young lady to me. He said I could have her!"

Tamar's stomach knotted. "He can't *give* her to you. She's a person, a child."

"Of course! I know that. But Father said he'd release her."

Tamar smiled. "She can live in Jarom and Sarai's quarters until they return. If they return."

"Thank you, Mother. You'd like her. I talked with her till late and watched her go to the women's quarters. Father never touched her."

Bile rose in her throat and she felt ill. *Lord, how many has he stolen virtue from? Why do you let him live this way?*

Limhi must have seen her blanch and reached out to steady her. "I'm sorry, Mother, to have reminded you." He took her hand and led her through the tree lined path.

"You recognize the way, don't you?"

"Yes. Grandmother used to walk this path with us when Hiram and Neriah were here. I've not been on it for years."

Snapping twigs alerted Tamar that someone else was behind her. She stopped, but Limhi was a step ahead of her and her fingers slipped from his hand.

Helam emerged from the shadows.

"My queen," he said with a slightly bowed head.

"Are you following us?"

Helam stammered slightly. "Mera asked me to watch over you and I'm afraid I'm not as quiet as I should be. Are you angry?"

Tamar sighed. "No, you might as well come along keep us company."

"Are you going to the spring?"

"Yes, it's been some time since I've gone there. It's been my refuge since I was a child."

"I know you've lived here all your life, but I know nothing of your family," Helam said.

"There's not much to tell, other than my parents came here with Zeniff. They left their families in Zarahemla and embarked on this journey with a spirit of adventure. They loved Zeniff. My father had come as one of his scouts. Father said it was one of the most beautiful places he had ever been."

"Why do I not know them?"

Tamar took in a deep breath, then let it out slowly, willing herself not to cry. She observed Limhi pushing branches away from the path and using a stick to remove webs along the way, and she realized that neither her father nor mother had met this fine son of hers. "Mother died years ago and was buried when the mound was much smaller than it is today. Father couldn't bear to be here anymore. He went back to Zarahemla. I stayed. This is my home. And I couldn't leave the place where my mother lay. Then I couldn't bear to leave Mera, who became like a mother to me."

"Have you had word of your father?"

"Traders have brought letters, but they have been few and far between." Tamar placed her hand over her heart. "It is my greatest desire that I see my father before he dies. I pray he yet lives."

"Zeniff and Mera have been good to me as well. I'd do anything for them." Helam changed the subject. "Who told you of the gathering today?" he asked as they walked.

Tamar stopped, nearly causing Helam to run into her. "What gathering?" she asked with some surprise.

"I thought you had been asked to come. Didn't Mera tell you?"

"Helam, what are you talking about?" Tamar asked, no longer hiding the irritation she was feeling. Limhi was now quite a ways ahead.

Over his shoulder, the answer appeared. Mera was making her way down the path, apparently unaware that Tamar was standing on the other side of the tall, muscular man blocking the path.

There were others with Mera. They talked in low voices, some men, some women. As they neared Helam, he stood with a perplexed expression, shifting on his feet. Tamar stood in stony silence. Tamar heard the friendly greeting as they came up behind him on the path only wide enough for one or two. Tamar must have been hidden to their eyes because they only greeted him and shouted ahead to Limhi. She was invisible to them.

As Helam turned, Tamar's presence was revealed.

Tamar's frustration was obvious.

"Don't be angry." Mera began. "We were going to let you know, but many were concerned that if you left the city it would make our meetings known to the king."

"Why? He doesn't even notice me anymore! We rarely speak and you think for a moment that I would betray my only friends to a man who feels the need to take every woman he meets to his bed?"

Helam had moved out of the way, backing into the underbrush, snapping more twigs and rustling the dry leaves.

"You're his mother," Tamar said. "Would there not be any concern there?" She waved her hand toward the trail and asked, "Is Limhi in on the secret too? How long have you been coming here?" She fired the questions in rapid succession.

Mera glanced at the faces of the others with her. Several were the old priests and a few were shopkeepers. One priest carried scrolls under his arm.

"Tell her," Yoseph, the master weaver, whispered. No one spoke, so Yoseph continued. "For some time, we have come here to pray for the Lord to give us guidance. Many feared meeting at the temple, that Noah would . . . well, like Melek."

It had been two years, but the image was painfully fresh in Tamar's mind. Melek falling to the ground, run through with a sword by Noah's hand.

"You should have trusted me," Tamar whispered. "I'm not like him."

"I know that, but others were not sure. I would have told you soon enough."

Tamar blinked. "I've begged to hear the word and have someone teach Limhi! I've waited so long . . ."

Limhi came walking back down the trail, a confused expression on his face as he scanned the trees, searching for his mother. A woman Tamar recognized as one of Mera's friends was at his side. "They are waiting to read the scrolls."

As Tamar looked at those she had known most of her life, their faces softened. Then Micah spoke. "We are sorry, dear queen. Please forgive us for fearing. We should have had faith in your integrity." He added, "Come with us."

No longer angry, she turned to her son. "Let's resume our walk to the spring and see what more this day will hold."

The tender green grasses grew like a thick carpet in the open bank overlooking the turquoise spring. The water was cold and clear as it flowed from deep within a cave back to the river that circled their city. The group of eager saints sat with rapt attention for several hours as Yoseph and others read from the scrolls.

When the sun reached the midpoint in the sky, Tamar realized that she would need to return, that her absence might be cause for alarm since the Lamanites had become more of a concern as of late.

She leaned over to Limhi. "We should go back home. Soldiers may come searching for us if many are gone for very long."

Limhi nodded and quietly stood.

Heads turned, noted the activity, then refocused on the high priest who was reading the scrolls of Melek.

Helam also stood.

"I'll return with you, my queen."

"No need. We'll be fine."

Helam looked from Tamar to Mera and back again.

"It's all right," Mera whispered. "Stay."

Tamar and Limhi slipped from the group and began the long walk back to Shilom.

Along the beautiful trail that led home, Limhi opened up to Tamar in a way he never had before.

"Mother, do you recall the day of the battle, when I was sent to keep watch on the tower?"

The memory was vivid. "Yes, why?"

"I was watching, but especially keeping watch on Uncle Jarom and Father. I wasn't sure for a long time, but I know now that what I thought I saw was true. Sometimes brothers can get so angry that they'd do something unthinkable. I think Father hated Jarom so much that he shot him."

Tamar's feeling of joy and light came crashing down around her. The reality of her life was like a yoke upon her back. "I always wondered what you saw that disturbed you, making you ill. I suspected it but never wanted to know for sure. So, you saw?"

"I did."

Tamar threw her arms around her son. "You've lived a difficult life. I wish it could have been different." Tears spilled down her cheeks, and her son, no longer a child, wiped them away.

"I'll always protect you, Mother."

# Blame

*Mera, 151 BC*

*Z*eniff shifted on the couch by the window, opening his eyes, searching the chamber until his gaze lit on Mera, who worked at a portable loom, pulling irregular threads back and forth. "You're weaving. I haven't seen you weave since we were young." His countenance lightened, taking decades off his appearance, if only for a moment.

Mera paused, twining a storm-colored yarn around her finger. "My pottery is not enough. I need to keep busy, keep moving my hands, or else I'll lose my mind."

Zeniff nodded. "I saw you in the gardens yesterday. The gardener didn't look happy."

"Of course he didn't. My small patch of the garden won't quite match all the others. But it will be mine, an order that is my own. He can't begrudge me that."

Zeniff clasped his hands. "Noah or the gardener?"

Mera wove the dark yarn through the lighter strings stretched down the length of the loom. "It's a small corner, just across from our window, beneath the peach tree. I can see it whenever I look outside. I just need something I can control, Zeniff. You can understand that. I pulled all the weeds. I don't know why pulling weeds has to be such a messy, painful job. I'd rather get straight to the flowers."

Mera felt a withered hand on her shoulder and looked up. While she'd been rambling on and weaving things all wrong, Zeniff had slowly crossed the room.

"You're a good mother, Mera. You always have been."

"But I . . . we weren't even . . ." Mera broke off, stifling a sob. "Wouldn't a good mother bear a good son?" She waved toward the window. "Don't peach trees bear peaches?"

Zeniff sank onto a hard stool beside her. "Peaches don't have agency, Mera. All you need to do is weed them, water them, and see that they get enough sunlight. Not so with children." He gave a heavy sigh, now looking older than ever. "We fed and watered our children, Mera. We taught them all that we know. We taught them to love God and showed them God's love. But they're not flowers and they're not peaches. Jarom and Noah both chose for themselves and so must we all. But there is no doubting you were a good mother. Still are."

"I pray for him every day." She dropped the yarn, letting it trail along the dusty floor. Her voice hushed. "Noah won't listen when I talk about things that really matter. The only relationship we have is based on empty things, like vases and window hangings."

"That's his choice, Mera. All you can do now is love him."

She bit her lip. "I had the weavers create a pattern of rings in Noah's curtains, a symbol of eternity. Surely his heart will soften. The Lord has a plan for Noah just like he has a plan for me. The scriptures tell of the Savior who will come to save us all. I have to believe He'll save Noah too. There must be a way."

A great clattering in the courtyard interrupted their conversation. Helam burst into their chambers. "Noah's in a rage. We need you both to help calm him. Tamar refuses to come. She won't have Limhi in there when Noah's like this. How she means to stop Limhi when he's seventeen years old, I don't know."

Zeniff stood and Mera tucked aside her weaving.

"What is it?" Zeniff asked, gripping Mera's shoulder for balance.

"The Lamanites." Helam's voice was grim. "Noah sent guards to chase them off our lands, but he didn't send near enough. They slew the men he sent and stole several dozen sheep, goats, and cattle. The people are angry and they're blaming Noah."

Zeniff's face tightened. "We must go. Noah won't take kindly to that."

"You have a way with Limhi," Mera told Helam. "Keep him out of this. Tamar is right to protect her son."

———————◆·——————

Noah slammed a cup of wine onto the ornate table by his throne, splattering the polished wood with crimson drops. The throne room in the new palace was full, despite its immense size. Stone idols crowded the corners. Smaller clay figurines stood in recesses in the walls, illuminated by a sickly light that streamed through thin leather hides filming the windows. Noah's image had been burned into the baked clay floor, consorting with gods of his own making. And women scantily clad lounged everywhere, satisfying the whims of the king and his priests.

Mera could hardly see any of it for the press of angry people thronging the chamber. She pushed through the crowd with Zeniff clinging to her arm. When had the people stopped parting for them? Angry voices rang out and she noticed several women among the men demanding recompense for their lost flocks.

Naomi stood with them, though she had no flocks of her own. In fact, the greater part of the people there were not shepherds or cattlemen. These stood calm and quiet, the blaze of determination in their eyes sending a chill down Mera's spine.

"I cannot restore your flocks!" Noah shouted over the general roar of complaints. "Those guards were weak. But they still put the fear of our gods in the Lamanites. They'll not trouble us again soon!"

Noah's most senior high priest and head guard, Amulon, stood on one side of him, his restless gaze searching the multitude for signs that it might erupt into violence. Alma guarded Noah's other side, gripping his sword, ready to defend his king.

Suddenly Mera understood Naomi's presence there. She was worried for Alma.

A great muttering broke out, like tiny rivulets working their way through a dam.

"The guards were weak?"

"He didn't send enough men."

"Weak, indeed."

"Weak with wine and glutting themselves while we slave in the fields."

"Noah doesn't care what happens in the fields so long as—"

Amulon stepped forward, his sword drawn. "Such murmuring against your king is treachery."

By now, Mera and Zeniff had neared the throne. They slipped behind Alma, who tensed at their passing, but recognizing them, did nothing. "Noah," Mera said in a soft voice. "I know you've done your best . . ."

He brushed her hand from his arm. "Go ahead, Mother, tell me what I should've done better."

She pulled back. "I didn't mean that."

"They've lost their flocks, son," Zeniff said in his slow, soothing way. "Some have lost sons or brothers. Just show some compassion and these people will be yours."

Mera could think of better reasons for showing compassion, but held her peace.

Noah's brow knit.

"It's because of the king that the Lamanites attacked at all!" a man toward the back shouted, waving at the statues lining the walls. "His idol worship, his defiance of the true God. He brought this on us!"

Noah's face darkened. He gestured to Amulon, who pressed through the crowd, several other soldiers falling in line behind him. Alma moved to follow, but Noah held him back. "Stay with me, son. I need your loyalty and your protection."

*Is it true?* Mera wondered. *Have Noah's sins brought destruction on them all? Is this the way God works, showering blessings on the good and woes on the evil? If so, what does that say about me?*

Noah saw her expression and rose to his feet, looking thunderous. The crowd went still, some staring at him, others watching the commotion in the back, where Amulon had cornered the man who dared defy the king. "If you think the God of your fathers can do a better job at defending our lands," Noah said, "the former priests can fight the Lamanites."

Near the front of the mob, an elderly woman gasped, clutching the frail man beside her.

Noah pointed at them. "Many of you cling to the old ways. But *old* means almost dead. And here, in Shilom, the old ways are dead. Anyone who denies this can fight in the next battle. Starting with him." The king cocked his head to the side, glaring at the old man. "I'm sure the Lamanites will tremble in fear when they see him."

The crowd shifted uneasily, but no one dared say a thing with Noah's guards standing ready to pounce. Mera noticed a minor disturbance in the area where she'd last seen Naomi.

Mera saw Naomi mouth the words, "No, Gideon."

Mera groaned. If Rachel found out her son was here, she'd find some way to blame Mera, especially if any harm came to the boy.

"You've made your point," Mera said to Noah, to distract him.

"Yes." He gave her a broad smile that did not reach his eyes. "I believe I have."

A few hours later, Mera addressed the believers who'd gathered at the old temple. The wooden walls gleamed in the warm light of the oil lamps, every surface burnished to perfection. "We've been meeting here for two years now, ever since Noah moved his priests and his religion into the new palace."

Naomi met Mera's gaze across the crowd. "Surely Noah is not ignorant of this. Continuing to meet only risks our safety."

Before Mera could answer, Lisha spoke up. She'd married Alma the year before and stood near Naomi, her mother-in-law. "From what Alma has said, I'm certain Noah suspects we meet here. But he and Noah are both too involved in the idol worship and"—she paled, as if her next words pained her—"their *unusual* lifestyle to really care. Up until now, at least."

Tamar's face tightened at Lisha's implication, but she said nothing.

Mera felt sorry for her and for Lisha, now that Noah was corrupting her husband as well. But what could she do? Her lectures accomplished nothing but to drive Noah away.

"Noah's *your* son, Mera," Rachel said, her body rigid. "Surely you have some influence on him."

Gideon stood beside his mother, looking uncomfortable. Clearly, he'd gone to the palace without Rachel's permission and didn't want Mera to tell.

"Your son is eleven, Rachel." Mera folded her arms. "When he's in his twenties, then you can talk to me about controlling him."

"I know it's not easy," Naomi said. "Many of us feel the same. My Alma stands at Noah's side, no matter what I say."

"I am sorry for that," Mera said.

Lisha twisted her dark hair around her finger. "Alma's heart is divided. He won't come here, not against the express wishes of the king. But if we met somewhere else . . ."

"I'm not sure we want Alma coming," one of the former priests said stiffly. At Lisha's and Rachel's shocked expressions, he raised his hand. "It's not that we don't welcome him. Indeed, we welcome all believers. But under Noah's influence, we don't know what Alma would do. We can't know how deep his commitment to the king runs."

"Alma wouldn't betray us," Mera said.

"Thank you, Mera," Naomi said.

"There's still the matter of the temple," said the frail priest who'd been at court. "This is the Lord's house. This is where we must worship."

Naomi spread her arms. "The wide world is the Lord's. Every bubbling brook and copse of trees. It matters not where we meet."

"The real question," said the first priest, a stout man with a certain softness about him. "I say, the real question is do we continue meeting at all, now that Noah threatens to send believers to battle?"

Hissing conversations broke out in the room, reminding Mera of the scene in the throne room the day before. "Of course we keep meeting," she said, though she felt a pang of fear.

"Easy for you to say," Rachel snapped. "You're Noah's mother. He won't harm you." Her expression was bitter, her fingers digging into Gideon's shoulder.

"What does Zeniff say?" the stout priest asked. "Can he protect us from your son? Noah already forces us to work in the vineyard and winepresses when we should be tending our flocks. This has weakened us and emboldened the Lamanites! So, I repeat, can you and Zeniff protect us from your son?"

Mera felt a hot flush of shame.

"Where is Zeniff? Shouldn't he be here?" asked the elderly wife of the frail priest.

"He's grown weak," Mera admitted. "After the uproar at the palace, he needed rest."

More grumblings filled the room.

"But please." Mera raised her hands in supplication. "I can't promise to control Noah, but isn't the truth worth the risk? Isn't it worth any sacrifice to teach our children and grandchildren?"

"I don't see Limhi here." Rachel shook her head. "Or any of his half brothers and sisters. How you let Noah cavort with all those women . . ."

"Rachel! Hold your tongue." Naomi moved to stand beside Mera. "Have you no respect for Mera, for the years she's spent among us, sharing our burdens?"

Rachel looked away.

"I stand with Mera. I say we continue meeting. The Lord will watch over us."

Mera nodded.

The gentle priest stood. "Let us continue in faith. Let the Lord soften Noah's heart. We must trust that if we continue to meet at the spring or secretly in the temple, the Lord will protect us." He closed his eyes and spoke a soft prayer. "Lord, please soften the hearts of our enemies, all of them. Strengthen our faith to do Thy will."

"Amen" rippled through the crowd.

# 15

# Attack

## *Tamar, 150 BC*

The Shofar horn rang out through the early dawn, confusing Tamar. Dreams ending too soon and the reality of waking were happening all at the same time. She sat up, shaking the remnants of sleep from her head. It was the sound of attack. The horn blew loud and long. Instinct told her to wait and listen. The next sound was a short blast. The Lamanites were advancing quickly. She turned to wake Limhi and realized he was not there. Fear gripped her. She remembered that he had spent the night at the palace. She could only hope that Noah was paying attention and would make sure their son made it safely to the cave.

She pulled her shawl over her long hair, drawing it tight around her chin. There wasn't time for a formal prayer, so her thoughts came quickly, *Lord, please protect us*, as she slipped her sandals on.

The streets were alive with activity. Strangers visiting Shilom didn't appear to know what the horn meant. Confusion washed across their faces as they watched soldiers and citizens arming themselves and running toward the fortifications between the Lamanite city of Shemlon and the Nephite city of Shilom.

The last time the city had been under this kind of attack, Mera had been the queen. Tamar knew it was now her responsibility. She closed her eyes and for a moment envisioned that last battle, when things were so much different. Simpler.

She steeled herself, cupped her mouth, and shouted, "To the cave!" The women and children were coming toward the old temple, and she stood by its doors. This was the gathering place when there was trouble. People always went to the old temple to get instructions, to find direction and for comfort. Truly this was a time when all would need just that. Even those who no longer believed recognized that this was where they needed to be.

"Care for the elderly—please take the hands of your children. No one will be left behind. Families stay together!" Tamar's voice rose above frightened cries. Mothers called to their children. Still in night clothing, women hurried to cover their infants with their long head scarves. Many ran in bare feet.

Men and soldiers girded up their loins, their legs exposed but better able to run quickly. They weaved through the throng to reach the battle's front, leaving the aged and very young to go to the cave for safety. Tamar's instructions mingled with the shouts of the men. People were listening. They were looking to her for guidance. *Help me be the kind of leader Mera always was.*

*Mera . . . Zeniff . . . Who will help them?* Tamar watched the people moving quickly toward the first bridge. Her eyes darted back to the old palace, where she knew Zeniff lay in a weakened condition. Mera would be by his side. Suddenly, several people branched off of the flowing river of people. Tamar couldn't see beneath the head scarf, but the hunch of age and the slower feet gave Avi away. Helam had her hand. Rachel and Gideon soon followed. The four of them made their way to where Mera and Zeniff would surely be.

Tamar, with concern, watched as more people than she had ever seen at one time attempted to cross the first bridge. It groaned beneath the weight of those fleeing the battle, each step bringing them closer to safety. So far, it was holding up, but she wondered for how long. There were so many people. She looked quickly back and saw not four but six people coming from the old palace. Relieved, she rushed to the edge of the river and slowed the people crossing so fewer were on the aging bridge at one time.

Once across, their pace quickened as they made their way toward the final bridge and then the cave. Should the Lamanites come, their path would be obvious. The lush green fields of pasture first held up to the feet passing over it, but it didn't take long for there to be a well-worn trail. Tall shafts of grain lay dead on the ground. She watched until everyone but Mera, Zeniff, Helam, and Avi safely crossed both bridges. The only face she hoped to see and didn't was Limhi's. Her stomach knotted in fear as she scanned the final faces. She was torn between seeking him out and doing her duty to her people, to lead them through this crisis.

*My first duty is to my son. He's not here, but he's also not a child. Noah is probably hiding in his fortress, ordering everyone else to go fight the battle while he sits safely in his palace. Lord, please watch over my family. I'll go to these, Thy people, and trust You'll be with mine.*

Zeniff was moving slowly, but with Helam's strong arm around him, they moved from the palace. Tamar waited by the bridge until they arrived. They would be the last to cross.

"How is Zeniff?" Tamar whispered in Mera's ear.

"This is not a good day to be in the cave."

"Is it ever a good day for war?" Tamar's words were strained.

"Where's Limhi?" Mera asked.

"With Noah."

"In the palace . . . in the city?" Mera fired back.

Avi piped in. "God will watch over them. He always has been good to that son of yours. He will be fine."

Zeniff's breathing became shallow and labored. His lips took on a bluish hue.

"Helam, can you carry him? I'm not sure he can make it the rest of the way, not without time to rest."

Zeniff didn't complain or resist. Helam whisked him up off his feet as if he weighed no more than a child. Zeniff put his arm around Helam's neck and rested his head on his shoulder. They made the rest of the journey in silence but for the distant sound of battle cries. The conflict was well underway.

Tamar had done her job well. Everyone was in the cave. Except this little remnant she was with, there was no one else in sight. She crossed the second bridge, the final one before reaching the cave, and looked down into the river. No longer a crisp clean blue, the water ran muddy and brown. A Lamanite soldier with arrows in his back floated beneath her feet, his blood staining the once pristine water.

Tamar averted her eyes and clenched them tightly closed. She wasn't sure she could ever drink from the river again, at least not for a long time. When she opened her eyes and glanced down the river, she saw another body, then another. She entered the cave, hoping the all clear blast from the Shofar horn came soon.

———— • ————

By the time the signal sounded, the river carried the tale of death and destruction through the city of Shilom. Young saplings growing along the river's edge snagged pieces of cloth that floated past. A few of the bodies wore Nephite robes. The journey back to the city was somber. The night was alive with sounds of frogs croaking and crickets chirping.

On any other night it would be a beautiful sound. On this night, it was noise, chaos. Tamar's head ached with the sounds of weeping, chirping, crying, croaking. It was too much. Added to that, she needed to find Limhi. She found herself no longer shepherding her people, but running past them, trying to get back to the city to see what had become of her son.

# 16

# Abinadi

## Mera, 150 BC

*M*era and Zeniff made their way from the cave back toward the palace, their progress slowed by Zeniff's weariness as much as by the soldiers celebrating in the streets.

"A thousand Lamanites," Amulon bragged. "Our fifty against their thousand and we killed 'em all." The men around him cheered. Amulon stumbled against Mera, sloshing wine down her robes and all over Zeniff, who leaned on her shoulder. They were both filthy from the cave.

Mera moved to the side, dragging Zeniff toward the old palace. She found herself wondering why Noah hadn't come to help after the battle. He knew his father was weak. She sighed to herself. More and more, Noah only thought of himself. Zeniff's foot snagged in a crevice in the road, halting their progress. Mera paused while he freed his foot. Her friend Rachel, the master potter, hurried over and slipped under Zeniff's other arm. Rachel's son, Gideon, lagged behind, staring in the opposite direction.

"Thank you," Mera said.

Zeniff nodded his thanks to Rachel, his face rigid with pain.

Gideon had been swept away by the crowd.

"Son," Rachel called out, "we need your help."

"But, Mom, did you hear that man?" He pointed into the shifting mass as he trotted back to his mother.

Rachel reached out and grabbed Gideon's arm. "Try not to listen. These are dangerous men."

The crowd swelled, pushing Amulon back into them. He gripped Zeniff's shirt front. "Bet you wish you'd been in the battle, old man. Blood running down the hills." He leaned close and Zeniff flinched back, looking disgusted. "We showed the Lamanites, slaughtered 'em all. And didn't need no God to help us." Amulon dove back into the ruckus, cackling.

"Are you all right?" Rachel asked, looking horrified.

"I'm fine," Zeniff said, though his voice sounded strained to Mera.

"He forgets you were once king," Rachel said darkly.

The furrows in Zeniff's brow deepened.

"We'll be home soon," Mera reassured him, moving a little faster as the crowd grew more wild. There was some sort of commotion near the temple, something different from the boasting and celebrations around them.

A strong voice soared above the others. "Wo be unto this people . . ."

The crowd surged toward the temple, shoving around each other to see what was going on. So many people were shouting that Mera could hardly hear. Zeniff raised his head, looking alarmed. Not far away, Helam and several of his men were trying to prevent an all-out brawl.

"That's him!" Gideon said, pointing. "The man I heard." He pulled free of Rachel and darted between the lawless soldiers, weaving his way toward the stranger.

"He'll be crushed!" Mera said.

Rachel released Zeniff and went after her son.

"Repent and turn to the Lord," the strange man cried, "or He will deliver you to your enemies!" He stood on an overturned pot, which raised him head and shoulders above the rest. He was thick, muscular, taller than Zeniff, though Mera thought Noah would've surpassed him by an inch or two. He moved with a languid grace that came only with years of training and a certain stiffness that hinted at old injuries. His unruly dark hair and beard shadowed his face. "I have seen your abominations!" he cried, his sure voice carrying over the restive crowd.

Amulon shook his fist in the air. "Who are you to threaten us? We just delivered ourselves from the enemy! We don't need your God." He nodded to armed men on the edge of the fray. "Seize him!" But the men couldn't push through.

"We've got to get out of here," Mera said, trying to move Zeniff forward by herself. The tenor of the crowd had shifted from raucous to menacing. It was only a matter of time before a fight broke out. "Let's go," Mera urged.

But Zeniff didn't budge. "I want to hear him."

"He's either brave or crazy," someone behind them said.

The stranger raised his arms overhead. His right hand reached higher than the left, as if he were pointing to heaven. "I am Abinadi, servant of the Lord. He sees your wickedness. You must repent and come to know the Lord your God."

"*Zeniff,*" Mera said, tugging his arm. "Come on!"

Zeniff turned to her with an elated look. "The Lord has heard our prayers. He's sent a prophet to Shilom."

Mera drew in a sharp breath and turned back toward Abinadi, seeing him in a new light. Could it be true? Had the Lord sent this man to soften their hearts, to change their ways? To change Noah? "He's come to save us," she said in a whisper.

"Except you repent," Abinadi cried, "you shall be brought into bondage. But the Lord can set you free." His gaze swept the crowd, pausing on Zeniff and Mera, the only elderly among them. And while part of the crowd grew restless, another part grew still.

Amulon's eyes narrowed, his face turning black with rage.

Mera gasped. "Amulon will hurt him."

Zeniff's weight lifted off Mera and she turned with a cry, but it was only Helam, sliding under Zeniff's arm.

"You must go to Noah," Helam said. "It won't take long for Amulon to convince him to kill Abinadi." Helam's eyes gleamed as he watched Abinadi preach. "Finally, someone who speaks the truth."

Mera hesitated, her gaze on the new prophet. If Jarom had stayed in Shilom, things would be different. There would be no need to cry repentance and prophesy destruction. Would she forever wonder what had become of her eldest son and his family? She shivered, drawing her shawl close around her body.

"Hurry," Helam said. Soldiers pressed toward Abinadi, spears in their hands. "I'll see Zeniff to your chambers."

"Helam's right," Zeniff said, his voice pained. "You must go."

Mera nodded and slipped away. At the edge of the crowd she paused, arrested by Abinadi's strong, reassuring voice. It was as if this new prophet had opened a window to her soul.

# Standing Tall

## *Tamar, 150 BC*

Tamar saw through the crowd that Mera left Zeniff and Helam. She was too far away to shout to Mera, and the noise of the crowd wouldn't have allowed it anyway. She was alone.

Tamar felt it before she saw it—warm blood trickling down her cheek. The soldiers had struck Abinadi as they dragged him away and she'd been standing too close.

"No!" she cried out. His obvious pain sent a shudder through her stomach. She lurched toward him. Blood dripped to her shawl and she reached up to wipe her face with woven cloth, only smearing it more.

There were so many questions in her heart and mind. She'd hoped to find answers through Abinadi. Her attempt at trying to get close enough to speak with him failed.

Amulon's voice rose above the shouts of the people. "If he escapes, his guards will die. We will have order in our city! We have laws to deal with these kinds of people. If he is found guilty, he will be punished. If not, he will be set free." His words placated both the believers and unbelievers, all nodding in agreement. "Until that time, he will be kept under guard, for his safety as well as our own. The council will meet and determine *if* he is guilty." He grinned at the *if*, nodding to the priests standing nearby.

The guards pushed closer together. Tamar could barely see the prophet. She knew where they would take him, so she slipped back through the jostling crowd. Her stomach began to knot in fear. Those she trusted and knew as friends had become separated from her. She was surrounded by strangers.

"Some queen," a ragged voice said. "You defy the king to support a madman?"

Tamar spun to find the voice, but her shawl blocked her vision.

"Traitor," came another voice.

Shoulders and elbows jabbed at Tamar and she realized that she was in very real danger. Amulon's threats against Mera felt tangible to Tamar now.

Abinadi still stood tall above the others. Tamar could just see the tight cluster of soldiers with him in the center, heading toward the palace chamber.

# Trials

*Mera, 150 BC*

*A*mulon reached the palace before Mera and was already whispering lies in Noah's ears, stirring him to anger as she entered the sumptuous throne room. She strode past the idols cluttering every corner, resisting the temptation to kick them.

"Who is Abinadi," Noah said, waving a hand in outrage, "that he should judge me and my people? He's just a rebel stirring up old feuds."

"My men are holding him now," Amulon said. His thick fists were clenched at his sides, still stained with blood from the battle.

"And who is the Lord to bring affliction on us?" Noah said disparagingly. "He's no more than some old fool's imaginings."

"Noah." Mera stopped several feet from the throne, not bothering to curtsy. "That's blasphemy. Have you no remorse at all?"

Noah sat back, plucking grapes from the polished wooden table at his side. "We defeated the Lamanites," he said, "without the help of the tottering old priests you and Father admire so much. And without the help of your imaginary God."

Mera rocked back on her feet. How could Noah deny God? Couldn't he see the terrible consequences of his choices, the pain he'd caused for so many? Couldn't he see that if he'd followed God's ways things would be better? She'd always thought he still believed, deep down in the recesses of his dark heart, even if he didn't obey. Maybe it was too hard to hold on to two conflicting ideas. *No man can serve two masters.* She stepped closer to the throne, as close as she dared. "Noah, don't you remember what we taught you? You know how to recognize truth."

Amulon stepped between them. "This is ridiculous. I'll send your babbling mother away."

"No." Noah brushed Amulon aside. "I decide what to do with my mother."

"I know you've felt the Spirit," Mera said. "Abinadi can help you find your way back."

A conflicted expression flickered across Noah's face. He leaned forward in his throne, his fine embroidered coat straining against his girth. "And how do I come back if I don't even believe?"

Mera clenched her robes in her fist, trying to not to let her hope show and ruin it all. "All you need is a desire, a tiny little desire."

Noah raised his chin, closing his hand around a goblet of wine on the table. "And what if there is no God?" He swigged the wine, wiping his mouth on his sleeve, then waving the goblet around the room in an expansive gesture. "There's no evidence. There's nothing I can see."

Behind him, a faint smile played on Amulon's lips.

"By their fruits ye shall know them," Mera said. "I know God exists. I've seen his hand in my life. I've seen the good in the lives of those who follow him."

"Like Jarom?" Noah said, his eyes devoid of feeling.

Mera wasn't sure what to say.

A young soldier clattered into the room, rushed forward, and gave a cursory nod to Amulon before bowing to Noah. "He escaped, my king." He paused to catch his breath. "The prophet escaped."

Noah struck out, knocking the boy to the floor. "Find this so-called prophet and bring him here. No one stirs up my people to rebellion! I'll slay him myself."

The young soldier scuttled backward, then sprang to his feet. "He's gone, Your Majesty. He left the city."

Mera felt like she was drowning. The new prophet was gone before she could even meet him, before he could speak with Noah and change everything. And now Noah, her once-sweet Noah, had threatened to kill him if he returned.

She looked up at the king, shouting from his jewel-encrusted throne, seeking to destroy a man who had the truth she sought, the one thing Noah refused to grasp. Mera stepped backward, shaking her head while he raged on and on. Noah wasn't her son anymore. Pain shot through her, an agony rivaled only by what she'd felt when Jarom had left.

She'd lost both her sons.

# 19

# A Prophet among Us

### Tamar, 150 BC

Tamar found Limhi outside the old palace and wrapped her arms around him. "I'm sorry I didn't come back for you. I should have, but I didn't." She stifled a sob. "Please forgive me. I went to the cave without my own son. I'm so sorry."

Limhi held his mother close, then pushed her back to look closely at her face. "What happened to you?" he said with alarm.

"I'm fine, it's not my blood."

Her response must not have been good enough. "I don't care whose blood it is, what is it doing on you?" His muscles quivered with fatigue. Tamar felt his arms shaking.

"I can explain, but for now, we must see what Noah plans to do with Abinadi. You, you've fought your first battle." Tamar had moved on from guilt to genuine concern. "How are you?"

"Mother, I fought well. You would be proud." He gently gripped her shoulders with his scraped and bloody hands. "Helam has been a great teacher. I don't glory in taking any man's life, but I fought to protect you. To protect our people." His eyes were moist. "I felt the Lord's protection and guidance. Instructions from Helam, words of warning . . . these all flooded my mind. It's hard to explain, Mother."

"I know. Just remember this day. The stories of our ancient ancestors were told to me as a child. I told them to you. Remember this day and tell it to your children."

Limhi nodded. "I will. Not to tell of killing other men, but how God watches over us."

"When we are righteous," Tamar added.

"Not all of our people are righteous, Mother. Certainly not Father and those who follow him."

"I believe that when we do as we should, the Lord's blessings spread over others. Like rain that falls on everyone, not just the good. It waters my crops at the same time it waters the gardens of those who worship idols and live wicked lives. The just and unjust receive the blessing."

Limhi nodded. "I still don't understand why some die in battle, good men, and others who live wickedly walk away and live on."

Clearly, he was seeking understanding, and Tamar knew she didn't have all of the answers. "God's ways are not our ways. We won't understand why things happen as they do, but we trust in God. Trust means not having all of the answers, but going forward in faith."

Limhi lifted his arms to embrace his mother.

Tamar buried her face in his chest. He towered over her, as tall as his father now. The same, yet so very different. This would be a time of mourning for all. She was just thankful her son had been spared in his first battle, and she hoped that Zeniff would not suffer from the exposure in the damp cave. More than ever, she craved the peace and comfort of the words on the scrolls. *Why did it take so long for me to realize their value, how precious they would be to me?*

Limhi pointed toward the old palace.

"You need some time to yourself. Let's go home." Limhi put a gentle arm around his mother's shoulders and urged her to leave. Together they escaped the sickening mockery of the soldiers.

Once inside their own quarters, Tamar collapsed into the pile of skins in the corner of the room and closed her eyes.

"What are you thinking about, Mom?"

"I'm sad. Sad for those who have lost loved ones and sad that our people have lost so much of their goodness. Can you hear them shouting and cursing the Lamanites?" She spoke without opening her eyes.

"I can," Limhi said quietly, "and I fear that the wickedness will grow worse once Grandfather is gone. His presence reminds the people of what we used to be." Tamar sat up, feeling a sense of urgency. Limhi's lip quivered and a tear escaped down his cheek. He brushed it away.

"I love that you're a man with a tender heart."

He took in a deep breath. "There's something else, Mother." In a quick movement, he was kneeling in front of her. He put one hand on her shoulder and grasped it tight.

"I was out at the spring yesterday. There was a new teacher. He talked of traveling throughout the Nephite lands. He's got scrolls."

Tamar's face lit up. "Where did you hear this? I heard a commotion in town but didn't stop to listen. I was trying to find you."

Limhi continued with greater excitement. "Many strangers pass through the city. There was one I kept seeing. He didn't seem to be here to trade. He never went to see the king. He spent all his time in the old shops, seeking out the former high priests. They told me he'd met them at the spring for a private meeting."

Tamar rose. "Who did you hear this from?"

"Yoseph, the master weaver."

Tamar stood up quickly, brushing the wrinkles from her shawl and pulling it over her head.

"I'm going to make Shiva visits now. If anyone is looking for me, you can say that's where I've gone."

"You're tired, Mother, come rest. There's time for that on the morrow."

"I must go."

"At least let me come with you."

"Not this time, I need to go alone." Tamar slipped out of the tapestry door, then peeked back in. "I need to make more candles. Take some wax and honey from the bees, but not so much that they swarm."

"I can do that."

"You know which oils to use, right?"

"Yes, Mother."

"I love you, son."

"Yes, Mother." He smiled.

Tamar vanished into the raucous crowd and closed her ears to the vile and angry words. With a scarf over her head and face mostly covered, she darted into the weaver's shop without anyone stopping to speak with her.

A stranger stood with the weaver and his wife. Micah respectfully addressed Tamar. "My queen, we honor your company and welcome your visit. However, can this wait till the morrow?"

Hagar smiled. "We will come to the old palace at first light."

The stranger slowly turned, his face obscured with a heavy beard and a woven head scarf. He gazed in Tamar's direction, acknowledging her presence, but said nothing.

"How did you get away from the soldiers?" A peculiar warmth spread through Tamar's chest. He still said nothing, but he smiled at her and his eyes shone.

She paused and addressed the weaver. "Thank you. You're always so good to me. I'll await your visit in the morning." Once again, before leaving, she looked at the stranger and felt the urge to reach out to him or ask him a question. Just to hear him speak.

The weaver kindly asked her to be on her way and reminded her that they'd see her first thing in the morning. Tamar turned and slipped into the twilight to continue her Shiva visits.

At each home, there seemed to be a peace and calmness she hadn't expected. The mourning consisted of expressions of gratitude for the person's life and talk of how the Lord had blessed them. After the third visit, she began to piece together bits of what had occurred prior to her coming. The stranger had been to each home. He must have followed the lighted candles in the doorways to find those families who were mourning.

The stories she heard as she sat with each family unfolded in her mind. He had prayed with them, encouraging them to do the same. He told them that they would feel greater comfort if they visited one another instead of waiting for comfort to come to them. He taught them to reach out in their pain, and in return their pain would subside as they gave comfort to others.

This was fascinating to Tamar. She sensed a palpable difference in the feeling inside their homes. She intended to bring comfort to them but found herself buoyed and almost joyful as she returned to her home.

"Mother?" Limhi said as she slipped inside their home.

Tamar sat upon her bed and shared the feelings in her heart. "There's something different in Shilom, a new spirit. Something precious. And it came with the new teacher."

Together, Limhi and Tamar prayed. Although the fire had died down to coals, their hearts continued to burn.

*Lord, how can one day be both terrible and wonderful at the same time?*

Tamar drifted off to sleep and somewhere in the night, her old nightmare returned, her vision full of smoke and fire, terror and fear, and with it a growing sense of purpose and peace.

———◆———

The palace gleamed in the early morning light and Tamar was surprised that Noah would even be up this early. Amulon had roused her from sleep, shouting at her from the courtyard, refusing to set foot in the old palace. She came at the king's bidding to appease him but slow enough to keep him from feeling he had control over her every move.

Her sandals glided on the polished floor. It glistened with morning dew. She willed herself to push through the massive doors that led into the palace temple hall.

She had never seen it empty. It had always been filled with people either complaining or celebrating. Today it was still and silent, except for the sound of bare feet slapping the floor, which she soon realized was Noah, pacing.

"What's wrong?"

"Lamanites. I need some advice."

Tamar was perplexed. "You get all of the advice you need from Amulon. What could I possibly offer you?" She looked around. "Where is everyone?"

"I sent them all away. I just want to talk to you."

"I'm listening."

"After the attack yesterday, we wondered how the Lamanites always seemed to know when we were most vulnerable. They seemed to attack right when the flocks were out to pasture or the guards weren't at their posts. Now we know why. There is a Lamanite lookout up on the bluff, hidden in the trees." Noah waved his hand above his head, pointing off in several directions. "I'm afraid they may have seen some of the Lamanite women come to the palace a time or two in days past. I think we made some of the warriors angry."

"Okay, I'm not following why you need my help."

"The people are upset with me, as if I had anything to do with it."

The depth of Noah's oblivion to the impact his choices had on his people and his family was pathetic. "You truly can't see it, can you?" Tamar could not stop the words from coming out. "It *is* your fault, completely. You've brought wickedness into this city. You've chased out or killed the wise men who led people to be good and do good. You've brought shame to our family with your many wives and concubines when you promised . . . you *promised* me. You lied to me, Noah. You've hurt me deeply, and Limhi too."

Noah was silent. For once he had nothing to say. He looked at Tamar, then at the floor. "You're different. I don't remember you being such a strong woman."

"Is that all you have to say?"

"Can you help me with this Lamanite problem?"

Tamar realized that his heart had become stone. She took a deep breath and willed herself not to cry. *Lord, thank you for giving me the words and the chance to speak them. I can move on now.* "What do you want me to do?"

"I need someone I can trust to watch from the tower. Someone who doesn't drink. I need sober eyes. Do you think some of your people would be willing to help protect our city?"

"Who exactly are my people?"

"I've seen you with groups from time to time." Noah's eyes took on a steely glare. "Shopkeepers—those who still worship at the old temple." His lip curled. "Groups of people leave the city, are gone for hours, and then come back and open their shops. If I were to possibly read from a list, which may or may not exist"—his grin grew more sinister—"it would be any of the old craftsmen, the former high priests, and anyone loyal to Zeniff." Noah rose and added, "Mother was here yesterday. I know about the stranger who preached openly in the city yesterday. He's gone."

A twinge of fear struck Tamar's heart and she worried for a moment about the safety of their continued meetings. She had hoped to speak with the stranger. Now that wouldn't happen. She felt a sadness that she'd not had the chance to hear his words. Tamar thought a moment about Noah's request and whether she wished to help. "Limhi has a sharp eye. He could take a few shifts. I think some of Limhi's friends would help also."

"Good. I would like to spend more time with Limhi. I don't know him very well, honestly. He's grown so much. I heard he fought well in the battle yesterday." Noah paused for a second and added, as if forgetting good men had died and his own son had been in danger, "I thought that giving him that young maiden would make him want to come around more, but I've not seen him at all."

"Where were you yesterday, during the battle?" Tamar asked with a touch of anger.

Noah's face flushed. He spat back, "I was there, at the battle!"

Tamar looked at his face, his arms, his feet—no wounds, no scrapes, no sign of battle. "You came through unscathed. Not a scratch."

"My men needed to hear my voice urging them on, so I maintained my position in the rear, as an archer and battle captain. You wouldn't expect me to be in the fray." Noah's words fell from his lips like the spittle that accompanied them. "I'm their king. I nearly got hit by a Lamanite spear! I heard it whistle as it flew past my head! I'm lucky to be alive!"

Tamar studied the man who stood in front of her. So different from their son—noble and proud in righteous ways—who ran to the battle's front. This man, in his fancy robes, with soft hands, was a stranger to her now. "No, you're right. You don't know him very well. He's as much a stranger to you as you are to me."

Tamar turned again to leave, and as she walked back toward the door, she spoke without even turning around. "I'll arrange the watch schedule."

She felt free. Finally. Free of the guilt of not living in the palace. Free of the pain of not being able to tell him how she felt. On her walk home, the sun shone bright. A new day had begun. With a lighter step, she nearly ran back to her quarters. There were several people standing outside when she neared her home. Yoseph, the master weaver, as well as others faithful to the old high priests and their teachings.

Limhi stood head and shoulders above them all. Their voices were hushed. No one saw her slip up to the back of the growing assembly.

"Gone?" one asked.

"Abinadi was going to teach at the spring today," another added.

Tamar spoke up, slightly louder than those in the group. "His life was in danger. I believe we are all in danger if we continue to gather." All heads turned. "I've spoken to Noah. He's aware of a movement in the city. He watches us. He knows who closes their shops."

Fear washed across their faces.

"I'm glad Abinadi escaped before there was trouble," someone said. "I don't think it's safe to meet in groups any longer. We must think of our families."

"Has anyone seen Mera? She needs to know what is going on."

"The healer has been with Zeniff. He's not well."

Limhi's eyes caught Tamar's. He nodded toward their royal quarters.

"Please return to your homes," Tamar said. "We will find a way to gather. Take parchment and write the words Abinadi shared with each of you. We need his message."

# Goodbyes

## *Mera, 150 BC*

*M*era summoned the healer to her quarters for the second time that day. Outside, the peach blossoms nodded in a faint breeze, their heady scent recalling years gone by, a time of peace and hope, back when Zeniff was strong.

Now he rested on his bed, his thin chest heaving with the effort it took to breathe. His breaths came slower and slower and the grip of his withered hand in Mera's weaker with every passing moment.

Mera swallowed a sob.

*Oh, Lord, can you not spare Zeniff, at least awhile longer?*

She mopped his feverish brow with a damp cloth. His eyes fluttered open, but didn't focus at first. The slight pressure on her hand increased.

"Mera?" he murmured.

The tapestry in the doorway swung aside and Aaron, the healer, appeared. He hesitated at the threshold, gazing at Zeniff. Then he bowed his head and came in. He busied himself at a table against the side wall, lighting a candle and opening a pouch of valerian root. "All I can do now is ease his pain."

Zeniff waved him away. "I would speak with my wife alone," he said, and then he coughed. His coughing continued, dry and merciless as a desert wind.

Mera slipped her arms under his head and shoulders, lifting him upright. He felt light as a feather, as if his body had wasted away so much that his spirit would soon soar free.

The coughs continued.

Aaron heated water in a small metal ladle and then poured it into an earthenware mug with herbs. "These will not dull your mind," he said as he brought the drink over, "but will soothe your throat and ease some of your pain."

Mera blinked away tears. It would not do to have her husband, the former king, see her weakness.

He swallowed a few gulps of herb tea, then rested back against his heather-stuffed mattress, raising his wrinkled hands to cup Mera's face. "Oh, my sweet, sweet wife. You've been so good to me and have suffered for so long."

"I will leave you now," Aaron said, gathering his things into his leather satchel.

"Send for Tamar and Limhi," Mera said, her voice breaking. She covered Zeniff's hands with her own, longing for the time when hers were lost in his, but their roles had reversed of late.

"Give us a few minutes." Zeniff cast him a sharp glance. "There is much Mera must know."

Aaron bobbed his head, lifted aside the tapestry and, with a regretful backward glance, left the room.

"Prop me up," Zeniff said after the healer had gone.

Mera shifted furs and pillows underneath him, raising him to a more upright position.

"Thank you." Zeniff smiled, his eyes glowing with a light she hadn't seen in years. "Abinadi came to see me," he said, his voice hushed.

"What?" Mera's breath caught. "What if Noah had discovered you? He would've killed you both." The words left her before she could shove the horrible thought away, confirming what she had so long refused to believe about her son.

"Noah won't find him." Zeniff lifted his head, then dropped it back to his pillow. "Abinadi's gone to Zarahemla to see his family. But he promised he'd return." Zeniff gave her a tremulous smile. "Mera, you won't believe . . ." He had another coughing fit. When he'd finished, his face was pale, his voice hoarse. "It was such a blessing to have him here. I am so grateful. When he returns"—Zeniff gripped Mera's hands—"you must seek him out. You *must* hear his words."

Mera nodded, tears tracing down her cheeks. "But I heard him already, in the city."

"He wants to speak with you himself. He'll open your eyes, help you change."

Mera blinked. "Help me change? We need him to change Noah." She studied Zeniff. "What did he say to you?"

Zeniff sighed. It was a long time before he spoke again, and for a moment Mera thought she'd lost him. Then he spoke in barely a whisper, "Promise me, Mera, that you'll hear him. Listen."

Mera stroked his cheek. "I promise."

The tapestry rustled and Tamar and Limhi stepped inside. Mera made room for them both beside the bed. Zeniff rested his hand on Limhi's head and gave him a final blessing.

"You're a grown man now, Limhi," Zeniff said when he was done. "Someday this kingdom will rest on your shoulders. You must lead the people back to the Lord."

Limhi nodded and then turned away to hide his grief.

"Tamar," Zeniff said. "You're the daughter I never had. You've stood by Noah. I must ask you to do so a little longer." He patted her hand. "I can only imagine the agony you've felt as his wife. The Lord will bless you for your faith and perseverance. He's blessed you already." He nodded to Limhi.

At that moment, Noah burst inside, nearly tearing down the tapestry in his haste. "Why wasn't I summoned?" He surveyed the room with narrowed eyes.

"We sent a runner for you moments ago." Tamar raised her chin and met Noah's gaze. Something in her had changed, Mera realized. "We know how precious your time is."

Noah sniffed.

"My son." Zeniff reached for Noah, who moved closer and took his father's hand, though he did not kneel. "I will always love you, even from the grave."

Noah's face tightened, not with sorrow, but jealousy. It shadowed his brow and showed in the tense line of his shoulders.

Zeniff clung to Noah's fingers, his expression earnest. "I've always loved you as much as Jarom. You know that."

"Never speak that name," Noah said through gritted teeth. "I've told you that."

Zeniff's breathing hitched. He clutched his chest, his face going white. He took another breath, then went still.

"No!" Mera grasped Zeniff's arm, but he did not respond. She buried her head in his shoulder, shaking.

Noah pulled away from his father's body. "Now no one will question who rules this people," he muttered.

Mera raised her face in shock and saw Noah glare at Limhi before he tossed aside the tapestry and stormed away.

She seethed with silent fury. This is what Noah felt at his father's death? Not sorrow, not remorse, but satisfaction? "We're lucky he didn't kill Zeniff himself." She clapped a hand over her mouth, then slumped against Zeniff in tears.

Tamar's slim fingers stroked Mera's back, then Limhi's arms surrounded her. They huddled together, the last of Zeniff's hope, mourning his loss.

"You're not alone," Tamar said, again and again.

Mera wondered if Tamar was speaking to her, to Limhi, or to herself. Maybe to them all. *Will we ever find peace?*

She looked up into Tamar's and Limhi's teary faces, finally understanding what Zeniff had been trying to tell her. "I can't change Noah, can I? No matter how I try."

"Only the Lord can change him," Tamar said, "and only if Noah is willing."

---

Mera held fast to Tamar and Limhi as the procession wove through the dusty streets of Shilom toward the burial mound, their faces forward, their eyes pools of sadness. She needed their strength to survive this day.

*Lord, help me through this. Help us all.*

Joyful memories of life with Zeniff flashed through her mind: the daisies he'd brought her in her youth to announce his intentions. His laughter at her surprise, followed by a flash of vulnerability when he realized what her surprise might mean. The tender way he looked at her across the altar on their wedding day. His joy as one son and then another entered their lives.

Faith-filled evenings spent around the fire, teaching their children, even after his long days serving the people as their king.

Images of sorrow crowded her mind as well: the losses their people had faced at the hands of the Lamanites. The unrelenting pain she and Zeniff had endured over Noah's choices as well as Jarom's flight into the wilderness with his family.

She gave a slight shake of her head, deliberately replacing those miserable memories with other, happier times: hours spent together in the temple, Zeniff's pleasure at a blanket she'd woven, his wrinkled hands cradling her face.

She would see him again. If what Abinadi said was true, she would see Zeniff again. Mera's heart burned within her. Tears rose to her eyes. But these were not tears of sorrow. Instead, joy filled her, confirming her belief in the world to come, where she and Zeniff would live together with the Lord forever.

Meanwhile, Noah appeared to be the perfect grieving son. He wept at appropriate times and took great comfort in his many wives and concubines. Wails filled the air from a group of women he'd most likely paid, judging by their glances seeking his approval.

Behind the royal family, Zeniff's old friends, the shopkeepers and craftsmen, each carried a ceremonial bucket of dirt from the valley below. The old high priests mourned silently, with a quivering chin or tear-filled eye, but nothing like the group following Noah.

Mera walked tall. Her inner strength carried her. "I will see him again. I know it," she whispered to Tamar. "God promises the faithful they'll not be strangers in the next life." She nodded to fellow believers as their eyes met, her confidence growing with each step.

"We walk not only this road, but life's road, together," Tamar whispered back.

Mera smiled. She'd thought she'd never smile again. She'd lost Noah to wickedness. Jarom was lost as well. And now her beloved Zeniff. But something had changed inside her, a blossoming of the faith she once had thought was enough. Now she knew there was more. Now she knew the Lord would heal her and transform her, if she allowed it. So she smiled, a small, quiet smile that hinted at her newfound inner peace.

This was something she must share. That was what Zeniff would have wanted. He'd made her promise to seek out Abinadi when he returned.

Until then, she would see that all who believed could share the truths they'd learned.

Out of sight of the king.

This was how Mera would honor Zeniff as he left this world for the next.

The funeral procession wound its way to the top of the mound. Zeniff's final resting place on earth was the eastern tip of the burial mound, overlooking the city once called Lehi-Nephi. The city of his dreams—dreams of peaceful habitation with their ancient brothers, the Lamanites. Dreams that were not fulfilled. Instead, they were shattered by hatred—jealousy between brothers.

Mera stood atop the hill, side by side with Tamar and Limhi. Their hearts sank as Zeniff was lowered into the ground. Those he loved completed his burial, one bucket at a time. A light breeze tugged at Mera's shawls. As she blinked back tears, her conviction grew. She would not let Noah's jealousy destroy their people. Her deepened faith, united with Limhi's determination and Tamar's steadfast hope, must guide the people until Abinadi returned.

# 21

# Believers

## *Tamar, 148 BC*

Tamar had gone to place flowers on Zeniff's grave, which was now covered by tall green grasses. Her mother was somewhere much deeper in the mound. She had come more often since Zeniff had been brought here and felt that the flowers, although atop Zeniff's resting place, were for her mother too. She whispered as her throat constricted with grief. "Mother, I miss you. I trust we will see each other again." Tamar placed a hand over her heart. "It still hurts though."

Passover. A time of renewal and change. It always brought her to this place—the burial mound. She came to place a new smooth stone on Zeniff's grave to remember the years since his passing. Two stones. Two years. So many tears had been shed, but the promise of a savior brought her peace. He would come at a future time, this Messiah. She knew the stories. Prophets of old had spoken of his coming.

*I have so many questions. Things I should have asked long before now.* The small tree she had planted near the top of the burial mound was now almost as tall as Limhi, whose height seemed to change as much as the plants she tended to regularly. She breathed deeply and closed her eyes, taking in the cool freshness of spring, tinged with the ever-present smoke from the potter's kiln.

She was relaxed and at peace knowing Noah couldn't see her from his palace window. He had made sure that any view only included beautiful buildings of his design and not reminders of the city's painful past. A burial mound would be such a reminder. He never came here to honor his father's grave, and it infuriated him that she'd planted a tree, signifying an end to this mound's growth.

The smoke reminded her that she needed to speak with Lisha, who had asked to meet her at the potter's shed. As Tamar traveled the well-worn path, she reviewed the teachings of Abinadi. Step by step, word by word she rehearsed them in her mind. It had been two years since his teachings filled the hearts and minds of the people. Two years since he vanished before the king's army.

Remembering. Such an important thing. The teachings he'd brought had been added to the scrolls of Melek and she hoped that someday Abinadi would return, but she doubted he could. Noah had his soldiers on high alert watching for any new teachers.

On her way, she planned to stop by the palace to find Limhi, who had been visiting his father. She entered the city just in time to see him exit the palace in a hurry.

"Limhi," Tamar called to him through the crowded street. He looked up and scanned the crowd until their eyes met. His eyes stormed and brows furrowed. He wove his way through the crowd. When he reached his mother, Tamar took his hand, pulling him aside, out of the crush of people. "What is it?"

He appeared as though he wanted to hit something. "He's taken back the young girl as a new wife. The one he promised to me. He just couldn't let her be. I care for her, Mother. What can I do? Will there be no end to his wicked ways?" A small ripple passed through his lip. The young boy whose heart had been broken by his father was now a man, still hurting, but for a different reason.

Tamar embraced him gently, as to not capture the attention of passersby. "God knows your pain," she whispered in his ear.

"That's great, but can't God do something about him? How long will God let this wickedness go on?" His eyes were blazing, his voice husky with emotion.

"Let's continue this at home. I'd like to sit down and talk privately." They joined the flood of shoppers and visitors. As they passed by the potter's shed on their way back home they overheard Alma and Lisha engaged in a heated conversation. Alma's voice rose above hers. Tamar paused. "Limhi, I'll be home in a little bit. Wait for me there, please."

"Mother, it's not your place . . ."

"Son, please go. I'll be home soon."

As Limhi strode away, Tamar heard Lisha's reply to Alma.

". . . I don't care what he does. It's wrong and you know it."

Tamar sucked in a painful breath. She felt as though the words were coming from her own heart.

"It's an honor to be a high priest and to help lead the city."

"Not in this way. It's simply wickedness. That's what Abinadi said. One wife. One God. One faith. One people."

"Unless I hear it for myself, how do you expect me to believe?" Alma asked.

"It's what your mother taught you. It's what Zeniff taught our people. God doesn't change. We do. You once believed."

"I still do," Alma said.

"You can't say that and act just like Noah. Will you become one of his lying, thieving, whoring puppets?"

Tamar stepped in just as it Alma raised his hand, as if to strike Lisha.

"Alma!" Tamar cried.

Alma's hand dropped. His head bowed. "My queen."

"He wouldn't have hurt me." Lisha appeared stunned. "We were both angry."

"Alma, do you wish to continue the conversation with me present, or are you finished?"

"I'm finished." He turned to Lisha. "I'll be at the palace." He turned and walked out, not bothering to say goodbye to his wife.

Tamar put her arm around Lisha and together they stood in the doorway of the potter's shed and watched Alma storm down the street. It wasn't long before a few of the palace women were following after him. Once or twice they glanced back toward Lisha as if they knew there had been a fight. Faster their feet flew until they all passed through the palace door like the king and his harem.

Tamar comforted Lisha. Probably more than anyone else, Tamar knew her fears, her pain, and her sorrow.

"Let's go," Tamar whispered to Lisha.

"Where?"

"To the spring."

As Tamar neared her quarters, Limhi hurried to her. "Mera already left. I waited for you."

Moments later, Tamar, Limhi, and Lisha vanished into the thick vegetation along the river bank, wary of Noah's guards. But the soldiers were enjoying their regular gift of wine. They lounged, oblivious to the royal family they were supposed to be guarding.

———— ◆ ————

Helam stepped out of the dense underbrush and startled Tamar, causing her to gasp. "Don't do that!" she said in a loud whisper. "What if I'd cried out? The guards would have come!"

"My apologies, my queen." Helam bowed his head slightly. "My job is to keep you safe. Pass on through and I'll make sure you're not followed."

"Thank you. You're a true friend."

Helam nodded again, disappearing without a sound as quickly as he had appeared.

"You said we could talk at the house. Can we talk now?" Limhi asked as they walked down the path, arm in arm.

"We can. What we say will be good for Lisha to hear."

Lisha's eyes still held worry, fear, and sorrow. She nodded and kept walking.

"You visit the graves each spring," Limhi said. "Tell me what you know about the souls of the departed. Where is Grandfather now?"

Tamar took a deep breath, then took her son by the hand. "I learned some of this from the storytellers. More from Abinadi. I don't know much, but I'll tell you what I do know. His body sleeps. Till Christ comes, all who sleep will remain where they were laid. One day all who die will live again. Zeniff was a good man, overzealous at times, but he repented of his wrongs. He lived according to the teachings of the prophets. I believe he will be redeemed." A warmth filled Tamar from the top of her head to her sandaled feet. She knew. Those words were sweet and she desired more.

Limhi's face was light. "Did you feel it, Mother? Did your heart burn within you?"

Tamar turned to ask Lisha, but tears were streaming down Lisha's face. Tamar stopped and faced her. "All is not lost. Alma will find his way back." Tamar felt a burning hope that Alma would rise beyond Noah's influence. She could make no promises, though. She knew that all too well. "Whatever Alma is battling, we will pray for him. God would surely find a way to reach him."

Lisha smiled. It was a genuine smile, but her eyes were still etched with fear. "Did you feel this way about Noah, I mean, when he was younger . . . that he would change?"

Tamar nodded. "I always hoped. I thought it was part of his growing up, that he would lose his youthful lusts as he got older. He didn't. I loved him, but not what he did." Tamar's heart ached. "He just became more lost and more wicked. He is beyond the point where my love could change him." Seeing the concern in Lisha's face, she added, "Alma is different."

"How? How is he different than Noah?"

"He's got a goodness that runs deep. He treats you well."

"He's following Noah's path. I fear I may lose him the way you lost Noah." Lisha's voice was pinched and it quivered as she spoke.

"Whatever happens, the Lord will help you through it." Tamar embraced her young friend and whispered again. "I believe it will be well with you and with Alma." Lisha appeared to relax some. "Now, let's go to the spring."

The gathering was large, several hundred at least. Every bit of grass was taken and the large stones were covered with men, women, and children of all ages. Tamar looked around, scanning the group for Mera.

The old high priests were small in number. Age and war had taken most of them from this life. Others, like Melek, had been put to death. Those that remained were often asked to speak. They spoke words of peace and taught about Christ and the redemption that had been prophesied. Several from the crowd shared the words Abinadi had taught them. The collective experience buoyed Tamar. She felt light and happy. This spring felt like a holy place. She wanted to sing. So she did.

At first it was humming a tune she had been taught as a child. She recalled it being a song sung by the storyteller from time to time. Others nearby must have been taught it also, because they joined her. A ripple of music cascaded over the crowd and soon their voices joined in a chorus of praise. Peace and understanding washed over her, and from the expressions of those around her, they had to be feeling it also.

*Please, Lord, let Mera feel this too. I hope she is here, somewhere.*

Tamar scanned the crowd and spotted Mera leaning against a gnarled oak, accompanied by Naomi and the master weaver. Her eyes were closed, her mouth curled in a faint smile.

Night was coming on. They had to make their way back slowly as to not draw the attention of the king's guards.

"We should be going," Tamar said to Limhi and Lisha.

Lisha shook her head. "I'll stay back a little while. I need to spend a few moments understanding what I've felt this night."

Tamar nodded and slipped through the humming crowd, each group making their own way through the woods.

"I felt it again, Mother," Limhi said.

"Me too."

"What is it?"

"I think it is God's way of telling me something," Tamar said, "that he hears me and it's going to be all right."

Limhi nodded. "That's how I feel too."

People walked back to the city, speaking only in whispers so as to not bring any attention to their movements.

As they neared the edge of the forest, Helam was not where he had been before. Tamar wondered why.

When she returned to her quarters, she passed the healer who was just emerging from the courtyard. Before she could ask what had brought him there, Helam also emerged, slightly bloodied.

"What happened?" Tamar cried, rushing to his side.

"The king's guards were spying and wandered down the path. I fought them off. But Noah will surely find out we've been meeting here. I may be able to bribe the guards to keep quiet. Or brush the fight off as a disagreement that rose to blows."

"I'll wait with you next—" Limhi quickly offered.

"No!" Tamar said without letting him finish. "He already sees you as a threat to his kingdom. Don't give him any reason . . ." Tamar couldn't finish. She could only shake her head, her eyes expressing the horrible thoughts she could not bear to imagine.

"God will protect me. That's what you've taught me. I believe it. You must believe it too."

Limhi gave Tamar a gentle embrace. It filled her with peace and comfort. Her heart swelled with gratitude for a wise and good son. *Thank You, Lord, for this son. Bless and keep him always in Thy care.*

———————◆———————

The figure running past Tamar's door would not have caused her to look twice had it not been followed by another. The second was dressed in the royal robes of the high priests. Alma.

Tamar chided herself for even paying attention to their obvious marital argument. But something urged her to step out. She resisted. It nearly pushed her off the bed. Spring was in full bloom, and no one left their tapestry doors closed anymore unless in need of privacy. So she stood and ducked out her doorway and began walking in the direction they had gone. It didn't take long to find them.

Their voices were laced with pain.

"Are you going to strike at me again?" Lisha cried.

"I'd never . . ."

"You almost did the other day, before Tamar interrupted you."

"I was angry." His head bowed. "More than I've ever been. But I'd never hurt you."

"You already have. It's too late."

Tamar walked up to a heartbreaking scene.

Alma and Lisha stood apart in a small forest glade, their backs turned against each other. Tamar knew the feeling. She also knew she could help. Hers had been the heartbreaking reality of a husband who loved others more than her and didn't love God at all. Fighting her desire to let them deal with this on their own, she cleared her throat.

They both acknowledged her presence and then turned back away. Anguish drew heavy lines in their faces.

"Can I join you?"

Silence.

"Do you want me to leave?"

Silence.

"I'm sorry. I'll go," Tamar said. She turned to leave.

"No, stay," Lisha whispered. She burst out in tears.

Alma looked as if his heart were breaking. He crossed his arms over his chest.

Tamar took Lisha into her arms. She felt the agony of Lisha's broken heart. A heart torn apart by her husband's choices. She felt the pain of her own years of betrayal. Her sorrow was tempered by the gift of a son. A noble and strong young man.

Lisha rested a hand on her belly.

"You're pregnant?" Tamar took Lisha's shoulders and held her away, looking down at the tiny bump evident on Lisha's slender frame. She pulled her close again, this time feeling the tiny bulge. "You've been sick! Why didn't I put together your conspicuous absence around town?" Tamar chided herself. "I'm so happy for you." Then realizing that this little forest glade meeting was anything but a happy occasion, aside from this revelation, she said, "We need to all sit down."

The three of them found comfortable spots on the soft green grass. Privacy was theirs. Only the forest animals could hear their words, and they wouldn't be telling anyone.

It was difficult at first to get Alma and Lisha to talk. Tamar asked pointed questions that made Alma squirm. The truth came out slowly, painfully. There were moments where Lisha buried her head in agony at his honesty. Tamar wasn't sure she could take the truth. After a time, light began to filter through the trees. It cast a glow on their faces. Alma and Lisha moved closer together. He put his hand on her shoulder. She winced, but only a bit.

"Alma," Tamar said, "do you love Lisha?"

"Of course I do."

"Lisha, do you love Alma?"

"More than life."

"God has commanded us to obey His laws. Alma, you must love God first and Lisha second. By loving God first, you'll obey the commandment to love Lisha more than anything else. No other woman can have your heart, Alma." Tamar's gaze was unflinching.

Alma looked away. "You don't know what it's like. Noah expects certain things of me. What am I supposed to do, refuse him?"

"Yes, stand up for yourself."

"That's easy for you to say when you have chosen to not be a part of the palace life. That choice didn't earn you the respect of the people, you know."

"Their respect means little to me when it's God I hope to please. You'd do well to consider that for yourself."

He shook his head. "You don't understand. My future is in Noah's hands. He can make life good for me, or miserable."

"Are you only thinking of yourself?" Tamar felt herself becoming irritated. "What about Lisha?"

They both looked at Tamar.

"I don't know how to fix this." His eyes were pleading. "I can't just walk away."

"I don't have all of the answers, but God does." Lisha's voice was stronger. "Can't you trust Him?"

"No." His eyes became angry again. "He doesn't speak to me anymore. I don't need a God I can't see or hear."

Tamar's eyes closed. "If I didn't know it was you, Alma, I'd think it was Noah saying those words. He'll destroy you if you let him." She opened her eyes and let out a long, deep breath. "You were meant for more than this. You'll lose the things most dear and precious to you if you continue on this path."

"I can't lose Lisha." Alma's words were almost a whisper, his voice strangled with bitter emotion.

Powerful impressions came to Tamar's mind. "God loves you both. I know He's pleased with your love for each other. Are you committed enough to be unified, no matter what you face?"

Alma and Lisha gave each other a shy glance, then nodded.

"Alma," Tamar said, "your sins are great. But the Lord can help you change. Perhaps someday you will help others who are struggling and love them in spite of their sins." She took a deep breath. "We face difficult times as a people. God will be with us to strengthen and guide us, I know this. Try to listen for his voice."

*Thank you.* She offered a silent prayer of gratitude.

Alma's expression softened, love replacing the fire in his eyes.

Tamar, not wanting to lose this powerful feeling, suggested they pray together. After a brief but heartfelt prayer, Alma stood and helped Lisha to her feet, then did the same for Tamar.

"You can't expect me to abandon everything I've worked hard for," Alma said. "I have to do something though." He squeezed Lisha's hand. "Please be patient with me." He turned to Tamar. "I wrote some of the words Abinadi spoke when he was here two years ago. The king wishes for them to be burned, but I felt they should be kept as part of our history. Would you like them?"

"Oh, yes. We have tried to piece together a record of what Abinadi taught. Thank you, Alma. That will mean so much to us."

"Don't let Noah know I gave them to you."

"Would it be easier to give the records to Mera or to me?"

Alma shook his head. "Neither. Your movements are known. If Noah senses that I'm sympathetic to you believers, none of us will be safe. I'll find a way to get them to someone though."

Tamar nodded.

"The king has taken Gideon to be one of his soldiers," Alma said.

Tamar and Lisha both gasped in surprise.

"He wants to convince him that his father was a fool and died because he was mad. He has a plan for changing the young minds of Shilom, to draw them away from faith in God."

Tamar felt the peace of moments before drain from her heart as she considered the danger they faced in opposing Noah. The thought came to her mind to take one step at a time and have faith. "God will watch over Gideon. He's a good boy and his mother has taught him well. We must trust and not fear."

Alma's expression revealed his shame. "I don't want to see him end up like . . . like me."

# Fettered

*Mera, 148 BC*

*M*era scraped all the dried-out bits of clay from the work table, sweeping them into a bucket of sludgy water. Behind her, Rachel pumped her wheel, churning out one masterpiece after another for the king's court. All the while Noah was trying his best to corrupt her son. Naomi worked in the corner, crafting different, smaller pieces.

Mera watched the clay settle into the water. The larger chunks sank while the dust clung to the water's surface. *Repent and turn to the Lord.* That's what Abinadi had said. And that's what Zeniff had said too, more or less. *You must listen to Abinadi. He will help you change.*

For two long years, Mera had clung to these ideas. That was all she had left, with Zeniff gone, Jarom gone, and Noah—well, Noah was a disaster. A tear splashed into the dusty water. Mera wiped her face and set the bucket in the corner. Over time the clay would set up and be useful again.

"Rachel—"

"I know what you're going to say," Rachel said without looking up from the vase she was throwing. She'd drawn a reed along its surface, creating a thin spiral that wound up the clay. "Pottery is my livelihood. The court pays well."

Naomi snorted but didn't say anything.

"Now that Gideon is one of Noah's guards, I don't see how you can continue," Mera said. "I know how angry you are. If you refused the king's requests, you'd find other customers." She took a ball of clay from under a damp cloth and placed it on her own wheel. "Until then, I could help you."

"I won't infuriate the king and I don't need your charity." Rachel's vase wobbled and collapsed.

"Enough," Naomi said. "I am tired of your cutting remarks toward Mera. Ever since Melek died . . ."

Rachel stood, jostling her table. "You mean ever since her son killed my husband?"

A pang of grief shot through Mera. She pressed her hand to her chest. Rachel blamed her. She was probably right too. If only Mera had taught Noah better or if she'd prayed harder. *Repent and turn to the Lord.* The phrase echoed in her mind in a voice that almost sounded like Zeniff. Or some combination of Zeniff and Abinadi.

"I'm sorry," Mera said, folding her hands in her lap. She felt very small. "I'm sorry," she said again, then buried her face in her hands.

"I—" Rachel stopped mid-sentence.

Mera looked up.

"It's not Mera's fault," Naomi said as she molded ropes of clay into a platter. "You can't blame Mera for Noah's actions any more than you can claim credit for every good thing Gideon has done."

Rachel's chest swelled. "I raised Gideon right! Even without a father half his life. We read scrolls every day. We've never missed our prayers."

Naomi's fingers dug into her clay. "You think Mera hasn't done the same? You think she and Zeniff taught Noah this idolatry, these wicked ways?"

Mera sat quiet and still, her breaths catching in her chest. *Repent and turn to the Lord.*

Rachel threw her hands up. "Of course not, but they obviously did something wrong. They must've opened the door!"

Naomi's nostrils flared. "And what of Jarom? No better man ever lived than Jarom and you know it."

Rachel gazed from Naomi to Mera, her expression dark. "Then why did he leave? Jarom was no better than Noah. He was a coward."

Naomi gasped.

Both women stared at Mera, awaiting her response. "Jarom was not a coward," she said. "Just like you're not a coward for making pottery for a tyrant king. But I *am* Noah's mother. So it must be my fault."

"That's not true," Naomi said, leaving her clay and moving to Mera's side.

Mera gazed up at her. "You remember what Abinadi taught?"

"Of course I do. It's all anyone talks about at our meeting at the springs."

"And everywhere else," Rachel added. She'd sat back down and was slapping her clay back into a usable shape. "Unless the king or his guards are nearby."

"He said to repent and turn to the Lord," Mera said in a quiet voice.

Rachel glanced up.

"He meant that for all of us, Mera," Naomi said, "not just for you."

Mera shook her head. "Zeniff told me to listen to Abinadi. He told me I must change."

Naomi nodded. "So must we all." She gripped Mera's hand. "Zeniff's last words to you were not an accusation. It was not a suggestion that you were a bad mother or, or . . ." she waved her hand, "that you're responsible for Noah's sins. How could you be?"

Mera swallowed back her tears, thinking of the hours she'd spent on her knees, begging the Lord for peace and guidance.

Naomi knelt at Mera's side and gazed up at her with shining eyes. "It was a message of healing and of hope, Mera. And we need hope now more than ever."

At the wheel, Rachel made a strange choking sound, something between a laugh and a sob. She shook her head. "Noah will corrupt Gideon. What am I supposed to do?"

Naomi's mouth thinned to a line. "I don't know. But I'm not giving up on Alma." She rose and with a last squeeze of Mera's hand, added, "And Lisha isn't either," before returning to her work. "What else can I do?"

"I truly am sorry," Mera said. "Even if I can't take the blame for what Noah's done, I still feel responsible. That's just something I have to live with or work through."

"Or give over to God," Naomi said. "That's what Zeniff was trying to tell you, Mera."

Rachel blinked and continued her work.

Mera felt a confusing mix of relief and disappointment. She sighed. At least Rachel wasn't shouting anymore.

There was a clatter outside and Mera flinched, leaving a long mark on her bowl. But it was only Alma pushing aside the curtain Rachel kept over the studio door after business hours and stepping inside, followed by Gideon.

Rachel rushed to Gideon, her hands white with clay, but he backed away. She froze, blinking. "What is it? I'm not good enough now that you serve the king?"

Gideon flushed. "I can't soil my uniform."

Alma cuffed him on the back of the head. "Lighten up and give your mom a hug." He pecked Naomi on the cheek, then grabbed a cake from her shelf and started picking it apart while Rachel and Gideon retreated to her workspace to visit.

"How's Lisha?" Mera asked.

Alma shot her a sharp look, then studied his roll. "She's fine. Why?"

Mera's brows raised. "Tamar mentioned she's with child."

"Oh, that." Alma colored. "She's pretty excited. At least, she says she is, in between throwing up."

"She should try mint tea," Mera said. "You can snip mint from the herbal gardens at the palace. Tell the gardener I said so."

Alma grinned and nodded, but his smile didn't last long. "There's a new teacher in town, stirring up trouble."

Mera's spirits lifted. "A prophet? Where's he from?"

Gideon's head rose. He and Rachel stopped talking.

Alma ate the last of his bun. "I overheard him in the market, talking to Yoseph, the master weaver. He wasn't shouting like Abinadi did. But still, a new preacher means new trouble. Noah won't like it."

Mera tensed and met Naomi's gaze, then glanced to Rachel, who hovered protectively beside her son. At fourteen, Gideon stood a full head above his mother.

"Is this true?" Rachel asked him. He nodded, his face shining.

"Better not let Noah see you that happy about a new preacher," Alma said, folding his thick arms across his chest. "Or Amulon, for that matter."

Mera rose and wiped her hands on a wet cloth. "Is he still in the market?" she asked while she cleaned her nails.

"No." Alma's voice was sharp. "That was yesterday. But I came here to warn you away from him. King Noah won't tolerate dissent. He's made that clear. And I don't blame him. We have enough problems with the Lamanites without trouble amongst ourselves."

———◆———

The next morning, Mera searched for the new prophet. Rachel and Naomi strode alongside her through the market, stopping at the weaver's stall. When Mera made her way inside, Yoseph, the master weaver, smiled at her over heads of an unusually large crowd of customers.

His daughter swept over and grasped Mera's hands, looking from Mera to her friends, her face aglow. "You've heard then? About the prophet come to teach us?"

"Yes," Mera said. "Where can we find him?"

"He spoke at the spring last night," the girl said.

Naomi sighed. "We wanted to come but . . ."

"Gideon let slip that guards were watching to see if we'd lead them to his hiding place." Rachel brushed off the front of her shawl.

Mera tensed, expecting her to say something caustic. "We didn't know if the new prophet would be there," she said, "but we couldn't risk exposing him."

"He promised he'd be in the market again today." A crease formed between the woman's eyes. "We warned him it wasn't safe, but . . ."

A strong, sure voice sounded in the lane, rising above the general chatter of shoppers and their children gamboling through the market.

Mera felt a thrill of hope mingled with anxiety. Could this be the new prophet? His voice sounded familiar, or was that just the whispering of the Spirit? She and the others rushed outside. Tamar stood across the crowd, gazing at the newcomer with rapt attention.

"Wo be unto this generation," he said, not shouting, but his voice still carried. "Thus saith the Lord: they have repented not of their evil doings; therefore, I will visit them in my anger."

*Repent and turn to the Lord.* There was that message again. Only this prophet gave it more forcefully as if the last message hadn't been enough. A tight, sick feeling churned in Mera's stomach.

A rough hand slipped into hers. "This condemnation isn't for you," Naomi said. "It's for Noah and his wicked priests." Her voice broke. "I just hope it's not for Alma. I hope he's changing his ways."

Rachel stood beside them, her body rigid. "He sounds so much like Abinadi. Perhaps Alma will listen to him. He's heard him teach once already."

Mera grasped Rachel's hand as well. "Don't worry, Rachel. Gideon knows the truth. He will hold strong."

Rachel gave a sharp nod, her gaze on the prophet.

Guards jostled at the edge of the market. A frisson of tension spread through the gathering. Mera, Rachel, and Naomi pressed closer to the prophet, united in their hopes and their fears, determined to hear the words of the Lord and share them as well, no matter the cost. Across the multitude, Tamar did the same, with Limhi close behind her and Helam guarding them both.

"It shall come to pass," the prophet continued, "that the life of King Noah shall be valued even as a garment in a hot furnace; for he shall know that I am the Lord."

Mera gasped. She met Tamar's tortured gaze. Still they pressed forward.

"It *is* Abinadi," Rachel said. "He's returned."

Naomi nodded. "He's been teaching in disguise. Gideon told me. But now he's come out in the open. Why?"

Mera felt a sudden understanding, as if the Holy Spirit spoke directly to her mind. "This message is for my son," she said. "Abinadi is risking his life to change the course of our people."

"I will smite this my people with sore afflictions . . ." Abinadi's voice rose and fell. While Mera tried to listen, her fears for him crowded out half the words. The crowd was growing angry. They didn't like being told to change. They didn't like hearing the consequences of sin. Someone threw a wilted head of lettuce at Abinadi, but he moved to the side and the vegetable sailed past him.

". . . They shall howl all the day long. Burdens shall be lashed upon their backs."

Mera strained to hear but only caught snatches of Abinadi's words over the chaos of the crowd.

". . . except they repent, the Lord will utterly destroy them from off the face of the earth!"

A garrison of guards, led by Amulon, forced their way through the crowd, knocking aside women and children in their quest.

A calm determination swept over Mera. She stepped in their path.

"No, Mera!" Rachel tried to pull her back.

Across the crowd, Tamar's eyes widened. Limhi pushed forward. Both were too far away to stop Mera. She came nose to nose with Amulon. "You will leave this man alone."

". . . They shall leave a record behind them," Abinadi shouted, ". . . for other nations . . . that they may know of their abominations!"

Amulon's face grew boiling red. "If King Noah weren't your son, I would've killed you long ago." His breath was hot and sour. The guards jostled behind him, unsure what to do. "You could die here and now in a riot, you know."

Rachel and Naomi stepped up beside Mera. She felt Naomi's strength and Rachel's trembling resolution.

"We'd tell Noah," Naomi said. "Everyone here would."

Amulon gestured for the soldiers to move around him. "I'll tell Noah myself. You've thrown your lot in with his enemies. You can't undo this defiance, Mera. I'll see that he never forgets."

Amulon shoved Mera back against Rachel.

A sort of madness consumed Mera. She lunged for Amulon's knife. He knocked her away, then pushed past her with ease, laughing as she stumbled into a pile of refuse on the ground.

An abiding hatred rose in Mera's chest.

"Don't let it consume you," Naomi said, helping Mera to her feet while Rachel dusted her off, adjusting her scarves.

The guards converged around Abinadi, pulling him down from the overturned box on which he stood. As they bound him with cloths, he didn't even struggle.

*Why doesn't he fight back?* Mera wondered. *Why not try to escape?*

Instead, a heavenly light shone around him. Beneath his beard and unruly hair, his expression was stoic and calm.

"You're going to your death, you know," Amulon said.

"No, he's not!" someone shouted from the crowd.

Others cheered as the soldiers dragged Abinadi through the market and to the palace.

Mera and her friends pushed through the angry crowd, joining Tamar and Limhi as they rushed to the palace. They entered Noah's throne room just behind the soldiers. Amulon deposited Abinadi in front of the throne where Noah reclined, a simmering hatred clear on his face.

Mera was shocked to see his expression and realized how close it was to what she'd felt for Amulon. Naomi was right. She couldn't let their wickedness turn her heart to stone. She was even more shocked when Amulon signaled for Alma to bring her forward.

Naomi and Tamar gripped Mera's arms. Limhi moved in front of her. She shook the two women off and forbade Limhi with a glance. Alma gave her an uneasy look as she accepted his outstretched arm and strode forward, her back straight. To her surprise, Tamar approached the throne with her.

For a brief moment, Noah's eyes betrayed his confusion, then his mask of anger and domination snapped back in place.

"Your mother defied me in front of your people," Amulon said.

Noah's expression darkened. His fists clenched and he raised his arm as if to strike his own mother.

Mera felt a surge of fear. She flinched, expecting the blow, but Tamar stepped between them. Instead of feeling relief, Mera's fear intensified. But Noah stayed his hand.

Tamar bowed her head in respect. "My husband, please have mercy. She only followed her heart."

Noah cast Mera a scathing look that only intensified when he saw how Abinadi stood boldly before him, his shoulders thrown back, his head held high. He waved Mera and Tamar away. "She is an old woman and is of no consequence. This man, however, must pay for his crimes."

Amulon stepped forward, eager. "It is Abinadi. He's been preaching in the city, disguising himself as a new teacher. But the people know his voice. I recognized his manner of speaking."

"You dare show your face in Shilom after I threatened to kill you?"

Abinadi started to answer, but Amulon interrupted. "He's prophesied evil concerning your people. He claims God will destroy them. He even said your life is worth nothing more than a garment in a fiery furnace."

Mera felt sick. She shifted slightly toward Abinadi.

Amulon laughed. "She thinks to protect him."

Noah sneered.

The knot in Mera's stomach twisted. Tamar slipped her arm through Mera's and pulled her a bit to the side, out of Noah's direct line of sight. "Don't push him, Mera," she whispered. "You know his temper as well as I do."

Mera nodded and wrapped her arm around Tamar's waist.

The chamber was full now. Rachel and Naomi had managed to move halfway up through the crowd. Limhi stood protectively beside them, but Mera could tell he wanted to be beside her and his mother. Only her warning glance held him back. *Noah must never see Limhi as a threat, or worse, see him supporting the prophet*, Mera thought.

"He says you're nothing more than a dried-out stalk of grass, to be run over by beasts." Amulon continued. "And he pretended the Lord has spoken it."

The crowd shifted. Several people gasped. Whether most believed the truth or believed Abinadi blasphemed, Mera didn't know. Regardless, Noah's face was growing more and more ugly.

"He says all this will come upon you except you repent." Amulon leaned closer to the king, his face a sneer. "But what great evil hast thou done?" He spread his hands, a gesture of innocence.

A gasp escaped Mera and she covered her mouth. *What great evil have they done? What haven't they done? What commandments haven't they violated? How could they be so blind?*

"What great sins have these people committed, that we should be condemned of God or judged of this man?" Amulon asked.

Mera flinched, realizing what Amulon was doing, how he was painting Abinadi as the sinner and Noah as the saint. Had she done the same, only in reverse? Was she just like Amulon? Blind to her own sins? Had she been so focused on changing Noah that she didn't notice her own weakness?

Noah nodded, now stroking his beard.

"We are guiltless, and thou, O king, hast not sinned. We are strong, we shall not come into bondage, or be taken captive by our enemies." Amulon's voice rose. "We have defeated our enemies many times before! Thou hast prospered in the land, and thou shalt prosper forever!" He strode to Abinadi and pushed him into a kneeling position, slipped his hands under the prophet's chin, and forced his face upward. "This man is evil. He desires to undermine our peace and destroy your rule. Behold, I deliver him into thy hands; do with him as seemeth thee good."

Noah slowly rose to his feet, his gaze on Abinadi, who stared back, unflinching, still wearing the same expression of calmness, peace, and hope. "Throw him in prison," he told Amulon. The high priest's mouth curved into a gruesome smile. "The council will convene and decide this man's fate. No one who tries to destroy what we've built can escape unpunished!"

# 23

# Council

## Tamar, 148 BC

Cheers erupted from the angry crowd and they turned back toward Noah. With the crowd distracted, Tamar slipped out the back without any trouble. Mera and Limhi were already outside.

Rachel slipped up beside them. "We need to stay together."

"Yes, it's not safe to be alone," Tamar said. "There are those in the city who would do us harm for standing up for Abinadi."

Limhi nodded. "Mother would like to change her robes. We'll be back soon."

Tamar longed to find answers, to find truth—peace.

She and her son walked arm in arm toward the old palace. Between buildings, they could see the slow procession of soldiers carrying torches, making their way to the bluff prison. Their lights cast long shadows through the pastures of sheep, giving the impression of fire spreading through the fields. By the time Tamar and Limhi reached their home, the soldiers were making their way up the trail to the prison.

"I'll be quick," Tamar assured Limhi as he stood outside her quarters.

She emerged a few moments later dressed in her work shawl.

"If you're trying to disguise yourself," Limhi said, "it didn't work."

"It might be safer for us to not stand out quite as much." Tamar pulled her scarf tighter around her face. "Would you know I was the queen?"

Limhi laughed. "You could put mud on a dove but you would always know it was a dove. Maybe there will be enough commotion that they won't be looking for you, but your presence is difficult to miss. It's not just how you appear, it's the feeling in the room when you enter."

Tamar looked at him, puzzled. "What do you mean?"

"Remember how you felt when Abinadi spoke, when we talked of Christ and sang the songs of the Redeemer?"

"Yes, but what does that have to do with me?"

"Mother, you may not see it, but you have a power and spirit about you. Mera sees it. Lisha sees it. Others have spoken of it as well. The people admire that in you."

Tamar shook her head, trying to make sense of her son's words. They began settling into place in her mind, fitting together like the pieces of a finely carved lintel. Her life was beginning to make sense, to take shape. "One moment." Tamar slipped back inside and came out dressed in her finest linens.

"If Abinadi is willing to let everyone know who he is, I can too."

There were many people heading toward the palace. Angry voices spoke in anonymity. Tamar didn't try to find the faces, to see whose lips had spat the vile words; she just moved with the crowd.

"How dare that man speak against our king."

"He's a stranger—how could he know what our city used to be? Look at the old palace, that tiny old house Zeniff died in. What did he ever do for this city? Nothing!"

"Truly, look at the grand structures Noah has built. We've not had a finer king, never in our history."

"Noah opens our minds to the good things in life. Look at the vineyards that line the hills. We have the finest wine in the whole of the country. Trade has made us rich!"

"Long live King Noah!" someone shouted.

Tamar's stomach churned. Where were those who believed Noah was wicked?

No one made room for her. She was pushed and jostled like everyone else. Limhi's hand was fixed tightly on her arm. Tamar felt sure he wasn't going to let anything happen to her. As they neared the palace, the crowd swelled. Mera and Rachel were not where they had left them on the steps, but had moved to the side and stood in the shadows to let the crowds enter the chamber.

Torches had been lit and burned on each pillar of the palace, illuminating it with a bright yellow light. "There is danger for us here, but if Abinadi was willing to stand up to Noah, we should have the courage to do the same." Tamar's voice was strong.

The four of them entered the chaotic palace chamber.

———— ◆ ————

The priests were all in their places. Noah sat on his throne, his robes stretched taut across his chest. His fists were clenched.

"Silence!" he bellowed as he pounded his scepter on the stone floor. The percussion reverberated off the walls and died in the murmuring of hundreds of voices.

"Silence, I say, or leave this place!" Noah commanded.

The murmurs turned to whispers. There was only standing room, yet more people pushed in the doors to see what the king would do about this stranger who spoke accusations against the king.

"Alma, take note of who is here. I want the names of all who speak, especially the traitors." Noah's eyes scanned the crowd. Tamar felt his gaze rest on her. His eyes burned with hatred. He didn't speak for a few moments. He just looked from her to his mother, to his son, and then to the mother of Alma. "On second thought, Alma, come down here beside me. I want to make sure every single name is written in the record."

The priests all leaned forward on their seats, their elbows resting atop the cushioned breastwork. Alma walked down the staircase, descending to the level of the people. Before his face was lost in the crowd, he looked at his mother. Tamar recognized the fear in his eye. He began recording names on a parchment scroll.

The wealthy who had built homes on the high places in the city sat beneath the priests. The priests lounged on their elaborately tufted silk seats.

Amulon spoke first. "Oh king, we know that thou art the finest king in our people's history . . ."

Before he could finish, clapping and shouts of "Long live King Noah!" echoed off the chamber walls. The corners of Noah's mouth curled, his anger easily cured by flattery.

". . . And our noble king has been chastised in the public forum by a stranger, one who came amongst us two years ago, causing divisions among our people," Amulon said. "The troublemaker escaped. He then came to Shilom in disguise and began pronouncing judgements on our people without cause."

The murmurs resumed.

Another priest spoke. "We have witnesses from the first time he came and the same who have heard him speak against our king and our people. Let those witnesses be heard."

Amulon leaned so far forward, Tamar thought he might topple off his seat and down to the floor below, landing right on the heads of some of the high and haughty merchants who were shoving each other in their eagerness to speak.

The first in line was a well-dressed merchant whom Tamar had seen in the marketplace many times. "Oh king, thou who art mighty and wise. The man Abinadi came to our city in disguise, hiding his identity from all so we didn't truly know who he is or from whence he came. Some say he came from Zarahemla, but we believed them not. This man called you wicked and vile. He said you've sinned in having many wives—and your priests too."

A gasp rose from the gallery and murmurs began again.

"Silence!" Noah bellowed. "I want to hear what this supposed prophet said about me!"

Another man pushed his way to the front and began speaking loudly. "Not only did he condemn you, oh great king, but us. He claims we have sinned too!" This brought on more murmurs and the crowd was becoming restless. More pushing to the front of the line.

"Names, I want names," Noah said. "Write the names of all who speak!"

Alma's hand worked quickly.

One after another, witnesses twisted the words Abinadi had spoken. Tamar watched with mounting anxiety as the crowd became angry, the priests' faces reddened, and Alma, poor Alma, blanched with fear.

"Idol worshipers," someone shouted from the very back.

"You've all become vain worshippers of idols, forgetting the One True God!"

All eyes turned to the source. A feeble old man in simple clothes. "I'll not stand silent while the words of a prophet of God are mocked."

Fear gripped Tamar's heart as the crowd turned on him, telling him he was an old fool, but he continued. "Abinadi said our people would become slaves, captive, delivered into the hands of our enemies. We shall be afflicted, driven, and tormented."

"Seize him. Cast him into the prison with Abinadi," ordered King Noah.

"Repent and turn unto the Lord God," the man managed to shout before he was swallowed up by the soldiers who carried him away.

Alma leaned over and whispered to the king.

The voices in the chamber faded as everyone watched this private exchange.

"Are there others who wish to speak?" The glare from Noah's eyes burned into the crowd.

Limhi stood.

Alma's eyes widened, the quill dripping ink on his parchment. His hand froze in midair.

Tamar felt as shocked as Alma. Probably more so. But it was too late to stop Limhi. He was already standing, drawing the attention of the crowd and his father, the king.

"How beautiful upon the mountains are the feet of those who preach peace, good tidings, and publish salvation. They are the seed of the One True God, the Messiah." Limhi let the words sink in. "Let me be counted as one of His seed." Limhi met Noah's glare.

Noah's face turned crimson with rage. He stood, using his scepter to lift his bulk. The carved, gold-encrusted throne disappeared behind his frame, his robes spilling out onto the glistening floor. All eyes were on him. "That has nothing to do with Abinadi!" Noah shouted, glaring at his son.

It was as if time stopped and so did Tamar's breathing. She braced herself against a copper-carved baluster that led up the stairs to the priests' chairs. She couldn't bring herself to look away from Noah's flaming eyes.

Through clenched teeth, the words came slowly from his lips. "Bring the prisoner."

# Testimony

## *Mera, 148 BC*

*M*era's fingers curved into tight fists at her side.

*Repent and turn to the Lord.* The words rang through her mind even after the soldiers dragged the old man away. It was as if Zeniff spoke to her from the dead, as if Abinadi still shouted in the marketplace instead of languishing in the prison.

"Bring the prisoner," Noah repeated. "I will hear him myself. If what you say is true"—he nodded toward Amulon—"he will die for his crimes."

Moments later the soldiers returned, shoving Abinadi so that he stumbled. The crowd parted as they dragged him toward the throne.

With a meaningful glance at Tamar and Rachel, Mera stepped away from their sides and followed the soldiers. Limhi gave her a worried look, but she wasn't about to stand by while her son interrogated the prophet and sentenced him to death. There must be something she could do. Even more, she wanted to hear his words. She longed for the feeling that came whenever she listened. And she'd promised Zeniff.

Someone jostled Mera as she came to the front of the crowd. She turned, expecting guards, but it was Rachel, her arm slipping through Mera's, with Tamar and Limhi just behind her.

Mera's throat tightened in fear. It was one thing for her to risk Noah's wrath—he was bound to notice her expressions, she knew she was easy to read—but why draw his ire on Rachel and Tamar?

Limhi's expression remained smooth and unafraid. "Whatever foolishness Father believes is beyond my control. I stand with the prophet. We all do." He nodded toward Rachel and his mother, whose face glowed with pride. He'd already made his stand.

Mera feared the only reason Noah hadn't struck Limhi down was because he was the heir, and to do something so horrific in public could turn the people against Noah. But in private, well, that was another matter. Mera squeezed Limhi's hand.

She turned back around to see the soldiers removing a gag from Abinadi's mouth and forcing him to bow before Noah. He winced as they squeezed his left shoulder. Once he stood upright again, he was slightly angled toward Mera so she only saw him in profile, but when he turned, she gasped.

His cheek was bruised and his forehead gashed, yet he still bore that calm lightness about him, a familiarity that resonated with Mera's spirit. Without thinking she took a step forward, meaning to give him comfort.

But three pairs of hands pulled her back. Mera blinked, realizing what she'd almost done. The prophet met her gaze with a sad smile. She found herself crying. Why hadn't she found him before it came to this? Why hadn't someone told her sooner? How would she keep her promise to Zeniff if Noah condemned this righteous man to death? But if she spoke against Noah here in his court, he'd see it as an outright betrayal. He'd kill her, if not now, later. She felt sure of it.

Mera felt a deep stab of sorrow. How she longed for Zeniff and Jarom. How she longed for the gospel and the peace it could bring.

Noah's furious gaze lingered on Mera, looking disgusted. Mera stared back, not wiping her cheeks, silently pleading that he would see reason, praying that the Lord would soften his heart.

Maybe if she said something just right, Noah would listen. Maybe he wouldn't be so angry. If she could use just the right tone of voice and have the spirit with her, he was bound to listen, wasn't he? Mera opened her mouth, but before she could speak, a voice rang once again through her mind.

*Repent and turn to the Lord.*

It wasn't up to her to change Noah. It wasn't for her to try to control him. He had his own agency and there was nothing she could do to change that, no matter how she wished she could. And in that moment of under-standing, the tension drained out of Mera. She closed her mouth. Now was a time to listen. Now was a time for her to learn. Let the Lord work with Noah. She closed her eyes.

*Lord, please forgive me. Forgive me for trying to control my son. Forgive me for not trusting You to make things right. Please soften my heart and help me turn more fully to Thee. Help me lean on Thee amid my sorrows as well as my joys.*

When she opened her eyes, she felt a lightness like what she'd seen rest-ing on Abinadi. She would submit to the Lord's will and trust in His timing.

And now, she would listen to the prophet.

At first, Mera feared Abinadi could not withstand the questioning by Noah and his high priests. They were as clever and remorseless as hungry foxes. But the prophet wouldn't be trapped. He answered them with bold-ness, confounding them again and again.

Mera's spirits rose. Perhaps he'd defy them all. And when he did, she'd understand what Zeniff said about her need to change and how she could find peace and joy. She'd learn what Abinadi meant when he said, "Repent and turn to the Lord." Wasn't she already following the Lord? What more did he know that she didn't? There was something. She felt sure of it.

Mera gave Abinadi a small smile of encouragement and he blinked, a strange expression crossing his face, something akin to sorrow and a depth of love she never would have expected.

Amulon moved between them, to a position of greater prominence, interrupting the moment of connection. "What meaneth the words which are written," he said, "'How beautiful upon the mountains are the feet of Him that bringeth good tidings; that publisheth peace?'" He paced in front of Abinadi, his arms behind his back. "If you believe this to be true, how can you breathe out such terrible threats and condemnations in our streets?"

Abinadi held his head high, surveying Noah and his comrades. "Are you priests, and pretend to teach this people, and to understand the spirit of prophesying, yet desire to know of me what these things mean?" His voice rang strong and true. "Ye have perverted the ways of the Lord. Ye have not applied your hearts to understanding; therefore, ye have not been wise. Therefore, what teach ye this people?"

The crowd shuffled, murmuring amongst themselves.

"We teach the law of Moses," Noah said, his voice carrying over the rest.

"Why do ye not keep it?" Abinadi asked.

Mera gasped. The crowd grew more restive. If Abinadi remained so bold in his accusations, how could he possibly survive? She glanced to Tamar, who shook her head just slightly. Helam had come up behind them, and was scanning the room, protective as usual. But he couldn't protect Abinadi. Only the Lord could do that.

"Why do ye set your hearts upon riches? Why spend your strength with harlots and cause this people to sin?"

Noah flushed but said nothing.

"Ye know I speak the truth and ye ought to tremble before God."

"My lord," Amulon pointed an accusing hand toward Abinadi. "He speaks such lies and blasphemy."

Noah took a deep breath. He leaned forward, about to speak, but Abinadi continued, ignoring the interruptions.

"What know ye concerning the law of Moses?" he asked. "Doth salvation come by the law of Moses? What say ye?"

Mera leaned forward herself. A quiet voice in her heart whispered that this was important, to sit up and take notice.

"Of course salvation comes by the law of Moses," Noah said. Amulon gave a sanctimonious nod.

"Then why have ye not kept the commandments? Ye commit whoredoms and worship idols even as ye claim to be holy. Ye know this to be true."

Noah nodded toward Amulon and the priests behind him. "This man is mad. We have no choice but to slay him in order to protect our people."

Amulon nodded agreement and gestured to several others, including Gideon, whose eyes widened as he took a step back.

"He's too young," Mera muttered. "He shouldn't be part of this."

Alma stepped forward, distracting Amulon from Gideon's frightened response.

Mera heard a soft cry from Naomi.

"He just saved Gideon's life," Tamar said in a soft voice. "Amulon would've struck him down where he stood if he defied a direct order, even out of fear."

Alma fidgeted with his dagger and seemed to be trying to look anywhere but at the prophet. His gaze flickered past Mera to Naomi. He flushed and turned away.

"He's looking for Lisha," Naomi said. "He needs her strength."

"He'll see her." Mera squeezed Naomi's hand. "She's in the back, near the door."

The men approached Abinadi, but the prophet thrust his hand toward them.

"Touch me not!" His face shone brighter than sunlight on water. The priests cast uneasy looks amongst themselves and backed away, visibly shaken. "God shall smite you if ye lay your hands upon me, for I have not yet delivered the message which the Lord sent me to deliver."

The crowd murmured.

"Look!" someone said. "His face is aglow just like Moses on Mount Sinai."

King Noah shot to his feet. "Who said that? I demand to know who said that."

"Ye have not power to slay me," Abinadi said.

Noah rounded on him, blustering, then stopped and sank in his chair, leaning back as if wishing to escape the spirit surrounding Abinadi.

"The truth cuts you to your heart," Abinadi said. "I will finish my message, then it matters not whither I go, if it so be that I am saved."

Mera tensed. *It matters not?* That sounded like Abinadi was walking to his death and was just fine with that small detail. But the Lord wouldn't let him die, not like this. He'd stop Noah, wouldn't He, if it came to it?

*But what about agency,* a voice whispered in the back of her mind, *the power to choose?*

Mera shook her head and Tamar cast her a questioning look.

"What you do with me," Abinadi continued, his voice unfailing, "shall be a type and a shadow of things which are to come."

*What did that mean?* Mera glanced around. Everyone seemed confused. Had Abinadi just threatened the king?

"Ye have studied and taught iniquity the most part of your lives," Abinadi told the king and his priests. He then expounded the law of Moses, the commandments given on Mount Sinai.

Mera's heart swelled. It had been too long since she'd heard such words. She'd studied them on her own and with the small group of saints she often met at the spring, but this was different. It was as if she were hearing them for the first time, straight from the mouth of God.

Beside her, Tamar slid her arm around Limhi. He glanced down at her, his eyes shining.

Abinadi paused, his piercing gaze on King Noah. "Have ye taught this people to keep these commandments? No, ye have not. Ye have said that salvation cometh by the law of Moses. It is expedient that ye keep the law of Moses. But salvation doth not come by the law alone; and were it not for the atonement, which God Himself shall make for the sins and iniquities of His people, they must unavoidably perish, notwithstanding the law of Moses."

*Repent and turn to the Lord.* This was what it was all about.

The court remained silent as Abinadi taught about the Atonement, sharing the words of Isaiah, an ancient prophet from the old country. "The Lord shall suffer for our sins. He shall rise from the grave and break the bonds of death. With His stripes we are healed. All we, like sheep, have gone astray; we have turned every one to his own way."

A strange peace came over Mera. At last she understood. The call to repentance was for everyone, even for prophets like Abinadi. She felt a sudden kinship with him, as if she'd known him for ages.

Other faces in the crowd seemed to glow. Naomi, Gideon, Yosef the weaver, Helam, Tamar, and Limhi. Some seemed conflicted, staring steadfastly at the prophet, many looking down as if afraid to meet his gaze.

Alma didn't seem to know where to look.

"Come on, Alma," Naomi whispered from beside Mera. "Let the words into your heart."

Mera glanced up to the throne, where Noah still strained away from the prophet, his expression dark. For once, she didn't feel she must save Noah. She didn't feel that all the horrors he committed weighed upon her shoulders. An incredible sorrow hung over her, yet she somehow still felt peace.

"He shall be called the Son of God, and having subjected the flesh to the will of the Father, being the Father and the Son," Abinadi said. "The Father, because he was conceived by the power of God; and the Son, because of the flesh."

Mera imagined what it might be like to see the Son of God, to hear his voice, to feel his love and witness the sacrifice he would make.

"Ye asked me what it means, how beautiful upon the mountains are the feet of Him that bringeth good tidings, that is the founder of peace, yea, even the Lord, who has redeemed His people; yea, Him who has granted salvation unto His people. These are the good tidings. The Lord lives. He will come. He will save us all, if we but believe and follow Him. He is the light and the life of the world; yea, a light that is endless, that can never be darkened; yea, and also a life which is endless, that there can be no more death."

Several of the priests seemed troubled. Alma rubbed his forehead.

Noah, however, looked furious. Amulon, noticing, moved to interrupt Abinadi, but Noah forestalled him. "Let him speak. Let him condemn himself."

A knot rose in Mera's throat. She gripped Naomi's and Tamar's hands, but she knew Noah and she knew what he would do. It would be up to the Lord to stop him.

"And now," Abinadi continued, his powerful voice rising, as if his message couldn't be stopped, "ought ye not to tremble and repent of your sins, and remember that only in and through Christ ye can be saved? Therefore, if ye teach the law of Moses, also teach that it is a shadow of those things which are to come. Teach them that redemption cometh through Christ the Lord, who is the very Eternal Father. Amen."

"He speaks blasphemy," Amulon hissed. "He teaches against the Law of Moses, as if it were meaningless. He claims you are wicked, as if you were nothing." The high priest cast a devious look to Noah. "What should we do with him?"

Noah rose from his seat. He moved like a raging river slowly escaping its banks. "The law is clear. This man blasphemes, he lies, he seeks to cause misery and unrest among our people. He must die."

"No!" someone cried out.

Shocked murmurs filled the room.

Mera searched for the source of the voice and realized, with a pang, who it was.

"*Alma.*" Naomi half whispered his name. Tears began filling her eyes, though she looked more proud than afraid.

He'd risen from his ornate priest's chair and was approaching the throne as Noah wheeled around to face him. Alma bowed his head in respect. "Please don't be angry with Abinadi."

"Don't be angry?" Noah threw his hands in the air. "He's trying to destroy everything I've built!"

Abinadi did not argue. Instead he maintained a steadfast gaze at the king, a gaze that made Mera long to examine her own soul. No question, Abinadi was a prophet.

"Let him leave in peace," Alma continued. "He'll do no harm." He turned to Abinadi. "You won't incite riots or stir up the people against the king?"

"I only speak the truth," Abinadi said.

Amulon moved quickly. "Listen to his silver tongue! This man challenges all we believe. He has accused *you*, my lord, of being wicked! You, the most respected man among us!"

Noah swelled, patches of red blooming high in his cheeks. "It is lies! All of it. Lies."

"If you please, King Noah, none of us is without sin," Alma said. "Abinadi speaks the truth. You know this as well as I do. You know how we've lived, the things we've done." His eyes flicked to the back of the crowd, where Lisha stood near the door. "We all must repent, my lord. All of us. It's not an insult. It's an invitation. Abinadi's trying to help."

Something flickered in Noah's eyes, and Mera felt a flash of hope. Then his expression hardened. "You will leave us and never return!" he boomed, not at Abinadi, but at Alma.

Alma turned and ran. His fingers trailed across his mother's shoulder as he passed. The multitude made way. He reached the back of the chamber in mere seconds. Lisha turned, as if she would go with him but he shook his head, gave her a swift kiss on the cheek, and fled into the night.

"Take this rebel." Noah nodded toward Abinadi. "Bind him well and cast him back into prison."

"But I thought you said slay—" Amulon sputtered.

"What you thought is of no consequence!" Noah roared. "I rule this people. I am the law!"

Amulon slid up next to Noah's side, leaning in close, whispering in his ear. Noah's color deepened.

"Send someone after Alma," he added in a voice too low for the bulk of the crowd to hear. "No one defies me in front of my people and lives to tell the tale."

Mera shrank back against Tamar and Naomi. "Alma's frightened Noah. If one of his priests can see the truth, who else may . . ." She looked to Naomi's tearstained face. "Alma knows these hills, Naomi. He'll make himself scarce."

Naomi made a hiccupping sound. "And what of Lisha? She's with child."

Tamar squeezed Naomi's upper arm. "We'll help her. She won't be alone."

The throne room was in an uproar. In the chaos, Helam slipped up beside Tamar and Mera. "I'm going after Alma, to warn him." His eyes flashed to Limhi.

"I'll keep my mother and grandmother safe. You've done your part."

Helam nodded, then rushed away through the crowd.

The guards bound Abinadi. He made no protest, not even a sound. As they led him through the restless crowd, he turned. Mera expected him to fix Noah with his perceptive stare. Instead, his dark eyes found her and stayed on her until he was gone.

She gasped, her promise to Zeniff filling her mind. He'd wanted her to listen to Abinadi. But he'd said more than that. He'd said Abinadi wanted to speak with her, that it would change her. He'd made her promise.

Mera raised her head, throwing her shoulders back.

She would find a way.

# 25

# Uproar

## *Tamar, 148 BC*

Limhi grabbed Tamar from behind, pulling her out of the crowd as she passed the home of Rachel, the master potter. Startled, she cried out. Gideon and Limhi stood in the shadows of the potter's stall. Without a torch, Tamar could barely discern their faces.

"I must go with my company to guard Abinadi," Gideon whispered. "Noah must not suspect I am a believer. He thinks he has won my heart and mind. But I will do anything I can to help the prophet." He paused and stepped into a sliver of moonlight that cut through the darkness like a knife. "The king has sworn vengeance on all believers. Tell everyone to pray for Abinadi, but to be secret about it."

The city was in commotion. Stories were being told and retold, each one more fantastic than the first. Some were completely false, others true, but damning to those who told them. The words Abinadi had spoken clearly stung more than just the king and his priests. Most of the city had long ago taken to worshiping idols and drinking wine to excess. Winebibbers—all of them. Tamar knew something must change.

She watched as Gideon stepped into the angry crowd. He stood tall, eyes scanning the crowd for trouble. Or was he looking for other believers?

Tamar couldn't tell. Torch lights cast a yellow glow on everyone. Angry faces were everywhere, hatred evident in the snarl of their lips.

The smoky smell of the potter's shed brought back memories for Tamar. From her earliest years, this was where she had first felt the inklings of truth. Those that cared for her after her mother's death often spoke of a messiah. Words she had only heard from time to time in stories now carried deeper meaning. Savior, Redeemer, Messiah. Looking back, she could see how, over time, her heart truly had changed.

Noah was never interested in these feelings. She had tried at times to share them, so he could have the same experience. He had mocked her questions. He scoffed at those who believed and seemed as though he tried to crush her faith before it had a chance to grow. There were a few moments of joy when she saw recognition in his eyes, as if he were allowing himself to believe. As those fleeting moments came, he pushed them away, buried beneath his pride. Tamar felt sad for him. She no longer felt hatred for the man who had betrayed and hurt her. Now she just felt pity. If he knew that, it would make him furious.

"Mother," Limhi said, "I'll go check on Grandmother. She's still in the midst of the crowd."

"Thank you. I'll go back to the palace. I'd like to hear what else is happening."

After a quick hug, they slipped out into the chaos. Tamar was jostled more than once as people pushed their way to the palace. Without her son to protect her and no acknowledgement from those in the crowd that she was the reigning queen, she felt lost and not at all safe.

By the time she arrived, the palace was in turmoil. Priests were talking in quiet whispers, nodding to one another, moving to speak privately with each other. They mingled on their upper level platform, looking down on the mixture of wealthy newcomers and humble craftsmen. Not many were left of the original immigrants to the once named city of Lehi-Nephi. Those few that remained were stoic. They stood in quiet groups while angry citizens milled about, yelling and shouting about the harm done to their noble king.

"Passover should be skipped—this is far more important," one merchant cried. There was nodding all around.

"We must have laws punishing any who preach against the king!" Cheers erupted from the crowd.

"Cast out troublemakers. Our city prospers. We don't need religion."

"Get rid of the believers!"

The small clusters of Abinadi's followers clung tightly together. They were outnumbered.

"There is one God," one man said. "You mock and revile Him with your words. That won't change the truth. He will come and redeem His people!" His voice was small, but emboldened another to speak out.

"Abinadi is a prophet of God. He has spoken God's word. No king can change what God's prophet speaks." People began looking around for the voices, obviously coming from believers. "He will break the bands of death. He will show mercy to even the vile sinners."

"Again the believers condemn us and call us wicked!" Angry voices again rose above the words of the believers.

"Believe, and become an heir to the kingdom!"

Noah's voice bellowed. "I have my kingdom and no prophet of a supposed God can take it from me!" He seemed pleased with the increasing uproar. He got up several times and walked the upper platform, speaking with the priests individually. Their hands waved, their fingers pointed, their eyes flashed.

Tamar watched. She waited. She had a feeling that this time, Abinadi might not escape with his life. As she observed the behavior of the people and the expression on the king's face, she felt like she had been here, in this setting before. Torch lights flickered and their smoke ascended in thin wispy columns. The faces of the idols were set in motion with the dancing firelight and shadows of people moving about.

The sounds of shouting voices faded away and she leaned against the cool stone wall and closed her eyes, wondering what Mera was doing and if Limhi had found her. She thought of the humble potter, Naomi, and how hard she worked to provide for Gideon and raise him well. She thought of Helam, his loyalty to their family. Sarai and Jarom, their sons—what a blessing these people had all been to her. In spite of the chaos, the noise, the uncertainty, she felt peace.

At first she didn't sense the change, but the longer she pondered on her blessings and those she loved, the calmer and more serene she felt. Warmth spread from the top of her head throughout her body like a welcome summer rain.

Limhi returned and grasped her arm, whispering, "Mother, I can't find Mera. They say she has gone to see Abinadi. I fear she may try to help him escape. If she does, her fate would be that of Melek, certain death for her and Abinadi."

The words "death for her and Abinadi" brought a sudden, violent memory to Tamar's mind. She *had* been here before—in her dream. Fiery images and swirling smoke rose in her mind, an echo of the horrors that had haunted her for so many years. She felt as if her dream were coming alive in the restless, furious crowd. And if it continued and played out to the end, it would be the terrifying fulfillment of her nightmare. How could she possibly feel peace?

# 26

# Revelation

## Mera, 148 BC

Two days and two nights had passed since Noah threw Abinadi into prison. Again. But this time, Mera sensed the outcome would be different. The riots throughout Shilom guaranteed that. Noah would never tolerate dissent, especially with Amulon whispering in his ear. The people were either outraged or empowered by Abinadi. Either way, Noah wasn't about to set the prophet free.

Mera strode into the throne room, which teemed with scantily clad women lounging on cushions or dancing for the king. The priests huddled around him or reclined in their chairs, enjoying the view. Mera kept her eyes forward, trying to ignore the laughter that rose as she passed.

*Disgusting.* These people cared for nothing but themselves. While Abinadi and the old man who'd spoken against Noah wasted away in prison, they celebrated. While Alma hid in the woods, scrabbling for food and shelter, they stuffed their faces and drank themselves silly. It was appalling.

Mera slowed in her approach to the throne, reminding herself to work on her own frailties instead of focusing on theirs, no matter how glaring they seemed.

Noah gazed at Mera, then waved away the priests and concubines nearest him.

Mera bowed her head. "Thank you."

"What do you want from me, Mother?" Noah sat back in his throne, folding his hands across his lap. "How can I possibly please you?"

Mera went still. "Noah. You know I love you."

Noah's cheek twitched. "I know you've spent the last two days trying to see that false prophet, but the guards turned you away."

Mera stared. "You should give him a chance," she said quietly, then held up her hand, for Noah showed every sign of being about to interrupt. "I won't lecture you now. Heaven knows I've done enough of that. And I'm sorry." She looked down at her fingers, now loosely clasped together. "Maybe if I'd listened more . . ." Noah gave a heavy sigh and she looked back up at him. "It's just, when I listen to Abinadi, my heart lifts, my burdens seem lighter."

Noah's eyes narrowed. "Your burdens? What burdens can you possibly be carrying? I'm the king! The whole nation rides on my shoulders."

Mera's mouth hung open for a moment, then she collected herself. "I've lost my husband, Noah. I've lost Jarom. And—" She stopped herself.

"And you've as good as lost me," Noah finished. "Because I refuse to bow down to your God and listen to your prophet and follow his stifling rules."

"Noah, please. I'm not trying to change you, not anymore," Mera said. "That's between you and the Lord." Noah's jaw tightened. "I'm just trying to change me. Just let me see Abinadi once. Just once. I promised your father I would. Don't make me break my promise."

Noah leaned forward, his expression sharpening. "Father met with Abinadi?"

Mera nodded. "Just before he died, Abinadi visited his chamber. I don't know what was said. But your father made me promise to see him, to hear him out."

Noah sagged back. For the first time, Mera noted the wrinkles time had etched into his face and a heaviness that seemed to hang over him. *Did he regret the terrible things he had done?* "Noah, you could come with me."

Noah stiffened. "It's too late for me, Mother."

Amulon glared at them from across the room and moved like he would return to Noah's side, but the king shook his head. He waved a scribe over and nodded to indicate he should start writing.

"Be it known that I, High Priest King Noah, grant my mother, Mera, permission to visit with the prisoner, Abinadi, for the space of one hour today."

Mera suppressed a cry of relief. "Thank you, my son."

The scribe rolled the scroll and dribbled hot wax along its edge. King Noah sealed it with his ring and sent the scribe scurrying away. "You know this won't change anything."

"I know."

His face darkened. "Do not defy me. And should you try to help the blasphemer escape, Amulon will execute the guards. Their blood will be on your hands."

Mera bowed before leaving Noah's chamber, her heart floating.

———— • ◆ • ————

Five men guarded the prison door, including young Gideon, who was staring out over the river when Mera approached. "I've told you, you can't go inside," said the head guard, a stocky man with beady eyes and thick reddish hair, who Mera knew to be named Koresh.

She handed him the scroll.

His slit it open and read, his eyes widening. "Noah gave his permission." He scratched his head. "That makes no sense."

"You're sure that's the king's seal?" a soldier asked. This one had a mean air about him and looked strong enough to tangle with a bear and come out on top.

"Of course it is," said Gideon. "You think the former queen would fake the king's seal?"

Head Guard Koresh shrugged. "She helped Jarom escape."

"Jarom wasn't in prison," Mera said. "Send a runner to the palace if you need further proof."

"I believe her," Gideon said, simply.

"Sure you do," said the grizzly beater. "She's best friends with your mother."

"Plus, you're a sympathizer," said another, smaller, swordsman, shaking his head. "Don't think I haven't heard you talking with Abinadi. I know you listen to his ravings."

Gideon squared his shoulders, ready to fight, but Koresh placed a hand on his chest. "Now's not the time. Enok"—he gave a warning glance toward

164

the imposing senior soldier—"run along to the palace, just to be sure. If she's lying, we'll drag her out of here."

The smaller man sighed, then ambled away, picking up speed as he went.

Koresh eyed Mera. "Or maybe we'll just lock you up. You've caused Noah enough trouble over the years."

Mera felt a spike of trepidation and flinched, but couldn't back down now. Not when she was so close to fulfilling Zeniff's request and about to be face-to-face with a prophet of the Lord. *What would he tell her? What was so important he wanted to speak with her alone?* She squared her shoulders and raised her chin.

Koresh spat on the ground, then opened the prison. He led her to Abinadi's room, which was immediately on the left. She ducked her head beneath the low lintel, her fear rising as she entered the dim room. A small oil lamp flickered on a shelf built into the clay wall in the far corner. There was no furniture in the cell, only a pile of moldy hay, on which Abinadi sat, his eyes gleaming.

"You came," he said.

Those simple words and his sweet expression were enough to break through Mera's darkest fears. She rushed over and knelt beside him, keeping a respectful distance.

"He promised you'd come."

"Zeniff?"

Abinadi nodded.

Mera felt a strange sense that she knew Abinadi as something more, or different, than a prophet, as if she'd known him all her life. His powerful voice reminded her of someone, though she couldn't think of who. She studied him for a moment, then sat back on her heels. "But why did you want to see me? Why would you care?" She wished she could take back the words, they sounded so rude. At the same time, she wanted to know. She needed to know.

Abinadi shook his head slightly, an odd expression on his face. "Do you really not know me?"

Mera cocked her head to the side, feeling that same surge of familiarity that she'd sensed whenever she'd seen Abinadi or heard him speak.

With a slight wince, he shifted his robe aside to show his scarred left shoulder. "It never quite healed up. Our journey was long, the packs heavy, and the wound reopened."

Journey? Heavy packs? A shoulder wound.

Mera felt as if her heart had stopped, its steady thumping shocked into stillness. She leaned forward, peering at the prophet in the shifting golden light. His beard was shaggy, his hair hanging into his eyes. But if it were trimmed, it would reveal high cheekbones, a slanted pair of dark eyes, and—Mera reached out and lifted his hair—a smooth forehead marked with a scar in the shape of a crescent.

She gasped. "Jarom? Is it you?"

The prophet smiled, his eyes shining. Then he grabbed Mera into a hug. His shoulders shook, and as he buried his face in her shoulder, he began to sob.

Mera felt as if she'd explode. Jarom, here, in Shilom. Jarom, here, in prison.

"I've missed you so much," he said, raising his tearstained face.

"We have to get you out of here, Jarom. Noah thinks you're Abinadi. He'll kill you. He's decided." She waved a hand wildly. "There've been riots, people fighting in the streets. He won't back down!"

Jarom sat back, wiping his face on his sleeves, streaking his cheeks with dirt. "I won't leave, Mother."

Mera blinked and shook her head, not meeting his eyes. "Of course you will. We'll convince the guards. Gideon can help with that. They'll need to come with us or Amulon will hang them." She glanced up. "Noah told me—"

"I *am* Abinadi," he said. "When Sarai and I reached Zarahemla, we learned so much. Their prophet, King Benjamin, taught us."

"But you already knew—"

"I learned more. These people"—he gestured toward the door—"have been separated from the proper authority for so long that the doctrines have drifted. We tried. But we need more. The Law of Moses must be observed, but there is a great purpose behind it. Mother, you must understand. The Savior will come. He will redeem us all."

"I know." Mera's voice was small. "I heard you in the throne room."

He grasped both her hands. "Then you *do* know. And you know it can change you."

Mera nodded.

"It has changed me. The Lord called me as a prophet to this people. He gave me a new name—Abinadi. I must complete my calling." He swallowed and his eyes took on a brighter shine. "When I came here, I knew I would not return to Zarahemla. Sarai and I have said our goodbyes."

Mera gave a soft cry of despair and the guards shuffled outside.

"Everything all right in there?" Gideon called.

"Shut up, boy," came the gruff voice of the huge guard, Enok. "I'm trying to listen."

"When this is through," Jarom said, "you must go to Zarahemla. Find Sarai and the boys—they're so big, Mother, you wouldn't know them. Find them and bring them comfort. Tell them I remained true to them and to the Lord."

Tears streamed down Mera's cheeks. "If I tell Noah who you really are—"

"He'll think I've come to claim the throne. Spare him the truth, Mother. Promise me that. And promise me you'll not turn against God. You'll be angry. That's okay. But don't become bitter. Don't give up your faith just because evil exists and strikes too close to home."

Mera stifled a sob. "But why won't the Lord save you? You've proven yourself to him. You've given your whole life to him. Won't he save you now?"

"The Lord will not violate Noah's freedom to choose, even if the choice is wrong. Our free will is the one thing God gave us that He cannot take away. It is also the only thing we can offer back to Him. Everything else is already His. But my will is my own. I choose to submit it to God." He squeezed Mera's hands. "This is important, Mother. I've made my choice and place my will on the altar of the Lord. If that means I die for Him, so be it. Others will hear my words and see my faith. Their hearts will burn inside them. They will turn to God and know His love and His strength. If this is God's calling for me, I will obey."

# 27

# Condemnation

## Tamar, 148 BC

Tamar woke early. The clouds were thick over the city, and fog covered the river and the trees along its banks. She rolled over, pulling the skin blanket under her chin. She inhaled the faint scent of sheep. She had known the ram this blanket had come from. He had been gentle and guarded his ewes and lambs with care. He was injured when a wolf attacked the flock and had to be put down. It broke her heart, but her consolation was this warm and soft skin she slept with each night. He was never far away.

She slipped from her bed, her bare feet touching the cold clay floor. She knelt and prayed. *Dear Lord, Abinadi is still in prison. It's been three days and I'm sure he's not had food or water. If he is to be freed, please let it be this day. His suffering has been sore. Lord, my dream, or vision, if it is to be, help me be strong.*

A sense of peace settled over Tamar and she knew the Lord would be with her, whatever may come.

The sound of feet scuffing on tile startled her. She stood quickly and realized it was only Limhi. He had moved to Jarom and Sarai's old quarters and had slipped in while she prayed.

"Mother, I'm sorry to disturb you, but I have news." His face bore lines of worry. "Gideon stopped by early this morning and said the priests were up till late in the night. Noah ordered them to bring Abinadi before the council today. The priests took writings and records from the old temple. They've put on their robes and they appear to be enacting one of the feast rituals. We must warn the people. If the king condemns Abinadi, would he also come after us, and the believers?"

"He might. We need a way to communicate." Tamar closed her eyes and thought for a moment or two. "The song. Someone should walk through the streets, singing it. After this, the song will be the sign to go to the spring."

"That should work. I'll start the word with the old priests and let them have responsibility for getting it out." Limhi left as quickly as he had come.

Tamar dressed and began her day. A prayer, tidying up her home, eating some fruit and bread. Her errands took her throughout town. She greeted friends and welcomed guests in the city, speaking kindly to all she met. Children and adults alike had come to love her as much as they admired Mera for those long years when she was queen.

Everything seemed normal, but the simple tune of the believer's song floated like a butterfly on a warm spring day. Lighting on one flower, resting a moment and lighting on another in seemingly random patterns. The song was going from believer to believer, unknown to all others, because they knew not what it meant. She smiled. In spite of the impending events she felt in her heart were coming, she was calm.

As she passed the old temple, the doors hung wide. King Noah's priests were coming in and out, taking things to the palace temple. Believers stood in the background. Tamar knew who they were. Concern veiled their faces but no one interfered.

Noah's priests were dressed in their finest robes, those reserved for the ancient feasts, the ones they kept in part because it gave them an excuse to add their wine, fine foods, and immoral acts to the celebration, completely degrading the purpose of the feast and the intent for it being held.

Tamar stopped as she passed between two of Noah's new buildings. In the distance, a line of soldiers marched up the path to the prison. It was now sealed with iron doors and surrounded by guards. Noah wasn't taking any chances of Abinadi escaping. It felt like the beginning of the end.

Tamar sensed that after this day, things would never be the same. The dream that had haunted her had also prepared her for what this day and her future might hold.

169

Groups of small children played with sticks and rocks in the common areas between homes, while older youths kept busy with chores: gathering firewood and sweeping. Chickens pecked about and sheep bleated in the pasture. The fires of the potter's shed sent smoke billowing into the cloudless sky. Young ladies sat in the shade around the weaver to learn the skill of making cloth. Normal life.

Tamar made her rounds from one end of town to the other, making sure the leading figures of their clandestine group of believers knew to listen for the song in case they needed to meet quickly. They had been forewarned by Limhi already and the news spread rapidly.

By noonday the procession of soldiers made it back to the city with Abinadi. As they came through, people followed, the crowd growing with each advancing step. Tamar joined them. She wanted to be as close to the prophet Abinadi as possible. Others must have felt the same way. Some were already weeping.

As the prisoner marched down the street toward King Noah's palace, a wind rose and fluttered his hair away from his face, revealing a crescent-shaped scar on his forehead. He turned to Tamar and their eyes met. They held, he paused, and recognition hit her.

Abinadi was Jarom.

Her feet froze in place. The crowd punished her for the act. Elbows struck her from behind. Someone bumped her from the back, nearly toppling her. Her thoughts were no safer. They fell from their places, breaking into a shattered mess. Tamar shook her head, trying to make sense of what she'd just realized. *Jarom, Noah's brother, is Abinadi, a prophet of God, sent to call the people to repent.*

She let the crowd carry her along. One by one, the pieces of truth in her mind came together. Her nightmare became even more painful to recall. This man was not only a prophet, he was family. He had a family.

"Sarai," Tamar whispered out loud as tears filled her eyes. The harsh faces of the people around her became soft and blurry. "Hiram, Neriah . . ." *Oh Lord, what will this do to them? He is their father.*

Gentle words from the Lord filled her mind, truths spoken by Abinadi. *They are all my children. My love is upon them. Trust . . . Believe. They will kill the prophets and they will kill me. But I come to redeem all mankind, even those who do not yet believe.*

Not *yet* believe? Tamar looked around her. These people? This angry mob could never believe. They were too far gone, too much like Noah.

*Judgment is mine. I look upon the heart.*

With new eyes, Tamar looked past the angry faces and swinging fists and saw a people who had been good at times but had been led astray. *What am I to do?* Tamar prayed. The answer was swift and filled her with the warmth of the Spirit. *Forgive. Love with your whole heart.*

Tamar was stunned, realizing that the love she had shown others had been reserved only for the believers. She had shut the rest of the people out. Her vision cleared and she gazed on the faces of mothers, fathers, children, young men and women. These were her people, whether she agreed with them or not. This was her home, her family.

A young woman in front of her stumbled on her own shawl and toppled into the man in front of her. Tamar avoided falling, then stopped beside the woman.

Clearly this was not one of the believers and the expression on her face almost made Tamar chuckle.

"Here, take my hand."

The woman looked around before accepting Tamar's offer. People continued passing. None stopped but Tamar.

"You're the queen, Noah's first wife who refuses to live in the palace?"

Her royal robes gave her away. "It is I."

People were pausing to look, whispering amongst themselves. ". . . A believer . . . the first wife . . . why would she . . . unthinkable . . ."

Their surprise puzzled her. She was kind, generous, and caring to everyone, although her closest circle had been small. She'd not taken the time to even get to know the newcomers or those who didn't have her same faith. A smile in the marketplace doesn't make someone a friend.

"Let me help you," Tamar kept her hand outstretched until the woman allowed her to assist. They rose together and before parting, the young woman gave a confused smile and soft thank you.

Tamar moved along with the crowd, anxious, along with everyone else, to be present when Abinadi was brought before the king.

A scuffle erupted at the entrance to the palace, so many people wanted inside. Tamar could see people knocking against each other, some backing out of the crowded chamber. Soldiers moved in and, as quickly as it began, it seemed to end. All were silent.

Tamar pushed ahead as others moved back down the palace steps.

Fear knotted in her stomach as she stepped inside the palace.

Abinadi stood, facing Noah. He had been beaten and bloodied and had only a cloth about his loins. Black and blue marks spanned his back, but the old scar on his left shoulder was jagged and white.

Recognition spread across Noah's face. No one dared speak. It seemed an eternity as the two just stared at each other. Abinadi's weary muscles quivered with the strain of holding his position.

Noah's pasty white skin turned shades lighter as the color drained from his cheeks. Then slowly his forehead creased, his brow formed a *V,* and his eyes narrowed, burning with hate.

"This is my kingdom. My city. My palace. You'll never take it from me." Noah's chest rose and fell as his breathing quickened. Drops of perspiration formed on his forehead. "You'll never take what I have built. I am the king."

Abinadi rose to his full stature, feet planted firmly on the cold hard floor. "God will take this kingdom from you. I am simply the messenger of truth, calling you, Noah, and this people to repent." His hands spread out. "*Repent,*" he emphasized, "and turn unto the Lord, or His vengeance will be poured out upon this people."

Noah's expression was as hard as steel. His hands balled into fists.

"Amulon, read the charges."

"We have found accusations worthy of death against you, Abinadi."

Tamar forged ahead to try and get Noah's attention. "Noah!"

Heads craned as she pushed through the remaining bodies pressed against the soldiers. Abinadi also turned, his face aglow. His expression was pure serenity and it took Tamar aback. Love in his eyes said what his voice could not.

Tamar's emotions could not be restrained and the words escaped her lips in a hoarse cry. "Noah, don't do this."

His expression went from hate to fury. "I'm tired of being told what to do by my traitorous *family.*" He spat the final word. "Silence, woman."

Tamar found two soldiers spears crossed in front of her, blocking her way.

"Amulon," Noah hissed. "Continue the charges."

His sneer widening to a sickening grin, Amulon continued reading. "You say that God Himself should come down among the children of men. For this you shall face the sentence of death unless you recall the evil which you have spoken against this people and our king."

Abinadi stood resolute. "I will not recall my words. They shall stand as a testimony against you." The apprentice record keeper who'd been called to take Alma's place paused in his writing. He looked at Noah, at Abinadi, and then at Amulon. Abinadi continued and the writing did too. "If you slay me, you shed innocent blood. This shall also stand as a testimony against you at the last day. I have allowed you to take me that you may know that the words I speak are true."

Noah had not taken his eyes off of Abinadi, until now. Tamar thought she saw a change in his expression. *He knows . . .*

A strange trembling came over Noah, and his face went pale. "Release him," Noah said, his voice so low Tamar almost couldn't hear it.

Amulon stepped forward, not toward Abinadi, but toward the king. "He has spoken evil against you."

"I said *release him*," Noah said through gritted teeth, leaning so close to Amulon that their noses almost touched. "You heard what he said. The judgments of God will fall upon us!" His eyes were wild, flitting to Tamar, then to his mother, who leaned against the opposite wall.

"Thank you!" Tamar whispered, loud enough for Noah to hear.

Amulon fidgeted, his muscles straining like a snake about to strike. "If you let a man like this live," he said in a low, threatening voice, "you'll be dead before Passover. The people will rise up." He pointed to Abinadi. "This man is an inciter, a blasphemer."

The other priests gathered round Noah, hurling accusations against Abinadi. Noah's expression hardened. Anger burned in his eyes. He scanned the room until his gaze met Tamar's.

She felt someone clutch her from behind. It was Mera, her face contorted with grief. "Oh, Jarom . . ." Her voice was hushed.

Tamar stared. "You know too?"

Mera nodded.

Tamar took a few steps forward, the crowd parting to let her through. Noah was still watching her.

Amulon broke the silence. "This man has reviled the king. He has accused our people of wickedness. He has been sentenced to death by order of the priests and the king!"

In that moment, the words of her morning prayer returned to her. *If he is to be freed, let it be this day.* And she knew that indeed, he would be freed. Not in the way that she had hoped, but in the Lord's way. Truly Jarom, Abinadi, was in His hands.

Amulon's voice carried through the hushed room like a death knell. Other priests chimed in, repeating his words.

Noah's temper ignited. He raised a clenched fist. "Take him to the temple courtyard," he shouted, "and prepare the flames."

# Sacrifice

## *Mera, 148 BC*

Mera stumbled through the crowd, bile rising in her throat. Noah could've commanded an easy death, but no. He wanted to make a statement. She paused, leaning against Tamar for support. They'd rushed out of the palace together, closely followed by Limhi.

Yoseph, the master weaver, came up alongside her and took her arm. By the time they reached the temple courtyard, it was packed with people, some cheering, others crying. Guards were dragging Abinadi forward through the angry crowd.

Not far from Mera, Rachel stood with Naomi, scanning the crowd. She flinched, her face an image of despair. Mera followed her line of sight and saw Alma crouching in the shadows of yew trees lining the courtyard.

Mera's stomach twisted. If Noah's priests saw Alma, they'd kill him on the spot. Still, she couldn't help but admire his bravery. Jarom would be proud, not just of Alma's bravery, but of his dramatic change of heart, his willingness to risk his life for what is right.

It still felt strange to think of Jarom's new name. Abinadi. The prophet. To Mera, he was now a jumbled fusion of the prophet and her little boy. Now that she knew the truth of who the prophet really was, sorrow threatened to consume her. How could she stand here and do nothing while one of her sons ordered the death of the other? Could she be strong enough to honor Abinadi's request?

Fear momentarily paralyzed her breathing, and she reached for Tamar's hand.

Abinadi was already tied to a stake.

"What should we do?" Tamar asked.

"We hold steady," Mera said, her gaze upon the prophet, tears pricking her eyes.

He turned and looked at her and her family, nodding to each in turn.

Limhi moved forward, but Mera tugged him back.

The priests laughed and shouted, picking up embers and scourging Abinadi's flesh.

He cried out in pain.

"No!" Mera stumbled again, leaning heavily on Yoseph. Beside them, Tamar sobbed into Limhi's shoulder. Tears ran down his face.

Abinadi cried out over the crowd, "Behold, even as ye have done unto me, thy seed shall cause that many shall suffer the pains of death by fire; and this because they believe in the salvation of the Lord their God."

Mera gasped, shuddering.

The flames ignited the dry twigs near Abinadi's feet.

Mera covered her ears to stop his screams. But she refused to look away. She could at least do him that honor, to watch him die for what he believed. And she couldn't help but wonder, would she someday do the same?

A hand touched her shoulder, then an arm slipped around her waist. A song from a single voice began to rise with the smoke of the growing fire. Mera's eyes were fixed upon this prophet, her son. More voices joined and as they did, she felt hands holding her, supporting her as her knees began to buckle. She stood. The song grew louder, nearly drowning out the sound of the growing fire. As Mera looked for the last time on her son, she saw in the billowing smoke a figure. She watched as it walked from one end of the altar to the other and appeared to place a hand on Abinadi's head. Abinadi raised his head one final time.

"Ye shall be driven to and fro," came the words from Abinadi's heaving chest, "and then ye shall suffer, as I suffer, the pains of death by fire. Thus God executeth vengeance upon those that destroy his people. O God, receive my soul."

At this, Abinadi fell.

Mera watched as two figures now walked along the edge of the altar. The same one used in all of the Passover sacrifices. This sacred altar was where her son offered his final sacrifice—his life. The figures turned. Mera gasped as she saw the faces of Zeniff and Jarom, gazing at her as the words, *Be at peace,* swirled in her mind. She could no longer see the flames, just two angels in white.

Mera collapsed against Yoseph.

"He sealed the truth of his words," Yoseph said in a quiet voice, stroking Mera's back.

She gulped and raised her head, searching for Noah. Wasn't he afraid of Abinadi's prophecy? Didn't he worry the flames would come for him? The smoke parted and Mera spotted him near the pyre, his jaw set, his eyes ablaze.

She shook her head. *I don't know him anymore. The boy I raised is already dead.*

*They both are.*

———— ◆ ————

Mera had no gift to bring. Nothing that would matter. Her tapestry, the threads knotted, the selvage tugged in at the sides, was not enough, no matter her tired eyes and bleeding fingers. She brought it anyway.

Her walk through the throne room was long, the guards shifting and nervous. What would Noah do when his broken mother gave him her broken gift? She carried it clutched to her chest like a shield, her ears shut to the tittering laughs of priests and concubines.

To her right, someone moved as if to help. It was Gideon, she knew it was, but she wouldn't look. How much longer would he be safe here? Jarom was gone. Zeniff, gone. All that was left were Tamar and Limhi.

And Noah.

*Go to Zarahemla. Find Sarai and my boys.*

Mera would find a way.

The king leaned forward, shrugging off his bobcat cloak. The gold ringing his fingers, lining his neck and even his girth glittered in the torchlight. Tamar stood across the room, her face a mask of fear. If he'd burn Abinadi, was anyone safe? She shook her head at Mera, a barely perceptible movement.

But nothing would stop Mera.

Noah could spot a challenge a city away, but even he couldn't have expected this. When she knelt before him, she did not bow her head. He motioned for Amulon to take her offering and toss it with the other gifts celebrating Abinadi's death.

"No." Her fingers curled into the fabric. "This is for you. Honor your mother, just this once."

Noah's lips tightened into a thick, angry line and a flush crept up his neck.

"Don't let her tell you what to do." Amulon grabbed the king's scepter from alongside the gilt throne and pressed it into Noah's hand. Amulon would banish Mera or forget her in the dungeons, the mother of the king.

Noah brushed the scepter aside and beckoned Mera closer. She rose, her knees groaning, though she refused to show the pain. Noah reached for the tapestry, let it unroll to the floor.

Someone gasped.

There, twisted into the fabric for all the court to see, was a scene of triumph. But not Noah's. It was an image of Abinadi, drenched in fire, his spirit rising to join the angels above him.

Noah roared.

Mera turned and walked away.

No one dared stop her. Not even the king.

# 29

## Gathering

*Tamar, 147 BC*

*T*he knocking was incessant. It was so early. *Who could possibly need something at this hour?* Tamar wondered. She pulled on a robe and scarf and tiptoed through the courtyard. The morning dew was heavy and her robe left swaths of dark green where everything else was almost white.

The figure at the gate was covered in a beautifully woven shawl, a gift made by Mera for her dear friend, Rachel. She'd never worn it before today.

As Tamar opened the gate, Rachel slipped in, looking both ways before she entered. She appeared frightened. No one else was out yet except a few roosters and chickens scratching for a morning meal. "Can we step inside?"

"What has happened?"

"Ever since the execution of Abinadi, Noah has been raging. He wanted to see anger from the believers, an uprising—something he could use as an excuse to order the soldiers to put down the rebellion. Gideon says he paces, shouts, breaks things. Everyone is afraid of him."

"Is Noah aware Gideon is sharing information with you?"

"No, he is cautious and only comes late at night when the rest of the guards are drunk. The priests have their . . . indulgences, and are occupied in the evenings. They never even ask where he goes. A couple of times he has

179

been offered the wine, refused, and been ridiculed." Rachel's brow wrinkled and her lovely face showed lines of worry ever deepening.

"He's a good boy. No," Tamar added, "a good man. He's no longer a boy. Does he ever have any time to help you?"

Rachel sighed. "No, the king has them patrolling the bluffs, watching for Lamanite spies. Noah doesn't want them to know what goes on in the city." She rubbed her shoulder, the one that lately always seemed to cause her pain.

"We must meet and talk to the rest of our people about this," Tamar said with a tone of defiance. "The spring is the only safe place, but the path is well-worn. It may reveal our movements."

"Noah has soldiers watching the temple," Rachel added. "Could we meet in the cave?"

"He would see us all crossing the bridge and pasture. I believe we will be safe at the spring. The path is the deer trail. We would not be the only ones there." Tamar paused with a look of worry. "We will need to watch for boars, though, since they're in season." She mused for a moment. "Noah hates the wild boars. He won't go into that part of the woods, but he may send soldiers."

"Maybe news of an attack would scare them away."

A smile lit up Tamar's face. "Brilliant idea! I'll ask Limhi and some of his friends to spread word of an attack near the spring and add sightings of several boars. Even soldiers would fear to go there."

Rachel smiled. "May the Lord bless us. I long to hear the words Abinadi spoke. Gideon said it was as if his face shone with light just like Moses when he came from Mount Sinai."

Mera emerged from her quarters and looked from Tamar to Rachel, smiling when her eyes rested on the shawl. "It looks lovely on you. It brings out the color of your eyes."

Rachel bowed slightly. "Thank you. I know how hard you worked on it to make the pattern just right. I should have worn it before. I'm sorry."

Mera gave her a light hug and stepped back to give Rachel her space.

"It was beautiful and, at the same time, frightening to hear the words Abinadi spoke to King Noah. His words pierced my soul." Tamar's voice carried a slight tremor. "When Alma stood up and witnessed that he spoke truth and begged for Noah to listen, to repent, I feared for him. But at the same time my heart felt such joy." Tamar took both of Rachel's arms. "I believe Alma's heart was changed. I want to speak with him but no one knows where he has gone."

"Helam has been gone as well," Rachel added. "He's not been seen since Alma left."

"I wish I had been there." Rachel rested a hand on Tamar's arm. "We have the Lord on our side. Abinadi's death can't be for naught."

"Thank you for your faith," Tamar whispered as she drew Rachel into a quick embrace.

"I must go. The dawn has arrived." Rachel slipped away as silently as she had come.

"Do you think that will work, to make Noah think the wild boars are on the attack?" Tamar asked.

"I hope so. We need something to keep the king and soldiers away from the spring," Mera said.

Tamar and Mera tiptoed through the courtyard to where Limhi slept. Tamar whispered through the tapestry to see if he was awake.

She pulled aside the door covering and saw he'd already dressed, his knees slightly dusty from kneeling to pray. Her heart swelled with love for this young man and instinctively she drew him into a tight embrace. "I love you, son."

"Is that all you wanted, to tell me you loved me?"

"No, but that was most important. I need you to start rumors of a boar attack and make sure the king's soldiers hear about it. Without telling an outright lie, make them think you were in danger and the path to the spring is dangerous."

"I can do that." Understanding lit his face. "Is it to keep the soldiers away from our meeting place by the spring?"

"It is."

"It'll be done today. Is there anything else?"

"Just be careful, please," Tamar urged.

"Yes, please come back safe," Mera said. "I'm so proud of the man you've become." She hugged her grandson, who now towered head and shoulders taller than her.

Mera went back to her quarters and Limhi left to do his cunning task. Tamar walked slowly back to her own home.

As she neared her doorway, a shadow passed behind the tree in her courtyard. A figure stood concealed among the cascading leaves of the tree, its silhouette revealed by the light of the coming dawn.

Tamar stopped. It didn't move. She walked toward it. Still, no movement.

As she entered the shadows, she immediately recognized the face. It was Alma. Helam also stood behind him. She ran to Alma and took him into her arms. "Lisha has been weeping for weeks, wondering where you've gone! Your mother has been worried but had faith you were safely hiding."

His beard had grown long. He looked hungry and tired. Helam looked about the same. "I knew if I didn't leave I'd be killed," Alma said. "I've been writing the words Abinadi spoke." He pulled a thick scroll out of his cloak, and a smile lit up his eyes. "I have it here. I want to begin teaching the people. His words are true, and the Lord has called me to preach them."

"Can I tell Lisha you are well? She's worried sick."

Alma's expression was full of concern. "Is she still with child?"

"Yes, but the time is coming soon. She'll want to see you if that's possible."

Helam stepped forward. "My queen, if we could use your home, could Alma and Lisha meet there for now, in case the soldiers are still watching his house?"

Tamar nodded. "I'll get her now. Please go in and find something to eat."

Still in her morning shawl, she walked quickly to Lisha's home and woke her. "I'm sorry to come so early. It's important and I need you to act completely normal. Trust me, my reasons are very good." They didn't come directly back to Tamar's home, but stopped along the way at shops in town to appear as though they were just doing their chores early. Tamar could feel Lisha's hand shake as they walked. She whispered assurances and reminders to be calm so as to not raise any suspicion from soldiers who were stationed all over the city. They nodded as they passed, doing all they could to not hold their attention.

When they entered the private courtyard, Tamar whispered instructions. "Come into my home as you would any other day, and be very quiet. I'll come in with you." Tamar smiled. Lisha just nodded. Her chin puckered and quivered, eyes beginning to tear.

Tamar held the tapestry and Lisha stepped inside. Immediately, she was swallowed up in the arms of her husband. After a long embrace, the four of them talked for some time, Lisha telling what had occurred in the city and Alma sharing the trial of hiding out in the wilderness. "Helam brought food and supplies so I could write," Alma told them, while giving a friendly slap on Helam's back.

Tamar gave them fruit, bread, and honey. After what seemed like just a few minutes, another face appeared in the doorway—Limhi. "Alma!" He crossed the room in one step and embraced the haggard guest. Helam was next to be taken into Limhi's embrace. "It's good to see you both. You need to shave, and bathe." He clapped them both on their shoulders with a chuckle.

It didn't take long for him to report, with a mischievous grin. "I've spread the word through the city and palace that the trails to the spring are now the most dangerous paths to take anywhere." He added a few details about a bleeding and dying fawn, which made Tamar flinch. It was evidence enough for the soldiers and they drew their own conclusions as they saw the torn, bloody clothing on Limhi.

Helam clapped the young man on the shoulders and held him there, gazing into his eyes. "You take after your mother in faith and obedience. She's taught you well."

Limhi nodded, resting his hand on his mother's arm. "The blood is dry. I won't get any on you, Mother."

Smiles lit the faces of everyone there, the tension disappeared, and this little group of believers felt the joy of being together again.

"Let's call the people to the spring. Alma, can you begin teaching today?"

"Isn't it dangerous to be near the spring?" he said with a mischievous smile, drawing a chuckle from everyone in the room.

As each one left Tamar's home, they hummed a simple tune. Only the believers would know to listen for the music, and what it would mean. It didn't take long for families and individuals to slip away from their work, their shops, their homes and take an early morning walk to the spring. A few stayed behind to keep enough shops open to prevent suspicion.

———— ◆ ————

The many paths to the spring began to show wear over the weeks as people met daily to hear the words of Abinadi, taught by Alma. Their love and trust for him grew quickly. Lisha's belly grew ever larger.

One day, a soldier met her at her door as she was leaving to go to the spring. Tamar had come to her home so they could walk together.

"Where are you two going so early?" He looked down at Lisha's belly.

She wrapped a protective arm around her growing child.

Tamar stepped between Lisha and the stout soldier. "Without her husband, I'm caring for her. We will be leaving now." Tamar pulled Lisha close and they stepped outside.

"I'll do my best to keep an eye on you, to make sure nothing goes wrong when that little one is born." The soldier was talking louder to span the growing distance. "The child's traitorous father is probably dead by now! If not, he will be if, or *when*, we find him!" His shouting drew the attention of others in the city.

Lisha began shaking. Tamar picked up their pace to distance themselves from the hateful words of the king's soldier.

Many of the city's residents were not believers and only saw the death of Abinadi and the absence of one renegade priest as one more way of keeping the city safe. They thought Abinadi was a crazy man and had deserved to die. Their comments had been overheard in shops and shared sadly in private amongst the believers. Tamar had heard them all.

She pulled Lisha closer. "Don't listen. We'll stop at my house before going to the spring. Don't worry."

Over the course of the morning, they watched as family after family left the city. The soldier stationed himself where he could see Tamar's home. She realized, sadly, that they would both miss the meeting today.

They used the time to sit in the courtyard, talking and studying. Tamar mentored Lisha in preparation for the birth of her first child.

As the sun rose and traveled across the sky, they went into town to do more errands. Wherever they went, the soldier followed.

After the setting of the sun, Lisha went home, saddened to have missed time with other believers, especially her beloved Alma.

———— ◆ ————

The market bustled with foreigners parading themselves through the streets, led by the king's servants. Tamar was sorting through herbs at the healer's hut when a larger group than usual passed through. There was barely enough room. She stood aside, pleasant and accommodating.

As the entourage made their way to the shops of the king's craftsmen, she could hear the exclamations of "what quality . . . never seen such workmanship . . . finest city in all of the Nephite nations . . ."

She shook her head, looking back through the kohosh, lobelia, witch hazel, and comfrey leaves for the freshest available stems. Lisha was close to delivery and she needed to make preparations. A small hand tapped her on the shoulder. The slight young woman had removed herself from the palace group and stood in the shadow of the hut's canopy.

"Do you remember me?"

"I'm sorry, I can't recall your name. Please tell me again."

"Dinah. I am one of Noah's concubines." Her eyes fell at this confession.

The awkwardness of the situation must have induced additional explanation because she continued after Tamar's silence.

"He has me dance and sing for him. He's not taken me yet as a wife. He has many others before me." She smiled a shy smile. "He once gave me to Prince Limhi."

"Oh!" Tamar grasped both shoulders and held her while she studied her face. "You have grown so much I didn't recognize you!" With a warm smile she added, "I enjoyed our talks. We miss you."

"Limhi?"

"I did say we."

The young girl blushed. "I'd like to learn more about the herbs you use. There are many women in the palace bearing children and I know what you have would help them in their time of travail."

"Would the king allow it?"

"I wouldn't have to ask. I am free to move about and have responsibilities that take me out of the palace. We could just meet."

"I'd welcome the blessing to teach you, but wouldn't want to put you in any danger." Tamar thought a moment and added, "Come at sunrise each day to the courtyard. We can study there where Mera and I have many of our plants growing."

The young woman beamed with joy. "Thank you!" She turned to run and catch up with the royal guests, then stopped to shout out a question to Tamar. "Tomorrow?"

Tamar nodded with pleasure. She watched her turn and run, clutching her dress in both hands so she could move faster. Her petite feet churned up dust as she hurried down the street.

With a sense of purpose, Tamar continued her trading. Her final stop was Lisha and Alma's home. She called at the doorway and asked to come in.

"Lisha?"

Silence.

Lisha came to the door, pulling the tapestry aside just enough to peek out.

"Are you well?"

"Well enough."

"Can I come in?"

Lisha shifted from one foot to the other. "No."

A voice from inside the house said, "Let her come."

Lisha parted the tapestry just enough to let Tamar poke her head in. She was surprised to see two men. Alma and Helam.

"It's time," Alma said with concern as Lisha stood slightly stooped over, clutching her belly.

"Do you want me to stay?" Tamar asked, puzzled.

"She does. She's just frightened of the soldiers. They've been watching for me to return when the baby comes."

Helam stood and walked toward the door. "I'll distract them."

Lisha's waters broke and pooled on the floor. She groaned with a wave of pain. "Alma, hold her." Tamar guided. He gently supported her beneath her arms and Helam looked around nervously.

"I should go."

"Do something to occupy the soldiers, but don't get caught. They're looking for you too." Tamar shifted her focus, speaking as she worked. "Can you somehow get word to Naomi and Mera that Lisha's time is close?" She worked quickly, tearing the leaves into small pieces, then chopping them with an obsidian blade. She stopped for a moment to gaze at Helam before he slipped out the back doorway into the dark shadows of the forest.

Tamar's focus returned to Lisha. She quickly prepared some tea, steeping it in the pot hanging over the fire pit in the center of the room. A poultice was her next preparation, mixed with lard from a small pot on the table. She took a scrap of cloth and handed it to Alma. "Wipe her brow and keep her comfortable."

Lisha's pains came more rapidly, but her groans were drowned out by shouting in the woods near their hut. Tamar heard heavy footsteps stop by the tapestry, then a big thud as Helam sat on the ground behind the house, concealed by stacked wood and baskets of grain.

Lisha, through gritted teeth whispered, "I don't want to have a baby anymore. It's too . . ."

"It's close, she's nearly done," Tamar assured Alma as he stroked Lisha's long hair.

He began humming and whispering encouraging words in her ears. Lisha grabbed his strong arms and arched her back, crying out in pain.

Alma's eyes teared up and he asked, "Is there nothing I can do?"

"She must do this herself. Keep encouraging her."

With all the tenderness a man could offer, he spoke words of comfort and faith while she travailed.

It wasn't long before a final cry was uttered and the child was born. Tamar's hands were covered in blood as she tenderly wiped the child clean and wrapped him up in the softest sheepskin. She handed him to the tearful parents.

A thumping on the adobe wall broke the spell of the moment.

"You okay in there, little lady?"

Fire ignited in Alma's eyes as he slipped from behind Lisha.

A sharp look from Tamar warned him to stay hidden.

Another thump, then a spear parted the curtain covering the door, and a sliver of light penetrated the darkness. Alma hid in the darkest corner of the small room beneath the table.

The soldier's scruffy face peered inside. "Looks like the little one's here now with no daddy. Poor child with no father around."

It was all Tamar could do to keep from punching him. "You cannot be here. The child has just been born. It's not proper. Leave."

Mera appeared in the doorway, pushing the soldier aside.

"Am I too late?" she asked breathlessly.

"No, I still need a few other herbs. Can you get the lavender and comfrey leaves from our little garden?"

"Yes, and I'll let Naomi know to come as soon as she can."

With a snicker the soldier added, "A child with no father won't last long in this place. Another attack just happened right here in the city. Big boar took down a full-grown man." He pulled his head out and his next muffled comment drew the ire of everyone in the room. "I'll stand here and keep watch. Keep you and that little one safe."

Tamar could almost feel Alma groan.

She helped Lisha clean up and settled her comfortably in her bed. Their communication consisted of nods and whispers. Tamar made more noise than necessary and the young child wailed cooperatively, covering any noise Alma might have made.

"What will you call him?" Tamar asked in a whisper.

"Alma" they replied in unison.

Tamar whispered a tearful reply. "Alma the Younger."

# 30

## Celebration

### Mera, 146 BC

*M*era pushed her way through the thicket leading to the spring the people called Mormon. Her shawls snagged on the leafy branches. She didn't mind the thick vegetation, however. It kept Alma well hidden.

Other believers followed similar paths through the woods, taking care not to be seen by the soldiers as they left the village. As careful as they were, a sort of trail was starting to form, a trail that led to Alma and the Waters of Mormon. Mera liked to view it as a trail to truth. Unfortunately, she knew Noah and his priests would view it as something else.

Mera nudged a low-hanging bough aside and entered the clearing. So many people had started coming to Alma's meetings over the past year that they'd moved to a larger area. Still, people packed the glade, some leaning against trees, others sitting on stumps, and still others on the ground. Everyone knew to keep as quiet as possible. But with so many people, and children running to and fro, Mera wondered how long it would be before Noah figured out what was happening.

She settled next to Rachel and Naomi on a makeshift bench formed from a log wedged between stumps. Across the clearing, Tamar and Limhi sat near Helam, who, as usual, scanned the forest for trouble. Tamar bounced Alma the Younger on her knee, while his mother, Lisha, listened to the prophet speak with rapt attention.

"We all must repent and turn to the Lord," Alma was saying.

"Yes," replied the master weaver's daughter, "but what does that mean if we're not committing grievous sins? I repent of eating too much berry cake or of taking too many steps on the Sabbath?"

Beside her, her father, Yoseph, stroked his beard, his brow furrowed.

Alma raised one foot onto a stump, placing an elbow onto a knee as he addressed her. "The Lord won't tell you every little thing. He expects you to sort some things out yourself. Perhaps for some, honoring the Sabbath means baking only the day before. Perhaps for others it means time spent with family."

The crowd murmured and Mera leaned forward, listening closely to Alma. This is what she was trying to understand. *Repent and turn to the Lord.* What did that mean for her, and did it mean the exact same thing for everyone? And if not, why? Wasn't the Lord the same yesterday, today, and forever?

"The Lord has given us commandments. Many of them are crystal clear. Thou shalt not kill. Thou shalt not commit adultery. But others, he leaves open to interpretation, such as honor thy father and mother."

"But why?" Limhi asked. He sat arrow straight, protective of his mother as always.

Mera frowned. How was Limhi to honor Noah? How could the Lord even ask that?

Yoseph met her gaze from across the clearing, his expression compassionate, almost as if he knew just what she was thinking. While the discussion continued, he rose and moved to sit beside Mera, giving her a quick squeeze of his hand.

Mera flushed as she scooted over to make room. She felt flustered and pleased and slightly confused.

"This is part of the great wrestle the Lord wishes us to have with him. We must ponder over these things. How do we best honor the Lord? How do we keep His Sabbath? How do we honor our parents?" Alma paused for a moment and smiled toward Naomi. "The Lord wishes us to discover this for ourselves, through study and fervent prayer, through practice, and yes, through repentance."

Mera nodded. This she could do. Keep trying. Seek the Lord's guidance. Repent. Try again.

"But this requires humility and a constant renewal of faith," Alma said.

Limhi bit his lip and Tamar slipped her hand over his.

"But what is faith?" Gideon asked as he stepped into the clearing, his guard's uniform crisp and neat. "How does it work?"

Alma inclined his head. "Faith is believing in things which you cannot see, which are true. Faith is a power. It builds within us strength to follow God's commands, even when life seems difficult and unfair. It gives us the ability to trust in Him, to turn our sorrows and our fears to Him. It is like a muscle: the more we use it, the more we trust and obey, the stronger our faith grows."

"And the resurrection?" Rachel said, her eyes on Gideon. "His father will live again?"

Alma's face seemed to shine. "I know it to be true. We will all live again."

Mera blinked back tears, thinking of Jarom. And Noah too. In the next life, would he have a chance to change, to repent?

Gideon cleared his throat, giving Alma a respectful bow. "King Noah still suspects you and Helam are near Shilom, preaching the gospel"—he wrinkled his nose—"although he calls it subversion."

"It's been a year," Lisha said, rising from a willow stump. "Will he never leave us alone?" She took Alma the Younger from Tamar and slung him onto her hip. "Will we never be safe?"

"I will not cease teaching the word of the Lord," Alma said simply.

Lisha's lip trembled.

Mera stood as well, feeling she should take some responsibility for protecting Alma, Helam, and the others. Naomi watched her with a pitying expression. Rachel worried, her arms folded across her chest.

"I cannot control my son," Mera said heavily. "The years have shown me this. But I know him well." Her gaze met Tamar's. "He fears the wild beasts. He excels with the bow, but fighting in close quarters terrifies him."

"It's true," Tamar said, her expression shrewd. "That's one reason why we've met here. He's unlikely to come where boars have attacked."

Mera nodded. "What if we covered Alma and Helam's clothing with sheep's blood, then brought them before the king?"

"That's a dangerous game," Rachel said, her eyes narrowing. "What if he discovers they're alive?"

Gideon shook his head. "Noah would never believe it. He still resents what Mera did after Abinadi died, throwing that tapestry in his face." He held out a hand toward Mera. "No disrespect meant, of course. I was glad to see you do it. But I don't believe the king would be forgiving now if he thought you deceived him."

"I'm willing to take that risk," Mera said.

Yoseph rose and gripped her arm. "As am I. I will go with her and share this burden."

Mera flushed again.

Gideon shook his head once more. "No. It must be me. It must be a guard or he will never believe."

Rachel shot to her feet. "Absolutely not!" she said at the same time Mera exclaimed, "I will not allow it!"

The two women stared at each other, Rachel's expression softening.

"Neither of you can forbid me," Gideon said.

"No," said Alma, "but we need your ears in the court."

"What if I went with them," Gideon said, "and told the king they'd shown me these things when I visited my mother? Then let him make his own conclusions."

Mera glanced to Rachel, who gave a slow and thoughtful nod.

Overhead, a starling hopped from one branch to the next, then trilled a simple tune.

◆

Mera strode into the throne room, once again passing numberless idols and concubines. This time, she gave them little thought. Noah's choices were his own. The damage he'd done to his people rested squarely on his shoulders. All she could do was try to undo it, if only a little.

Gideon and Yoseph marched alongside her, Yoseph casting her nervous looks while Gideon stared straight ahead. Her arms were full of torn and bloody robes, her cheeks wet with tears. That part was easy—Mera's heart was so full of sorrow anyway.

Noah rose from his throne, towering over her as she approached. "What is this?" he demanded.

She dropped the ruined robes at his feet.

"I am sorry, my lord," Gideon said stiffly. "She insisted on bringing these here herself." He made a helpless gesture and gave a tight smile. They'd agreed beforehand that it was best if he acted as if she were a bit crazy. "You know how she gets."

Noah threw his hands in the air, casting an irritated look at Amulon, who had a grin playing about his mouth. "All right, Mother." Noah sank back on the throne with a sigh. "What is it this time?"

Several women in the court snickered.

"These robes belonged to Alma and Helam," she said. "I wove the trim myself."

Using two fingers, Noah picked up the shredded garments, examining the many rips and stains. "They are dead? You are certain of this?" He looked to Gideon, who shrugged. "Where are their bodies?"

"There are many wolves and wild boars in the forest," Gideon said.

"And plenty of Lamanite bones," Amulon said with an ugly laugh. "Let Alma and Helam's remains mix among the rest of the filth."

"You shouldn't have chased them away," Mera said, and there could be no doubt she meant it.

"This is no more than they deserved if they chose to live among wild beasts, scrounging and hiding like traitors." Noah spat on the baked clay floor.

Mera leaned on Yoseph's arm. The deception was wearing on her. Even after all Noah had done, she didn't like hiding things from him. She longed to tell him the truth. Not just that Helam and Alma were alive, but that Noah should listen to Alma, that he should repent. But she'd be casting her pearls to be trodden under his foot.

Some of the conflict must've shown on Mera's face because Noah narrowed his eyes. "Look, I know Alma was your friend's son and Helam always watched over our family." He pursed his lips. "A little too closely, to say the truth, but there's nothing to be done now. Be off." He waved Mera and Yoseph away. "Gideon, you shall be rewarded for bringing this wonderful news."

---

Alma laid low in the weeks that followed Mera's subterfuge, never coming into town, only seeing his wife and son when they met him at the spring. Helam stayed with him, vigilant and loyal.

Life continued for believers and nonbelievers alike. People loved, married, and died. Children were born, crops came in. And the believers still gathered in Mormon, their numbers swelling as Alma taught them to hope for a better life.

Mera only hoped the meetings could continue without Noah's notice.

"His new wives should keep him busy," Tamar said as they gathered at the spring one autumn afternoon, though her voice showed no anger. It seemed she'd gone past caring about what Noah did anymore, as if Alma's words and the new hope in her heart had healed her pain and given her more important things to think about.

Nearly two hundred people filled the clearing, embracing one another as they arrived, their faces aglow with excitement. Alma had spread the word that an important change was coming and all the believers should come.

"Why isn't Limhi here?" Mera asked Tamar.

"Noah demanded that Limhi help him with some business at the palace." Tamar glanced at the trail, then back to Mera. "I hope he doesn't keep him long. Limhi needs to hear Alma teach. We all do."

Once they'd all arrived and settled down, Alma held his arm out to the bubbling pool behind him. "Behold," he said, "here are the waters of Mormon. And now, as ye are desirous to come into the fold of God, and to be called his people, and are willing to bear one another's burdens, that they may be light . . ."

Mera's heart warmed inside her. Something special was happening. She wasn't quite sure what, but she didn't doubt that comforting feeling.

"Yea," Alma continued, "and comfort those that stand in need of comfort, to be numbered with those of the first resurrection, that ye may have eternal life . . ."

Mera looked to Yoseph, who beamed back at her, then to Helam, Tamar, Rachel, and Naomi. Hadn't they borne one another's burdens? Hadn't they made one another's hearts light? She had no closer family than those believers who now stood together in the grove.

"Now I say unto you," Alma said, his voice soaring over the water and the rustling of a light breeze, "if this be your desire, what have you against being baptized in the name of the Lord, as a witness before Him that ye have entered into a covenant with Him, that ye will serve Him and keep His commandments, that He may pour out his Spirit more abundantly upon you?"

Mera's heart swelled until she felt she might burst. A pattering sound spread through the clearing, from one person to another, until all clapped their hands for joy. Mera found herself joining in, forgetting to be quiet, forgetting any danger. All she felt was incredible happiness and peace.

"This is the desire of our hearts," Helam said, speaking for them all.

Alma held out his hand and entered the water with Helam, beseeching the Lord to pour his spirit upon them. Then he baptized Helam in the name of the Lord, submerging himself as well.

After that, one believer after another stood forth to be baptized.

Tears welled in Mera's eyes as Tamar was baptized, but she couldn't help glancing to the trail, hoping to see Limhi hurrying through the brush to join them. The faces of those who came out of the water seemed alight with love and with the Spirit. She wanted that for her grandson. She wanted it for herself.

Finally, Mera took Alma's hand as he led her into the water. She bowed her head, filled with a calm sense of purpose as he prayed. The first thing she saw when she rose from the water was Yoseph, his dark eyes shining.

The baptisms continued through late afternoon. Those who were finished seated themselves in the clearing to witness the rest.

Mera's eyes filled with tears. "Limhi's not going to make it. But surely he'll have another chance to be baptized?"

Tamar's chin quivered as she stifled a sob. "Noah will forbid it. He'll do anything to keep Limhi from the truth, even if it means assigning him meaningless tasks until Noah's men drive the believers from this land and from my son's heart."

Mera squeezed Tamar's hand in a wordless gesture of support. Both women turned their attention back to Alma, who'd resumed teaching.

"We are the church of Christ," Alma told the congregation. "We must continue to gather and worship." He urged them to keep the Sabbath day holy and to care for the needy. He explained the priesthood, the sacred power of God on earth, then ordained many—including Helam and Yoseph—charging them to preach repentance and faith on the Lord.

Mera felt the Holy Spirit confirm the prophet's words and felt a deepened commitment to follow the ways of the Lord, no matter the cost. She also felt certain that someday, someway Limhi would have his chance to be baptized.

As the months passed, the group of saints continued to grow, both in number and in faithfulness, meeting together often to worship in homes, shops, or gatherings at the Waters of Mormon. Mera found a peaceful kinship among them, each giving of their substance to the other, each laboring for the good of them all, including the priests. They flourished in the borders of the land.

Out of sight of King Noah.

And it was there, in the borders of the land, away from her cruel son, that Mera found love again, this time by the side of a weaver, whom she married at the feet of a prophet.

# 31

## Discoveries

### Tamar, 145 BC

You're with child?" Tamar exclaimed in a hushed tone. "That's wonderful!" She embraced Lisha, pulling her close, then whispered, "The king will know Alma is alive when you begin to show. Keep it hidden as well as you can."

Lisha nodded. "I thought of that too. I'm already three months. I won't be able to hide it for long."

Little Alma tugged at his mother's shawl, pulling it down over her eyes. "Alma, be patient. We are walking with the queen."

"Queen?" He pointed at Tamar.

"Yes, and my friend, so be my good helper and hold her hand while we walk so I can get what I need at the market."

He slipped his hand into Tamar's, tugging her along through the street. "Faster."

"You have your hands full with this little guy. He's growing so much each day."

"I do. He never stops. I'm exhausted."

"I'll entertain him for the day if that would allow you to rest."

Lisha sighed. They were nearing the weaver's shop and Tamar realized she needed to stop and pick up a dress she had asked Yoseph to make for her. They stepped inside, fighting the tugging of the young Alma to stay outside. "Alma, please come with us for just a few minutes. Then we will go do something fun."

"Want to play with Daddy!" he exclaimed, to the shock of both Tamar and Lisha.

"Shhh, don't talk of Daddy when we are in the streets. It's not safe."

Tamar noticed Mera standing beside Yoseph. "Oh, here you are! We were going to stop in to see you. Alma's going to spend the day with me so Lisha can get some rest."

Mera's eyes immediately dropped to Lisha's midsection. "Are you . . . ?"

Lisha nodded.

"This will certainly change things. The soldiers will know Alma is still around."

Tamar, not wishing to cause Lisha any undue stress, smoothed over Mera's comment. "We just need to have faith that the Lord will watch over us, right, Lisha? Alma has taught us a great deal. My faith has grown so much over the years he has led our group. I don't doubt we will all be fine."

Mera nodded. "Yes, but with Noah knowing Alma is alive, he will grow suspicious again. He assumed Alma and Helam were dead."

"Did you come to pick up your dress?" Yoseph asked, changing the subject.

"Is it finished?"

"Yes, it's in the workshop, I'll get it."

Yoseph emerged from the workroom with a beautiful cream-colored linen dress with a pattern along the bottom and around the neck. The lines were perfect and the pattern precise.

"Oh, it's more lovely than I imagined!" Tamar said.

"Mera did the weaving," he said with a bowed head. "She's quite gifted."

"Thank you," Mera said, gently touching his arm. "You taught me well."

"We should probably leave you to your work," Tamar said with a knowing smile. "Lisha, you go home and rest. I'll watch little Alma today."

Relief washed over Lisha's face and she thanked Tamar for the respite.

Tamar struggled to keep hold of Alma's little fingers as they left the shop. He wiggled and tugged to try and escape her grip. "I also had a little boy once and know how to keep hold, Alma. We will do something fun, I promise."

Tamar mentally went through her list of chores and thought a walk to the pasture to see the shepherd would be good for Alma the Younger.

"Let's go see the sheep," she offered.

"Sheep!" he exclaimed and he tugged even harder, almost dancing around Tamar as she walked.

Tamar was making her way toward the bridge when she looked down the street toward Lisha and Alma's home. Lisha had been stopped by the soldiers. Two stood on each side of her. The one who was always watching her had her by the arm. Fear washed over Tamar as she suspected there was, or would be, trouble. She bent and swooped little Alma up into her arms. He resisted and began kicking.

"Sheep, see the sheep!" he cried.

"We will, in a moment. Mommy needs help."

They ran toward Lisha, Alma still kicking and wiggling to get down.

"Is there a problem?" she asked the soldiers directly. "Did Lisha do something wrong? If not, release her."

"Oh we're just checking on her and her son. He needs a father to help him learn to be a man."

"Daddy! Let's go see Daddy!"

The words had escaped his mouth before anyone could stop him.

"So, you want to go see Daddy?" the soldier said. "Where is your daddy?" His eyes burrowed into Lisha's as he asked the question. Her protective instinct must have kicked in as she placed a hand over her belly. His attention was drawn to the slight bulge beneath her hand. "Why, yes, there is a daddy and he must not be far away. I'll be sure to let the king know."

"No!" Lisha cried. "He's not done anything!"

"That's not what I hear. I've observed the movement, people coming and going, like an uprising in the works. Maybe you'll be wanting to take over the city and get rid of Noah." He sneered. "Maybe Alma wants to be king?" His grin revealed stained and rotting teeth from the constant exposure to the wine Noah provided them nightly. "Noah will reward me handsomely for this information." He punched the other soldier in the arm. "Let's go."

They walked away, leaving Tamar and Lisha stunned and gripped with fear.

"What will we do now?"

"We need to prepare to leave the city. I don't think any of us will be safe meeting, worshiping, or living here any longer."

Tamar took Lisha by the hand, still holding the wriggling Alma in the other arm, perched precariously on her hip. He had begun to fuss again, fighting her as they went back to the weaver's hut instead of the pasture.

"How did the soldiers find out?" Yoseph asked.

Everyone's eyes went to the now inconsolable child. He cried for freedom to run and see the sheep.

"I'll go to Alma," Yoseph said. "He must seek the will of the Lord. I'll leave immediately, before soldiers are stationed around the city to watch or follow us."

Lisha began to cry. "Alma, my dear boy, why did you say that?" She took him by the shoulders and looked deep into his eyes. "I know you're only two, but what you said put us all in danger."

"He can't possibly know what he did. He's young and impulsive." Tamar reached down to smooth Lisha's shawl. "I'll take him to see the sheep."

Alma's weeping ceased and he smiled through his tears. "Sheep?"

"Yes, let's go see the sheep. Go home," she added to Lisha. "Prepare for a possible journey." She gave her a tight hug.

It didn't take long for word to go out to the captains of fifty, the leaders of their growing congregation. "Gather immediately at the temple," was Alma's message to Yoseph. "Prepare tents, food, seeds, tools, and bedding for a departure from Shilom." They would leave as soon as they could. All supplies would be stored at the spring and were to be taken there today.

Tamar missed the meeting, not wishing to fight Alma's strong will. She instead walked through the pasture, thinking about what she would do. Would she leave? She looked across the river at the city she had grown up in, the only place she had ever called home. She was the queen. Her eyes went to the vineyard-covered burial mound. The tree she had planted there for Zeniff at the highest point swayed only slightly in the wind. It stood nearly twenty feet tall now and had sunk its roots deep.

*My roots are deep too. Lord, must I leave? Should I stay? What would thou have me do?* Her eyes rested on the opulent structures throughout the city: the palace, the large homes, the marketplace, and then the temple. The old temple. Her heart swelled with love for what she had been taught through Abinadi and Alma. *Stay and fulfill your role here, with Limhi. I have a work for you to do.*

Tears sprang to her eyes as she pondered how life would surely change if she stayed behind with Limhi while so many of those she loved went on to somewhere else, maybe even back to Zarahemla.

Within a short time, soldiers had taken up positions around the city, watching for more than a few people coming or going. An announcement was made that anyone caught in a group larger than ten, the size of a family, would be punished.

Fortunately the word had gone out early and supplies had already been taken. Now they would need to carefully make their way one at a time to the spring to receive instructions.

As night fell, darkness filled the space below the canopy of trees. Those who made their way through the darkness knew the path well, every tree root, every stone. At those difficult spots where the terrain was rough, the bark of the trees had been worn smooth from hands seeking support from their anchored position along the river. Sounds of water cascading over stones and roots masked any sound their feet made. The people rarely got together all at once. In the past, they were careful to not appear as though masses were coming or going to the same place.

That had all changed now.

# 32

# Fleeing

## *Mera, 145 BC*

More than four hundred and fifty souls gathered at the waters of Mormon, on the edges of Shilom, out of sight of the king and his army. But the army would surely find them if they didn't leave soon. The bleating sounds of sheep and squawking of chickens removed from their nightly roosts all mingled with the easy laughter of children while parents tried to corral them. Captains double checked their packs for essentials such as water, blankets, and seeds.

Mera and Yoseph loaded a mule with their tent, tools, clothing, and cooking supplies. Tamar and Limhi helped tie the bundles to its back.

"I still don't understand why you won't come with us," Mera said for what felt like the hundredth time. She scanned the huge crowd for signs of trouble—soldiers, spies, anyone tied to Noah—unable to shake the feeling that he'd find them.

"I am the future king of this land," Limhi said. Mera was glad to hear him say it with only a sense of responsibility instead of greed or pride. "I won't abandon my people to the cruelties of my father. And if I were to leave, he'd never cease hunting us." He tightened the straps on Mera's mule. "I can make a difference here."

"Then I will stay with you," Mera said simply.

Beside her Yoseph rubbed his forehead. "I'm not unpacking and repacking again, Mera."

"You mustn't stay," Tamar said. "He's ordered your death."

Mera felt the blood drain from her face. "He issued the command then?"

Tamar nodded, her face tight. "As we knew he would once Alma's presence was discovered."

Mera swallowed a sob. "He's my son."

Tamar shook her head, resting her hand on Mera's upper arm. "He's not the same, Mera. He's not the man I married or the man you raised."

Mera blinked, nodding. Still, it sickened her to know her own son would command she be killed, even if she had misled him about Alma and Helam. "And what of you, Tamar? He knows we are close. He knows you worship with the believers. You are no safer here than the rest of us."

Tamar stood straight and unafraid. "I've given this great thought and prayer, Mera. I will stay. As much as I long to leave, the Lord needs me here, with Limhi."

Helam stepped up beside them. "Alma's given the call to move out. Naomi and Lisha are with him. And Lisha's mother too."

"Avi's coming?" Mera said in surprise. "But she's so frail."

Helam nodded.

"But you're not coming," Mera said shrewdly, noting his conspicuous lack of trappings.

Helam's face darkened. "I promised Jarom I'd watch over your family. You will be safe now. But Tamar and Limhi need my aid now more than ever."

Tamar gripped Helam's cloak. "Noah will never believe your story."

Helam gave her a grim smile. "I can be persuasive when I need to be. And I will do all I can to protect you and Limhi." He ducked his head in respect.

The caravan of believers moved out, calling their flocks, hauling handcarts, and driving their beasts of burden. Alma and Lisha moved among the crowd, helping where they could and offering encouragement.

Helam raised his head. "Alma."

The two embraced like brothers.

"I understand you'll be staying behind," Alma said.

Helam nodded.

"There are many believers who could not leave," Alma said. "Some sick, others afraid. Watch over them."

"Of course."

Mera pulled Tamar and then Limhi into a tight embrace. "If things grow too hard here in Shilom, come find us."

Tamar nodded, then turned to hug Lisha, who cradled her round belly.

"I shall miss you terribly," Lisha said. "I can't thank you enough for your encouragement when Alma"—she shot him a look—"well, when Alma was living a different way."

Tamar squeezed Lisha's hand. "I'm so glad I could help."

"And I'm glad she waited on me to wake up." Alma threw an arm around Lisha. "Now, we better get back before young Alma runs his grandmothers ragged."

They waved and moved quickly to the front of the crowd.

Mera watched them go, feeling a strange mixture of joy and grief. Alma had returned to the Lord. Why hadn't Noah? Could she ever find peace over that? And what about all the people she was leaving here in Shilom? Tamar, Limhi, and other believers like Gideon, who had refused to flee, despite his mother's tearful pleading.

Tamar and Limhi embraced Mera one last time. "We'll send word if we can," Tamar said, her eyes brimming with tears.

Limhi wiped his eyes.

Then Mera took Yoseph's hand and turned her back to Shilom and all she had ever known.

*Lord, you told me to follow Alma. You told me to leave Shilom behind. I offer this supreme act of faith, leaving it all in your hands.*

———— ◆ ————

The next few hours were terrifying. The sun set through the trees, painting them the color of blood. The lowering light made the path treacherous. Roots grabbed at Mera's feet. Brambles tore at her clothes. Up ahead, someone stumbled and gave a soft cry of pain.

As the caravan inched forward, Mera saw who it was. Ophir, the painter's wife, sat heavily on the ground while her wispy husband bound her ankle with strips of cloth.

"It's just a sprain," he said in a quiet voice when Mera paused to help. "We'll be along in a moment. Our son's finding a staff to help her keep going."

"God protect you," Mera said, dropping a kiss on Ophir's head.

They continued onward, Mera searching the dim woods for signs of pursuit. But the shadows were thick and confusing. Small creatures scurried through the underbrush. Fireflies hovered in the bushes, drawing Mera's gaze from other, darker things that might lurk in the forest.

Mera had thought she'd feel some relief once darkness descended, hiding the believer's exodus from Shilom. But the caravan's animals and children could not be kept quiet. Instead of protecting them, the darkness blinded them to their enemies.

Mera noticed Yoseph's hand going to his blade every time a strange sound came from behind them or from somewhere deep in the woods.

"Alma promised we'd be safe," she told him, although she still felt uneasy.

Yoseph nodded, his expression grim and wary. "I believe him. But I'll keep a friendly hand on my knife, just the same."

Other men seemed to have the same idea, some carrying atlatls, others farm implements or daggers.

Mera rubbed her arms. As soon as Noah realized they were gone, he'd send out his men to bring them back—or worse. Would his army sneak through the woods and surround them? Every rustling tree could cover the sounds of pursuit. Perhaps they'd charge through the forest, shouting and shooting arrows or throwing spears, confident that they could outpace the plodding caravan and easily overpower them.

Mera shivered and picked up her step, nudging the mule to move along.

"Won't matter," Yoseph said. "If they come after us, we'll just have to stand our ground."

"And be slaughtered by Noah's army?"

Yoseph reached out and tucked Mera's hair back under her shawl. "I will defend you with my life. If we die, we die faithful to each other and to the Lord."

Murmurs of agreement rose from the other families around them.

The believers knew what they were risking in fleeing from Shilom.

Were they walking to their deaths, like Abinadi? What purpose could that serve? What purpose did death and destruction ever serve? Was it just a horrible part of this world? A side effect of the freedom to choose? Why would God allow such horrors? Why did he let Noah murder his own brother, the prophet?

Mera shivered again, uneasy about where her thoughts were taking her.

Something cracked in the woods and Mera jumped. "What was that?" She peered over her shoulder. "I see something, there, in the woods."

Yoseph moved in front of her, pulling out his knife. Two younger men ventured into the forest, searching. Mera held her breath and waited.

Moments later, they returned, shaking their heads. "If someone was there, they're gone now," one of the men said.

"Could've been Ira's son," Yoseph said, but the set of his shoulders was tense, like a snake ready to spring.

*Oh Lord,* thought Mera, *please guide and protect us. We come here at Your bidding, following Your prophet. Keep us safe. Shield us from harm. Hide us from Noah's men.*

She paused, realizing she was now trying to control God, to tell Him what to do just as she had tried and failed to control Noah. A small huff of air escaped her lips. Then she grasped Yoseph's hand and began anew, this time aloud.

"Dear Lord, thank You for the faith of these believers and for the hope Alma has shared with us. Thank You for Yoseph and the joy he's brought in my life. Please Lord, if it be Thy will, protect us. Noah will send his armies before long. If it be Thy will, guide us to a land where we can serve Thee. But if not, we will serve Thee now, even unto death."

Mera finished and smiled into Yoseph's gentle eyes, peace blooming in her heart.

# *33*

# Gideon

*Tamar, 145 BC*

Tamar climbed the tower, clutching her robe as she did, one careful step at a time. Her left hand lifted the woven fabric and her right clung tightly to the rungs of the ladder. Each peeled wooden step, worn smooth from daily use, took her back to the first time Limhi had climbed here, alone, to warn the city of a Lamanite attack. The darkness of the moonless night shrouded the city in shadows. She knew what was moving in the darkness tonight. Her friends. Her family. Fellow believers. Silently escaping the city of Shilom and the tyrannical reign of King Noah.

Her chin quivered, not from cold, but from fear. The tower stretched ever higher and the buildings disappeared. Something caught her eye. Torch lights. Off in the far distance they moved slowly through the valley far beyond the city, away from the Lamanites, away from opulent structures lining the streets of Shilom and away from the empty humble huts in their shadows—devoid of the faithful believers who followed Alma. She knew where they traveled, toward Zarahemla, the land of their fathers.

Tamar finally made it to the top, clinging to the railing and the rope lashings that held the structure together. Gentle breezes caressing the city below had become stiff winds upon the tower. They whipped her hair and scarf, drying her tears before they fell.

She stayed till the torchlights blended into the starry cloudless night and she could no longer discern their movement. They were safe, for now.

It didn't take long for Noah to discover what had happened. Soldiers, all who were left, were summoned with a blast of the horn to the palace. Tamar stood above, watching them scurry about, running from house to house.

"Find them!" Noah bellowed. His face strangely illuminated by torchlight appeared to have no eyes, just puffy jowls.

"Captains, call your fifty."

A half dozen armed guards stepped up.

"Where are the rest?" Noah shouted over the shuffling of feet and clanking of swords and armor.

"Gone, Your Majesty."

Tamar watched with increasing interest. There had been a few soldiers in the meetings because they were family members, trusted to be loyal to Alma. No one questioned their presence at the Waters of Mormon, the spring where the people had come to learn about Abinadi's message, taught by Alma.

Noah's voice rang out over the deafening chirping of crickets and locusts, as if they were all competing for the melody in this nighttime choir. "Find them. Kill the soldiers and bring Alma to me, alive! I'll do with him what I did to Abinadi." His heaving chest rippled in the light of the soldiers' torches as his robes struggled to keep up with the movements of his arms.

The army, less than half its size, formed ranks. Each soldier held a torch, fanning the meager light as they walked. Tamar knew they were looking for signs of hundreds of footprints, animal droppings, and bent grasses. Tamar looked away to where she knew they had gone. The soldiers moved as slowly as a snake on a cold day, back and forth, this way and that. *Please lead Thy people to safety. Bless Alma to find the way home. Please Lord, protect Thy people.*

People had come out of their homes, watching the scene unfold, indiscernible voices rising to Tamar's ears. She looked down the ladder, turned, and slowly began her careful descent from the tower. The whispers became louder the closer she came. Limhi came from the pasture, the direction the soldiers were now going.

"Did you watch them leave?" he asked.

"I did. Where were you?"

"On the other tower."

Limhi took his mother in a tight embrace. "I'll miss Grandmother," he whispered.

Tamar just nodded, unable to speak.

"Bring her." Noah ordered to his priests. Tamar turned to see robed men coming toward her. She stood her ground.

"The king wishes to speak with you." Amulon's gaze was deadly serious.

Tamar and Limhi walked together to where Noah stood, seething, on the palace steps.

"Where have they gone? Mother has left with them." Noah's nostrils flared. "I always knew she would turn against me."

"It wasn't easy for her."

"She never loved me. I'm not surprised she left after her beloved Jarom, or Abinadi, whatever he decided his name was, died."

"You mean, when you killed him."

Noah's face shimmered with perspiration in the torchlight. "He was inciting rebellion, like Alma."

"They did nothing wrong."

Some who remained in the city were coming to hear the conversation between the king and his first wife. Other wives and concubines were slowly coming out of the palace. Dinah stood in the shadows.

"What will become of our city, now that most of the craftsmen have left?"

"Who knows the skill of pottery?" People began looking around. Indeed, most of the artisans were gone.

"Rachel and Gideon stayed," Tamar offered.

A voice from the darkness rang out. "Maybe Noah should do some work now that he's driven the people away." Priests moved menacingly toward the man who spoke out against the king.

"What if the rest of us leave?" someone threatened.

"Where have they gone?"

"Where *have* they gone?" Noah screamed, looking from face to face and finally resting on Tamar. His eyes were crazed and wide—bloodshot from wine and lack of sleep. "Tell me now if you know where they've gone." He stepped quickly toward Tamar, and Limhi moved between them.

"You'll not threaten her."

"I'm the king. Move aside. You'll do what I say. Everyone must do what I say!"

He began ranting, looking from face to face.

"All of you. Do what I say. Find them, bring them back!"

The people stared at him.

Some of Noah's wives had moved back into the palace, hiding inside the doorways. Children had long since been put to bed. Dinah's eyes, round with fear, peered out of the darkness.

"Who else will leave me?" Noah shouted.

Tamar felt a twinge of guilt. She hadn't moved into the palace. Had she left him or had he left her? He was so unhappy. Everything he did, he was motivated by pride, money, and power, leaving him bitter, angry, lonely, and empty. She felt pity that he couldn't feel the joy of Abinadi's message. In spite of her sorrow of seeing those she loved leave the city, she felt joy knowing that a Savior would come and redeem all who were willing to follow Him.

"Noah, will you not yet believe?"

She looked at him with new eyes. He was miserable. She knew in her heart that even in this state, if he chose to, he could change.

"Never. God could never love someone like me."

He turned and walked away. People watched him in stunned silence.

One of the prominent wealthy merchants turned to Tamar and Limhi. "Does your God love me?"

Tamar's heart swelled with joy. "Yes, yes he does!"

A woman stepped forward. Clearly she was a woman of the night. "Would your God love me?"

"God loves us all, and because he does, he wants us to follow Him. Obey His commandments. Because of that love, He will soon come down to teach us His ways. If we follow Him, He will lead us home."

"I'll follow him," she said with head bowed.

"Nonsense," another spat. "This is the rambling of visionary men and wishful women." He walked away, shaking his head. "I'm with Noah." He headed to the wine cellar where Noah had gone.

Once Noah was out of sight, a few of the wives approached Tamar and Limhi. The eldest, a dark-haired young woman who was great with child, spoke. "Dinah has told us many things. We want to learn more of what you've taught her."

Dinah stepped out of the shadows.

"Is this true?" Tamar asked.

Limhi smiled. "I'm pleased that you've shared what Mother taught you."

She blushed at his compliment.

"You'll make a great king one day," the elder wife said to Limhi. "You're not at all like your father." Her eyes dropped. "I would like to have my sons be like your son." She looked at Tamar. "How can my sons be like Limhi when all they see is Noah?"

An idea formed in Tamar's mind. "We can meet at the spring, like the others did. We still have leaders here. Some stayed behind. We can study and learn together."

A smile crept across her face. "What about Noah?"

"God will watch over us, like he did for Alma's people."

She nodded. "Can we come with Dinah?"

"Yes."

Noah was fully drunk when the group finished talking. He and his high priests walked from the wine cellar built into the sloping hillside of the burial mound. As the mound had grown, so had the vineyards. The hill, topped with Zeniff's tree, was nearly as tall as the palace.

"Wives. Line up. Let me choose one of you to come to my chamber tonight."

Reluctantly the women filtered back to the palace steps.

His head bobbed, eyes scanned one after another until he got to the end of the row. Dinah.

"You, down there. I've not been with you yet. Tonight you're mine."

Her face drained of color. She backed up.

Limhi stepped toward Noah.

"You'll do no such thing." His eyes steeled over. "You once gave her to me and I will claim her now."

Noah's laugh was menacing. "I don't think so, my son." Chuckling he added, "The king always gets his way."

"Not this time." Limhi stood tall and firm next to the swaying, unsteady king.

"Who'll stand by me and teach this boy of mine a lesson?" Looking around, no one moved. "Cowards! After all I've built here and made you all what you are?" A few wealthy merchants slowly stepped forward.

"Bring her to me."

As they slowly approached her, several others stepped to block their way. Lines were drawn. Those who supported the king and those who saw how they had been led down a path that they were no longer comfortable traveling.

Limhi positioned himself directly in front of Dinah. "She's mine."

"Take him. Take her. Cast them all into prison!"

What began as taking sides quickly became pushing, then shoving until the city was all in commotion. People who had remained in their homes, watching from the doorways, were now taking a position, neighbor against neighbor. Some arguing that Noah had crossed a line and didn't need to take any more wives. Others said Limhi showed no respect for his father, the king.

Tamar watched as the remaining people in her city rose up in anger one against another. She cried out. "Enough!"

"Kill the king!" someone shouted from the darkness. Murmurs erupted and Tamar scanned the crowd for the source of the threat.

Gideon, in full armor, stepped out of the shadows.

"I stand as an enemy of the king. It is time for a new king." He moved deliberately toward Noah, people parting as he passed.

"Arm yourself, Noah."

Noah fumbled and grabbed a sword left behind by one of the soldiers. He had been one of the best archers, but not the best swordsman. Still affected by the wine he had consumed, he stumbled toward Gideon, stabbing his sword into the dirt. He pulled it out, then ran. His steps were heavy. His robes tripped him, and he nearly fell. He was gasping for breath as he lumbered to the only place he felt safe. The tower.

Shuffling drunkenly to the base of the tower he had built near the temple, he grasped at the ladder.

Gideon was pursuing him with strong, slow steps. Noah stopped, regained his footing, and lunged at Gideon. The young man easily sidestepped the king. The king swung his sword wildly and missed Gideon completely.

Noah's first step up the ladder was a miss. His foot slipped and he cracked his shin on a rung, shouting and cursing. He managed a few more steps.

Gideon climbed after him. Noah threw his sword at Gideon, nearly piercing him through, but Gideon ducked. It passed over his head. Now unarmed, Noah scrambled awkwardly with both hands fumbling to keep hold. With each slip, the crowd gasped.

Gideon methodically climbed. Like a mountain lion stalking prey, he moved. His eyes never left the king.

Tamar held her breath, not wishing to see either meet their death. Noah kicked at Gideon, his other foot slipping as he did so, leaving him dangling from his hands. He cried out in terror.

Gideon continued his pursuit. When Noah reached the top, the crowd released a collective breath. Tamar's shoulders eased slightly. At least the threat of seeing the king fall to a gruesome death had been avoided for now.

Noah fixed his gaze beyond the bluff. The crowd looked as well. Noah swung his head around first at the approaching Gideon, then to the people. In a hoarse, breathless voice, he shouted, "Blow the horn! The Lamanites are invading."

Tamar looked at Limhi with questioning eyes. "Surely it's a lie."

"They couldn't be coming now," Limhi agreed and returned his gaze to the unfolding drama on the tower.

No one moved. Gideon reached the top. He came toward Noah with sword raised. To Tamar they were shadows, silhouetted against the starry night. Noah faced his attacker with arms waving wildly and speaking words lost in the wind.

Gideon's sword rested on Noah's chest, poised to pierce him through. Then strangely, Gideon's sword dropped. They both turned, gripping the railing. Gideon picked up the horn. The blast echoed through the night. Lamanites.

Tamar held her breath. The next blast was brief. They were advancing quickly.

Noah's voice rang through the night. "Gideon, spare me! I must protect my people!"

Gideon remained atop the tower while Noah cowered from him, never turning his back on the young soldier who had threatened to send him into the spirit world. As Gideon leaned into the wind whipping his cloak, facing the land of Shemlon, Noah made his escape. He climbed down and as he did, he shouted orders. "Soldiers are gone. All who have swords, arm yourselves and let us flee to the cave."

# 34

## Coronation

### *Tamar, 145 BC*

Tamar's years of preparation took over and she called to the mothers to get their children. Elderly were to be carried if they could not go on their own. The warmth of the season wouldn't require blankets, but the cave would be cold.

"Take only what you have with you. Come let us escape!" she cried.

She watched as families worked together, helped the elderly, and moved quickly toward the bridge. Noah ran out in front while his wives were left to fend for themselves and bring all of their children. Little ones were wailing as they'd been taken from their beds.

Near the back of the crowd women began screaming that they could see Lamanite soldiers coming through the city. This made the escape even more frantic. Men carried their children, women hurried the older ones along, but the pace was slow. The agile and swift Lamanite soldiers were advancing quickly.

Shrieks of pain filled the night air. Death came too soon for the young and the old as the attacking soldiers cut their way through the fleeing Nephites. This time it was Nephite blood that flowed in the streets, blending with the inky darkness on this tragic night. Noah was at the head of the crowd, Tamar closer to the rear. She had stayed back to make sure all were safe. They were anything but safe. As one after another fell, she felt herself becoming ill. "Keep running," she shouted over the screams.

Tamar thought she heard Noah shout an order to the men. She stopped to listen.

"Leave your wives. Come with me!"

A few placed their children in their wives' arms, and to Tamar's horror, they began running ahead of the crowd, following Noah into the woods beyond the cave. The Lamanites would find them and slaughter them inside of the cave. *We are doomed. Lord, what can I do?*

"Stop!" she cried.

Puzzled, the people looked back at Tamar as she stood atop the bridge. "Send your daughters to me."

Those women whose husbands had fled with Noah were truly terrified and their daughters resisted for a moment. It was Lamanites on one side of the river, Tamar on the bridge, and the people she was responsible to protect in the pasture behind her. She stood with arms outstretched.

She could see the bodies of many lying dead in the street behind the Lamanite soldiers and knew they would all be killed if this didn't work.

She motioned for the daughters to come forward. Her eyes never leaving the faces of the Lamanites, painted black with war paint, spears and swords ready for battle.

"Plead for our lives," she whispered to the girls who had trustingly made their way to the bridge behind her. "We will ask for mercy."

Slowly the trembling girls, led by Dinah, made their way to the bridge beside Tamar, tears streaming down their faces. They wept and pleaded with the soldiers. Slowly the swords were sheathed, spear heads lowered, and the leader of the Lamanite army came forward.

He looked from one face to the next, gently reached out to Tamar, and touched her hair. He then felt the cloth of her shawl.

"We are tired of Noah taking our women. We will take his women. You spin soft cloth. Make these for our women. You are now our slaves. Come."

He pointed at Tamar. Limhi, who had been carrying the only remaining living high priest who served with Zeniff, finally reached his mother. He stood beside her, hunched over, catching his breath.

The soldier spoke to Limhi, while pointing at Tamar. "We will hunt and find Noah. Our king orders Noah's death."

Shock was evident on Limhi's face as he jerked upright. "Why?"

"Our king wishes to rid this country of this evil king. Our people watch. They begin to act like your people. Noah must die."

"We don't know where he has gone," Tamar blurted.

"If you hide him from us, you will all die." The anger in his voice was not lost on anyone listening.

Tamar spoke gently. "We don't wish to be slaves. Can we live in peace, like we did in the beginning?"

A regal, white-haired Lamanite and his guards—painted loin cloth clad soldiers—slowly walked toward Tamar. He stood boldly before her and the soldiers parted so he could come close. "I was a young man when Zeniff took possession of this land. He was good to us. I'm now the king of the Lamanites. We don't wish to harm you. We want to rid the land of the evil ways of Noah. He takes our women and defiles them. We have killed, and will kill, any who get in our way. Noah must die." The lines in his face were deep. In the light of the torches there was a flicker of pain in his expression.

Tamar wondered what else Noah had done to bring pain to this king. What personal connection was there? She knew she may never find out, but whatever it was, she wanted to right the wrongs of her husband. "We will do as you wish."

"You give half of all your goods to us. Soldiers will guard your city. You spin, weave, make pots, and grow food to take care of soldiers and families who guard."

Tamar dropped her head, then asked, "Can we worship our God?"

"Do what you want as long as you give us what we ask."

Peace filled her heart. They could worship. *Thank you, Lord. We can have joy in our tribulation.* She smiled a faint smile and took Limhi by the arm. "Let's gather our people and bury our dead." She gazed with sorrow at those who had fallen, whose bodies lay scattered through the city.

The Lamanite soldiers stepped back, giving space for the Nephites to begin the grim task of buying their dead. A new mound was started out in the pasture where the sheep grazed. It was a beautiful resting place.

———— ◆ ————

Tamar sent word throughout the community to gather at the temple. It had been a very long night with little sleep. Even the Lamanite soldiers were weary looking. Their replacements had not come yet and they'd been standing guard all night long. The soldiers at first stayed right with the people, walking with them and watching their every move. Now they stood at the edge of town, leaning against trees or sitting on stumps.

Limhi stepped up on a rock wall and addressed his people. "I'm not ignorant of my father's sins. Truly he led our people astray, but I don't wish to see him die. We will do what the Lamanite king orders and live as slaves to our ancient brothers until the Lord sees fit to help us be free once again. We must do our part to be obedient. Who is willing to make the changes and live as God would want?"

Reluctantly, some raised their hands halfway. Others' shot up enthusiastically, in spite of their weariness. Many of Noah's wives raised their hands. Several of the wives whose husbands had abandoned them to flee with Noah also raised their hands.

"We will grow into a righteous people once again," Limhi said with a hopeful smile.

"Let us go about our days doing good," Tamar added. "Caring for each other, working and learning." She looked into their faces. "We have many women and children without husbands and fathers. Let us be thoughtful with our words—and tender in our hearts for their pain."

A number of the women whose husbands had fled wiped tears from their cheeks.

"This is a difficult time of mourning, each with different reasons. We will help those whose hands hang down and hearts are broken." She stepped down and embraced one mother with several children clinging to her skirts. "We will be here for you." The woman burst out in tears, sobbing on Tamar's shoulder.

Her words were halting, broken by sobs. "How could he leave us? What has become of him? What has become of all of those who followed Noah?"

Tamar addressed the crowd. "Go to your homes, let us begin to rebuild our city yet again."

After allowing the woman to weep for a time, Tamar gave her a tight hug and urged her to get some rest. Gideon and Limhi remained close by, watching the last of the people slowly return, some to huts and others to finely crafted mansions. The first day of their life of slavery had begun.

Tamar sat down on the temple steps. Limhi sat beside her and Gideon sat a step below. "We need to find Noah. The Lamanite king has ordered he be found and turned over to them."

Gideon spoke in a whisper. "I'll send some men to search for him. Many are no longer loyal to the king. I'll leave through the back pass as if I'm adding to the burial mound. We will search for him."

Tamar looked worried.

"I won't kill him. I'll bring him back alive if I find him."

Relief washed over her face. "His blood need not be on your hands."

"Am I going to be the new king?" Limhi asked quietly.

"Are you prepared to lead in righteousness?"

Limhi nodded.

"Act in that role until Noah is found. Gain the trust and respect of the people. Lead them the way you know you should."

"We will begin by making thank offerings. I can teach those who don't understand the old ways—how we look for the coming of the Savior, how we show gratitude for His blessings."

The excitement was evident in Limhi's face. Tamar smiled from deep inside her heart. In spite of hardship, she had hope.

As two of the guards fell asleep, Tamar saw Gideon slip behind the small burial mound, and with a small contingent of soldiers, he vanished into the tall prairie grasses.

———◆———

The people slipped into their routines, and life began to take on a cadence of normalcy. The grain was harvested and half went into woven baskets left by the Lamanite guards. Each day, the baskets filled with cloth, cuts of meat, fruits, and grains were taken to Shemlon.

The soldiers had already taken half of the people's goods and used them to create homes for the families of the guards who would spend their days keeping the Nephite people contained inside the city. The treasures of the temple were raided and taken back to the palace of the Lamanite king, and the less opulent palace was slowly being transformed into a home where children of Noah's many wives were being raised up and taught things of God that had never been spoken of before.

Tamar was teaching a group of women on the steps of the old temple when a cry went out from the tower. A watchman shouted, "They are coming. Our men, led by Gideon, have returned."

Several of the women whose husbands had fled to follow Noah, stayed behind the rest of the crowd. The approaching group of men snaked through the pasture, around the fresh burial mound, and toward the bridge. Rachel pushed to the front and stood on the bridge, Gideon led the group. Tamar scanned the faces. She recognized many of them: traders, shop owners, craftsmen, and soldiers. Noah was not among them. She watched as the final soldier at the end of the row crossed the bridge.

"Where is Noah?" Several Lamanite soldiers moved in close to the group, obviously wondering the same thing. At first some of the men whispered to their loved ones, eyes darted to Tamar, then hands covered mouths in shock.

Gideon's voice hushed the whispers. "Let us gather at the old temple, the temple of the One True God."

Without waiting for Tamar to respond, Gideon ordered the soldiers to stand back and let the men find their wives and rejoin their families. It was awkward for a moment as men who had left their wives to follow Noah returned with tearful apologies.

Gideon spoke loudly enough for all to hear. "Noah is no more. He is dead."

Tamar was surprised at her response. She clutched Limhi's arm and felt ill. He wrapped his arms around his mother and held her tight. It was almost as if a weight had been lifted off Tamar's shoulders. *He's in Your hands, Lord. He can do no more harm here to these people.*

"Justice has been served. Noah's death was the fulfillment of Abinadi's words."

A memory, a vision or nightmare, whatever it was came suddenly into Tamar's mind. "He died by fire," she whispered.

Gideon looked at her with surprise. "How did you know? Who told you?"

"I think I always knew how his life would end." Tamar nodded her head. "I just hoped I was wrong."

The vision that had haunted her for years now made sense. It had been a mixture of Abinadi's death and Noah's death mingled into one terrible vision. They lived so differently, but they died the same: one a martyr, the other a traitor.

"Noah tricked us," one man cried out. "He told us our families would be protected if we left with him. We were cowards to run. We know that and are ashamed." He crumpled to the ground cradling his head in his hands.

Another man spoke out. "We have obeyed the king for so long, we no longer thought for ourselves." His face twisted in anguish. "Until we realized what we had done."

The men's tears were bitter. They wept through clenched teeth, hands knotted into balls. The first who spoke cried out loud enough for all to hear. "We killed Noah, just like he killed Abinadi." Silence settled over the crowd as the reality of his words sank in.

"We were ready to come back and avenge our wives and children, had they been killed by the Lamanites." The Lamanite guards grabbed their spears as they listened to the words the men spoke. "We would have died fighting if it came to that." The expression on the guard's faces turned hard and their spears lifted.

"Do you wish to die now?" one particularly angry guard shouted.

With hands raised the man responded with humility, "There's been enough killing."

A woman's voice, small but piercing, asked the question everyone must have been thinking. "Who will be our king?"

"We want Limhi to be king," one man shouted.

"Yes, Limhi will be a good king," another voiced.

Tamar squeezed her son's arm. "You will be a great king," she whispered.

Limhi stepped forward. "I've learned through watching my grandfather Zeniff rule and my father Noah rule that not all kings are good. I've been taught well."

---

The excitement was palpable. There would be a new coronation and Limhi would become the new king. It was near enough to harvest time that a feast would be held along with the ceremony. Sacrifices would be offered and worship would be in the open, no longer in hiding.

"Do you want to be king?" Tamar asked her son as he stood alone in the courtyard.

"Yes . . . but . . ."

"But what?"

"Don't I need to . . . have a queen?"

Tamar smiled. "Just ask her."

Limhi sighed. "You make it sound so easy." Then, after a pause, he asked cautiously, "How did Father ask you?"

Tamar closed her eyes, going back to a day when they were young and life was much simpler. "I loved him. He loved me. He took me to the base of the old tower and we climbed up. He was so careful to make sure nothing happened to me. He was very protective then." Tamar's eyes opened and she continued. "He spread his arms out and said he would give me as far as my eyes could see, that he would someday own it all and drive the Lamanites out of the land. He said he would fill the valley with the most beautiful and grand buildings and give me anything I wished for." Tamar shook her head. "All I wanted was to be loved and to live my life with honor. Zeniff and Mera were like parents to me and taught me well. I guess Noah didn't understand . . . I grew, he didn't."

"I'll remember."

"Go find her and ask her to be your wife."

Limhi took a deep breath and with a huge grin left the courtyard and headed for the palace of the former king. Tamar held back, but stayed close enough to watch the moment that would change her son's life.

Dinah was leading a group of children through the street toward the stream. They were carrying small baskets of cloth.

"Dinah, can I speak with you?"

She paused and smiled. "Of course."

Limhi shifted from one foot to the other and clasped his hands in back, then in front.

She smiled wider, "I'm listening."

"I'd like to be your king."

"You already are." She smiled knowingly.

"I mean, I'd like for you to be my queen."

The children began giggling and tugging on her shawl.

"What I mean is that I'd like to have you for my wife."

"Now that I can agree to. Yes, I'd like that very much."

Before the end of day, a simple ceremony was held and Dinah became the wife of Limhi, who then became the king of the Nephite people in the land of Shilom. If the people of Alma had not been so far away, they might have seen smoke ascending from the altar of the old temple. A sacrifice had been made in righteousness. A thank offering to the God of Abraham, Isaac, and Jacob. The God of Israel—the One True God.

"Thank you, Helam," Tamar whispered to the man who stood beside her on the temple steps. "Those words don't come close to expressing the gratitude in my . . ." She placed a hand over her heart, unable to speak. Limhi stood: a man, a husband, and the new king.

Helam smiled. "No, my queen, it is you who taught him. I was just there to support you."

A new vision opened to Tamar's eyes. This one wasn't filled with horror or flames, but instead was peaceful. She had other children and grandchildren. She'd never seen Zarahemla but thought that this might be where she saw her family. She was there, with Sarai, Neriah, Hiram, and Helam. It was a happy time.

But right now, she was a slave. Her people were now slaves. Her son was a king in captivity—but she was filled with hope and peace.

# Epilogue

## *Mera, 145 BC*

*E*ight days was not such a long time. But eight days walking through untamed wilderness, fearing pursuit, driving cattle and mules, while carrying shoulder packs felt like an eternity. Despite her weariness, Mera felt an inner strength like none she'd ever felt before. The songs of the believers, which had begun at a safe distance from Shilom, had carried them all through the hardships and heartache of leaving their home.

The caravan slowed and Mera heard excited murmuring from those ahead of her. Yoseph turned to her, his angular face alight. "We've come to the place where Alma intends to stay."

They crested a hill overlooking their new land. A slow smile spread across Mera's face. "It's beautiful," she said. A crystal river wound through rich fields ready to be groomed for planting. Thick groves of trees wove along shimmering streams and dotted the meadows, casting welcome shade.

Mera and others ran down the hill in their eagerness to greet their new home.

The believers pitched their tents, started cook fires, then gathered for the evening songs and stories. As the voices rose around Mera and golden flames embraced the evening sky, a warmth filled her chest.

She rested her head on Yoseph's shoulders, content to soak in all the sensations of the evening, the rich scent of roast venison, the sweet perfume of honeysuckle vines dripping from the bushes behind her, and even sweeter, the calm sensation of peace and hope that had so often eluded her.

This was a new start, not just for her, but for them all, a chance to build a city that would keep God's commandments and live in peace. She sighed, scarcely listening to the planning that was happening near the center of the celebrations—where would they build the temple, the forge, the potter's shed?

These were minor concerns compared to what they'd been through. Mera trusted Alma to solve them with the help of the Lord.

It felt nice to simply trust the Lord and not have to make these decisions herself. But she'd learned her lesson well. Do not try to control others. Righteousness cannot be compelled. Trust the Lord to work in their hearts. Trust His atonement to heal them all.

Repent and turn to the Lord.

Mera sighed again and Yoseph cast her a bemused smile.

"I'm just so happy. There is nothing here to trouble me." She sat forward. "Just think. We can spend the rest of our lives doing good, worshipping the Lord."

Yoseph raised his brows. "You've already spent your whole life doing good and worshipping the Lord."

Mera gave an embarrassed wave.

On the other side of the campfire, Alma the Younger tossed dry leaves into the flames, while stories of faith and bravery hung in the air.

Mera smiled.

No, there was nothing here to fear at all.

# Afterword

This is a fictionalized account of a true record kept by real people. The full record is called the Book of Mormon. There are important doctrines, principles, teachings, and lessons contained in that sacred text, and the most important message is that there is a living Christ who knows us, loves us, and is involved in the details of our lives.

We know there were noble, valiant, righteous women involved in the Book of Mormon, but we rarely see them or hear mention of them, and it's not because their role is not important. It was in fact vital! These great women must have faced tremendous trials, suffered unimaginable hardships, and experienced their own crises of faith.

How they faced it, we don't know exactly, and that's why this is a work of historical fiction. Their story isn't told. Put yourself in their shoes. Put yourself into the Book of Mormon and ask, *What would I have done?*

We face similar difficulties today. Seeing how someone else struggled and made it through with their faith intact can help us when we encounter hardships that try our faith today.

Don't substitute reading this story for reading the Book of Mormon, but maybe seeing the events from a woman's perspective will help it come to life for you.

# Discussion Questions

1.  When have you questioned whether God was real and if He truly heard and answered prayers?

2.  Who can you talk to about how they have received answers to prayers?

3.  What examples in the scriptures show how someone prayed and got an answer to their prayer?

4.  What can you do to follow that pattern of prayer?

5.  Do you question your success as a parent when your spouse or child acts in conflict to your beliefs or standards?

6.  Do you struggle to feel love for a child who is disobedient?

7.  How did Mera and Tamar deal with these struggles?

8.  Were their struggles resolved quickly? How did they endure their trials?

9.  When have you listened to the Spirit, cautioning you to not respond to what seems like a bad situation, and later you found that the Spirit's restraint kept you from judging wrongly?

10. What are ways you can show or express love to someone that lives a very different lifestyle?

# Acknowledgments

When I kept pulling my little plant up to check it's roots, worried about Oxford commas and sentence structure, Renee patted the soil down and helped me see that leaves and branches had already formed. Together we nurtured this little garden and in our collective hands we pass on to you, our readers, friends, and family a bouquet representative of our harvest: faith in Jesus Christ, testimony of His love, and recognition of the value each of us has inherent in us as His children.

—Mechel Wall

Thanks to the many people who have influenced my faith, my writing, and my belief that I could complete such a vast creative project as a novel. There are too many to list them all, but a few stand out—my husband, Matthew, our children, Amanda, Chad, Jose, Josh, Jessica, Ivan, and Drake, my parents and other family near and far. Thanks to the many friends who asked about my writing and forgave me for the times my mind wandered off to Shilom while they were talking. Also, thanks to William Bernhardt and his writing workshops as well as writing friends who've cheered me on and given timely critiques on various projects—Grace Wagner, Doris Degner-Foster, Ann Christine Fell, Debra Renollet-Ferris, and Jessica Cox. A special thanks to Mechel Wall, for your brilliant ideas and persistent energy in seeing this project through.

—R. H. Roberts

Our hearts are full of gratitude for the team at Cedar Fort for helping this novel see the light of day. Thanks to Briana Farr for taking us on and shepherding us through the publication process, Shawnda Craig and the design team for their beautiful cover art, Kaitlin Barwick and the editing team for their sharp attention to detail and valuable insights, and the marketing director, Vikki Downs. And thanks to you, dear reader, for sticking with us through our story. We hope it means as much to you as it has to us. Finally, we offer our gratitude to the Lord for the gifts in our lives and this great chance to share some of what we feel and believe with you.

# About the Author
## Mechel Wall

*M*echel Wall recently celebrated her third decade as Barry's wife and mother to their eight children. Her education began at the family's private school at age four and simply never ended. Mechel's writing, whether poetic and funny or novel-length and serious, will often reveal interesting tidbits of their family life if you look hard enough. Country living sounded like a better option for their last three sons so they bought a small farm. Learning to care for chickens, pigs, goats, sheep, cows, and now commercial-cut flowers has made her writing rich, deep, and often comical in its content.

Scan to visit

writingonmechelswall.com

# About the Author

*R. H. Roberts*

*R*. H. Roberts lives in rural Oklahoma, raising kids and cattle at the same table. She majored in psychology and mastered in health at Brigham Young University before embracing her true love—literature. She has written several award-winning short stories and novels, which serve as a remedy for a life of devotion to family and faith. She loves hiking, traveling, and attempting foreign languages. Visit her at RHRoberts.com for book extras and life insights. She'd love for you to join the conversation!

Scan to visit

rhroberts.com